Advance praise for *The Plaintiff's Lawyer*

"The Plaintiff's Lawyer *introduces international intrigue to courtroom drama and creates a match made in legal thriller heaven.*"

— Gary Taylor
Pulitzer Prize Nominee Journalist
Author of true-crime bestseller *Luggage by Kroger*

"The Plaintiff's Lawyer *is a true page-turner. At the same time, it is a realistic courtroom novel. The lawyers do what lawyers would do in real life.*"

— Lynne Liberato
Past President, State Bar of Texas

"*When you finish* The Plaintiff's Lawyer, *you will come away with a far better understanding of real lawyers and real trials. I know because I, too, am a trial lawyer and author of legal thrillers.*"

— Larry D. Thompson
Law Firm Founder
Award winning author of *Dark Money*

"*David Crump describes the reality of a trial better than anyone! After 30 years as a trial lawyer and 14 years as a trial judge, I have had the same experiences.*"

— R. Terence Ney
Past President, Virginia Bar Association

"Lawyer books and movies usually don't get the lawyering right. Happily, David Crump gets the lawyering right and tells the tale in a compelling manner."

— Charles W. Schwartz
 Former Chairman of the Board, State Bar of Texas

"David Crump writes a legal thriller as only he can. It is both a thrilling story of lawyers pitted against often shadowy entities . . . and a tale of real law in action. Crump knows and understands how law works . . . and he understands lawyers and their lives. It is a great read!"

— Rex R. Perschbacher
 Former Dean, School of Law,
 University of California—Davis

"After reading the first chapter, I was already hooked!"

— D. Hull Youngblood
 Former Chairman of the Board, State Bar of Texas

"No one writes more realistic legal thrillers than David Crump. The Plaintiff's Lawyer *is proof. I enjoyed every page."*

— Scott Gerber
 Professor of Law
 Author of *The Art of the Law: A Novel*

THE PLAINTIFF'S LAWYER

THE PLAINTIFF'S LAWYER

David Crump

QP BOOKS
New Orleans, Louisiana

Published in 2020 by QP Books, an imprint of Quid Pro Books.

ISBN 978-1-61027-401-2 (paperback)
ISBN 978-1-61027-402-9 (ePUB)

QP BOOKS
Quid Pro, LLC
5860 Citrus Blvd., suite D
New Orleans, Louisiana 70123
www.qpbooks.com

This is a work of fiction. The characters, names, events, dialogue and circumstances are imaginary or are used fictionally. Any resemblance to real
persons or actual events is purely coincidental, fictitious, or imaginary.

qp

Cataloging-in-Publication Data

Crump, David.

The plaintiff's lawyer / David Crump.

p. cm.

ISBN 978-1-61027-401-2 (pbk.)

1. Trials—United States—Fiction. 2. Law Firms—United States—Fiction. I. Title.

PS3540.R3927C8 2020

872' .25.3—dc21
2020159867
CIP

To my Susanne

Author's Preface

As in my other courtroom novels, I wanted this one to show the law and lawyers the way they really are. Most lawyer stories don't attempt to do this. And that's too bad, because most people get most of their information about our justice system from fiction.

In this story, you'll see lawyers wrestling with doubts about accepting a new case. You'll see them trying, with incomplete facts, to forecast how the law might fit with the client's goals. The lawyers in my novel struggle to prepare the right kinds of suit papers. They take depositions, which are pretrial examinations of witnesses. They argue motions. And they spend long hours preparing for all these battles. They negotiate hard, and they try to settle in mediation. They pick a jury the way real lawyers would. They ask questions and make arguments realistically. And they "sweat the jury" during deliberations just as lawyers would in real life.

But a novel has to follow conventions. A lot of what lawyers do is boring, but no one wants a boring novel. And so I've shortened some of the procedures here, and I've tried to suggest the not-so-interesting hours without putting you, the reader, through them. And at the end, as I've done in my earlier books, I've added a postscript to tell you what's real and what isn't.

But now, let's get into our story. Imagine you're a new lawyer at the firm of Robert Herrick and Associates. You're about to embark on an adventure involving international intrigue and a claim about theft of secrets from the American space program.

THE PLAINTIFF'S LAWYER

1

The countdown was sharp and precise. It was the familiar backward set of numbers, 5-4-3-2-1, but announced in Persian. The language of Iran.

"Pene . . . chehar . . . seh . . . do . . . yek!"

The missile ignited. The Ayatollah's excited grin flashed white behind his binoculars. "It's going to fly!"

The rocket exhausts wobbled and shook. Then: "Liftoff. The *Kharramshar* is off!" The flame was an exploding orange-white, but the missile lumbered up by what seemed only an inch. Then, between the bare, lifeless humps of the Alborz foothills of southern Iran, it crept two inches higher, then more, and more. And then, it kept accelerating.

"But now we're facing a bigger challenge." The Aerospace Commander stood close beside the Ayatollah in his starched Revolutionary Guard uniform.

"That's right. The missile will make a turn in a few seconds."

"Yes. The rollover. The missile will make a slight turn. It's always a critical step. And even then, we can't be sure of success, because this two-stage craft has to separate, and the second stage has to ignite. All within a narrow trajectory."

The Ayatollah responded with the indifferent confidence that only those close to heaven can know. "The *Hwasong* of our North Korean allies is a reliable missile, and our *Kharramshar* is a faithful replica of the *Hwasong* they sent to us. This missile is going to do what it is supposed to do. God wills it, because God wants to show us magnificent success."

The Commander was excited too. "And, beloved Ayatollah, our version of this missile has the capability to target Israel, when that is needed. In fact, it can reach infidels beyond Israel. Like the American military base in Qatar."

The missile seemed to slow when its guidance system performed the rollover. The path of the projectile bent slightly, almost imperceptibly, to the observers' right. Soon its slanted trajectory soared above the jagged whiteness of Mount Damavand and touched the lower clouds, diaphanous enough to see through. And then, there was a sharp plume of rocket exhaust to signal the takeoff of the second stage, as the first stage fell into the ocean.

In less than a minute, the missile was a speck of gray.

"Like a well-watered rose," said the Commander, using a familiar Iranian figure of speech.

"*Ziba!*" the Ayatollah exulted. "Just beautiful. After this, everyone will know the lovely, terrible power of the Iranian people. Everywhere in the world, the believing and unbelieving."

"And they will be careful and polite to you, dear Ayatollah, knowing that you can turn the continents into seas of fire if they insult you. All peoples across the everlasting globe will know."

But the only people the two men really had in mind were those of one particular country. A country across the Atlantic.

"The Americans are bumbling amateurs at rocket technology." The Ayatollah snickered, with his nose in his floppy white sleeve. "Our missiles rained fire and death upon their air bases in Iraq, and the Americans were powerless to stop us."

By now, the missile was invisible.

"Praise Allah! The Prophet—peace be upon him—would be full of joy to see this." The Ayatollah high-fived the Commander, and they faced each other with grins wider than two scimitar-shaped crescent moons.

The Ayatollah had once prohibited the high five, on the ground that it was too Western. And as quickly as a switch could have flipped, the inner circle and then the people had obeyed the great man's order by abolishing this decadent custom. But then the Ayatollah had changed his mind, and instantly, the cheerful gesture had become acceptable again. The entire nation had reversed course a second time, just as quickly, to follow the Ayatollah's signal and use the high-five with everyone about anything.

* * *

Two hundred miles to the south, in the waters of the Arabian Sea, Admiral Laurencio Williams stood in the conning tower of the aircraft carrier *Gerald R. Ford*. This was the biggest carrier in the world, commissioned in 2017. The *Gerald R. Ford* could launch more aircraft, and do it faster, than any other ship.

Just as importantly, the Ford was also the most heavily equipped intelligence ship in the United States Navy. The admiral was using its snooping capabilities, now, by watching a bullet-shaped image on a screen that tracked the Iranian missile as it flew over the little town of Bandar-al-Jask and cleared the rocky country coastline of the Islamic Republic of Iran.

"That *Kharramshar* is going to pass right over us, isn't it?" The map on the monitor was what he called a dog-and-pony projection, with big simple shapes. There was the Gulf of Oman, and below it the Arabian sea, with a red track showing the path of the missile.

"The first stage is going to fall into the ocean thirty degrees east, in front of us," said the captain. "The second stage is going to pass overhead, to starboard."

The admiral nodded. "Keep us looking at it."

"Aye aye, sir." The voice that greeted the admiral was remote and metallic. "It's approaching maximum height now."

"All ahead three quarters," said the captain. "Yes, we've got it. Our guys are going to be able to dredge up this elegant piece of Persian trash."

"Both stages of it." The admiral shook his head, partly from disgust at the Iranians' behavior and partly in admiration of the American technology that would retrieve the missile. "This Iranian spacecraft is nuclear capable. Who knows how long it will take these outlaws to finish developing the Islamic bomb, once they start up again?

"This illegal missile is the Iranian version of a North Korean model. The *Kharramshar* is a version of the *Hwasong*. Which means Mars, in Korean. The planet Mars, that is."

"Mars? That's a whole lot of wishful thinking by the North Koreans. They're making plans to shoot a rocket to Mars? They're a hardscrabble third-world country, but they have master-race delusions. But anyway, we've got this sorry Iranian missile pinpointed for retrieval."

"Like a well-watered rose." And everyone on the bridge laughed at the translated Iranian words.

The sailors on the *Gerald R. Ford* knew the enemy.

* * *

Around the circular desk in the United Nations Security Council, the Russian delegation almost faced the United States ambassador. They watched each other across a curved empty space that only hinted at the real distance between the two countries.

"It is an internal matter for the Iranian sovereign nation." Even through the translation, the speaker's words were blunt, flat, and heavy, as one would expect of a Russian voice. They came from a face with a squat, wide nose and bulbous eyes. "My country cannot order them to stop their missile program or interfere with their national defense."

The American ambassador lifted her hands over her head in frustration. "You know that it is not an internal Iranian problem. You know it as well as the rest of us in the Security Council. It is an international problem, and it is a danger as big as the end of the world. But it can be solved. Your country can stop them instantly by refusing to supply them. It's imports from Russia and your allies that keep this pariah regime in business. Even the centrifuges for their nuclear program and the parts for their missiles come from Russia."

"We have no lawful reason for an embargo," answered the Russian ambassador patiently. "Such an act would amount to a siege that would cost the Islamic Republic of Iran its economy, and ultimately it would cost lives. We do not want to violate international law."

"We've already put some sanctions in place. The Iranians have defied them and used black markets. They continue to violate international law by the missiles they are developing. Our conventions make them illegal, because they are capable of carrying nuclear weapons. The Iranians are violating all sorts of provisions of international law, including the actions of this Council. We need to be more forceful."

"It would not be lawful for Russia to act. Whether the Iranians have defied the Council is a matter of interpretation."

"Well, to solve that, all you have to do is to vote in favor of the resolution now before this Council. Then, your actions will be as lawful in your eyes as they obviously are already in our eyes."

The American ambassador shook her head. "And you know as well as I do, that you can embargo military items and luxuries first, then prohibit economic items like construction equipment until these outlaw activities stop. Here in this Council, if you prefer, you can abstain from voting on the resolution. But your single negative vote, of course, is a veto."

"I cannot violate the principles my nation holds as fundamental, by meddling in the lawful affairs of a smaller country."

"Why must this reckless behavior be protected as if it were lawful, when all it would take for us to do something about it, would be to adopt this resolution?"

"Because it is an internal matter for the Iranians." The Russian ambassador's face was deadpan, oblivious to the irony in his response.

2

The Chase Bank Building was the tallest building in the city, and Robert Herrick's office occupied a top corner. His desk was a long block of carved mahogany, and behind him the greenhouse-style, floor-to-ceiling windows gleamed with brilliant sun. Outside, light splashed from the downtown spires in colors of brown, gray, and white, and the green swath along Buffalo Bayou stretched through Memorial Park to overlap the fog of the horizon.

"I'm sorry." Robert Herrick faced the three men sitting in front of him. "But I doubt that you can file a good lawsuit based on this problem about your turncoat employee. I mean, you wouldn't have a chance to win it."

The president and general counsel of the Nova Aerospace Company sat in matching desk chairs in front of him. In the third chair sat Tom Kennedy, the partner with whom Robert worked most often. Beneath them, a huge oriental carpet gleamed with bright triangles, diamonds, and circles in every color. Farther away, by the window, a hundred geraniums bloomed in pink, red and white.

"Why is it not a good lawsuit?" asked Nova's president. "This guy—his name is deTravanian Wrenger—he quit our company and left five projects in a state of total turmoil. And now Dravos Corporation has hired this same deTravanian Wrenger. Our most aggressive competitor. They know that deTravanian Wrenger signed an agreement not to go to work for anybody else in our industry, and they're deliberately breaking that agreement."

Robert nodded. "But Mike—may I call you Mike?—and I didn't catch your last name."

"Martin. Mike Martin," the president answered, a little defensively. "We thought it was a very good lawsuit, based on their hiring a guy who agreed to a contract. A covenant not to compete. I mean, he signed an agreement not to go to work for a competitor. And Dravos Corporation knows that deTravanian Wrenger signed it, and they hired him anyway."

"I'm sorry." Robert shook his head. "The law just isn't very helpful on this."

"This guy, deTravanian Wrenger, worked with us on a lot of projects for American missiles. Guidance. Propulsion. A rollover device. And Dravos, in the past, has not only competed with us. They've also done all kinds of work for other countries, including some that aren't friendly. Like Iran."

"Iran? Good grief. But none of that can change your chances in a lawsuit."

Robert Herrick's eyes were a sky blue color, set deep, and when he was serious, people swore that he could see through them. At six feet two, he had a commanding presence, even behind a desk. A shock of black hair hung over his forehead, giving him a perpetual too-young look, so that his opponents named him "the Baby-Faced Assassin" for his youthful appearance and his ability to beat them in trial. Women jurors loved him, and the men respected his ability to concede weaknesses in his cases without showing weakness.

"I'm sorry," Robert shook his head again, "but there's no law against quitting work, of course. And if you filed suit on the covenant not to compete—the contract Dravos Corporation has broken by hiring your ex-employee—I'm afraid the deck would be stacked against you."

"How so?"

"The short answer is that the courts have made it really, really difficult to enforce covenants not to compete. Impossible, in cases like yours. First of all, the covenant has to be limited geographically. That means, even if the courts might enforce an agreement covering the same city where your outfit, Nova Aerospace, is located, they'll throw it out if it locks down an ex-employee, all across the country."

When he had graduated from law school, Robert Herrick had turned down all of the lucrative job offers from big law firms because he had wanted to go it alone. Today, his law firm had well over a hundred employees, including an audio-visual department that made models and videos for use in court. His clients at the beginning were so-called "little guys" who had been injured or had their relatives killed by carelessness. Now, his firm's attorneys represented some businesses, too: usually small businesses that had been mistreated by bigger ones.

The big-firm lawyers traded jokes with Robert when they agreed to settlements that paid his clients multiple millions and built his law firm along the way. "But the money is never enough to make them better off than if they hadn't been injured," he was fond of saying.

Now, Robert faced his clients to deliver the bad news. "So, a covenant not to compete has to be limited geographically. But that's not all. Second, the agreement has to be limited in time duration. If it stops competitors from hiring an ex-employee for a year or two, maybe you can enforce it. But not if it's an agreement that lasts forever."

"That's crazy," Mike Martin protested." Dravos is competing unfairly against us, right this minute, with knowledge this guy got from us while he was our employee."

"I know. It's wrong, especially in an industry like yours. But the bottom line is that your covenant not to compete is broader than anything the courts will come close to enforcing. It covers the entire country, and it lasts for ten years. And this competitor, this Dravos, is located in Atlanta, which is where deTravanian Wrenger works. He's not close to you geographically."

"But . . . the covenant not to compete has to be written that way, or it won't work." Mike Martin's eyes narrowed in disgust. "We compete with companies located in California and New York. And for that matter, in Milan and Tokyo. A one-city covenant not to compete wouldn't do us any good at all. And a trade secret that we have today may be the key to a development five to ten years in the future, so what about a covenant not to compete for one year? Useless."

"I understand. It was Shakespeare who said that the law can be like a scarecrow. It threatens, but it doesn't always work. We can't assume that the law will produce justice. It's only law, and law isn't the same thing as justice. I'm just telling you the way it is."

Mike Martin frowned and chuckled at the same time. "We heard that you were the best plaintiff's lawyer around, Mr. Herrick. That you could make lawsuits work when other lawyers couldn't."

"Thanks for that." Robert smiled. "But the plaintiff's lawyer can't do what can't be done."

"Well . . . , maybe we could file suit and just try it." Mike Martin's voice sounded hopeful. "There's always a chance. And, we could put Dravos to a lot of trouble, which they deserve. We could teach them a lesson, even if we don't win."

"But that's not a good idea either." Robert's voice was firm. "First of all, I've never filed a lawsuit that wasn't based on the law, just to give someone a lot of trouble. And second, filing a lawsuit wouldn't be cost-free for you. Dravos would come up with a counterclaim of some sort."

"How can they do that?"

"Competitors have rights. They'll probably sue you back, even if it's based on phony made-up facts, or facts-according-to-Dravos. You wouldn't like the result. It would cost you a ton of money to defend that counterclaim. It would take all kinds of time away from your employees' work. The lesson you want to teach Dravos will be the same lesson they'll try to teach you."

Robert smiled sympathetically. "And I know that this is absurd, but you could even lose Dravos's suit against you, because there would be a jury. With a jury, there's always lots of unpredictability. And you'd have expenses for presenting your own claim."

"Well . . . all of that stuff would be awful, of course."

"I don't like telling you this. I'd rather right wrongs in the world. And I certainly agree with you that this situation is an injustice, because your employee signed an agreement, and Dravos is using what your employee learned with you to take business away from you."

Robert looked out the window to the blurry line where the green of Memorial Park merged with the sky. "I don't like telling you this. But I think it's my job."

*　*　*

On the other side of the globe, the United States Navy had deployed the destroyer *Cincinnati* into the shallows of the Arabian Sea.

"Now, pay attention to Admiral Ellison, here," said the captain. "Our mission is to pull up the missile that those bad guys in Iran tested a few days ago."

"And yes, we've found that missile." Admiral Ellison tapped the map with his pointer. "How many of you remember the mystery of Maylasian Airlines Flight 370?"

The crew of the Cincinnati looked blank. There were sonar analysts in the crowd who nodded, but most of them were clueless. What was Malaysian Flight 370?

"The disappearance of Flight 370 is the biggest mystery in aviation history," the admiral explained. "It was a passenger flight from Kuala Lumpur to Beijing. It fell off radar. There was an international search across the Indian Ocean."

Admiral Ellison turned to face the crew. "Pieces have washed up, but the wreckage has never been found, and neither have the bodies of the 239 passengers and crew. I mention Flight 370 because we've used the same techniques that they used in that search."

He held up a hand and said, "But there's a big difference. The hunt for Flight 370 was enormous—and international. In this case, we, the United States, have conducted our search alone. In secret."

He looked toward the map. "We've used two kinds of underwater vessels, just the way they looked for flight 370. But we knew where the *Kharramshar* splashed down, even if not exactly where it ended up.

"Our first undersea vehicle," he went on, "was what's called a '*towfish*.' That's a sonar device tied to our ship by a cable. We pulled the towfish back and forth, sort of like cutting grass with a lawn mower.

"So, that was our first asset, the towfish.

"Then, we used what are called '*AUV's*.' Which stands for '*Autonomous Undersea Vehicles*.' We didn't tow them. They sailed under their own power, while we guided them electronically."

"And during all of this, we analyzed the sonar onboard," added the captain. "But the pictures tend to be obscured by this thick, gnarly vegetation."

"Right. And that's what the AUV's are for," said Admiral Ellison. "We could send them to take a closer look. Momentum and currents moved the wreckage on the way to the sea bed."

He moved to the center of the hall. "And that means . . . yes, we've found it. Any questions?"

"How do we get it up?" one seaman wanted to know.

"Balloons," said the admiral. And the silence that followed made him chuckle.

"Yes, the plan is to use balloons." Now, the monitor showed boxes holding floppy orange objects. "These are huge balloons. This is the technique, when the recovery is undersea."

The monitor changed to show a mass of blackish-green seaweed. "There's the missile, there."

"We were lucky with the splashdown," he added. "The first stage of the *Kharramshar* hit the water at latitude 15.400 and longitude 62.337, just southeast of the Gulf of Oman. This is shallow ocean, at a depth where divers can get to the missile."

The naval officers on board strained to see.

"The first stage broke into three main pieces." The admiral pointed, again, at the monitor. "And it'll be easy, compared to some salvage operations. The divers will attach empty balloons to each piece. Then, we'll pump air down to fill the balloons. When we float a piece of missile to the surface, we'll use a barge with a high crane to pick it up."

He grinned. "And that's how we're going to find out how well the Iranians are doing with their Death-to-America campaign."

3

Tom Kennedy wore his "uniform": a brown suit, a tan shirt, and a brown tie. He had many of each, in solid, houndstooth, glen plaid, striped, and tone-on-tone versions. It was a convention that made life easier for a busy man who didn't want to take time choosing clothes in the morning.

Now, he shifted in his chair. "Robert, you sounded a little unconvincing in talking to Mike Martin about the contract. The covenant not to compete. Like, you just didn't want to take on a big case. You having a midlife crisis or something?"

Robert looked across his big mahogany desk at his partner. The day outside was spectacularly bright, with sun blazing through the floor-to-ceiling windows and spotlighting the multicolored circles, boxes, triangles, and scimitars of the huge oriental carpet. The meanders of Buffalo Bayou were bordered in sparkling green, and beyond it, the trees, roads, and homes sprawled to the west until they were welded to the sky in a blur, without a joint.

He winced. "Midlife crisis? No. Not exactly."

"Something post-menopausal, then?"

Robert's eyes wrinkled as he smiled. "Not that either."

"Listen, buddy. This is Tom. I know you. You don't seem to want to do anything and you're drinking too much. Normally, you would have jumped at the chance to take on a big case that promised something new. There probably are ways to enforce that covenant not to compete, such as getting the court to limit it instead of throwing it out."

"Possibly."

"I saw you when you turned down that case with Nova Aerospace. The employee who broke his contract and went to work for—what was it?—Dravos Corporation. In the old days, you would've wanted that kind of case."

"We don't know how to handle a case like that. We've built our firm on personal injury claims. Besides, it would have been a hard, uphill slog to win that case."

"No. That never stopped you before. You've liked difficult cases. It's something to do with you."

"Well, I guess so. I'm not up to a challenge right now."

"Also, that case had something else that you usually like. It wasn't just a dogfight. It had to do with the well-being of the country. What that turncoat employee did was dangerous. It would weaken the space program."

"Right now, I don't want new challenges, I guess."

"Yep. I see that. You've been president of the bar association and all kinds of blue ribbon committees. And now you can rest on your laurels. You don't want anything new."

"That's right."

"The fire's gone out."

Robert smiled again. "I guess. I just want some good cases involving thoughtless corporations trying to take advantage of injured workers and gullible customers."

"Instead of a case against a thoughtless corporation taking advantage of inventors and hurting the national defense of the United States?"

He sighed. "That case would be really difficult. It's a loser."

"You know as well as I do that sometimes cases that look like losers turn out well, and you like that kind of case if it's an important one and you're on the right side."

He sighed again. "This is turning into another one of those 'Why do we do what we do for a living' talks. A philosophical debate about, 'What should the plaintiff's lawyer do?'"

"Maybe. But you're also drinking enough so that you don't feel good in the morning."

"All right. All right! Let me think about it."

* * *

When Tom was gone, Robert looked out the window again.

Maybe Tom was right.

He was right at least to this extent: I don't have the fire in the belly I've had for some earlier fights. Fights for little guys who were right. Fights for what I felt, all the way, were about righting injustice.

But that gets said so often that it's a cliché. "Righting injustice." What is injustice? Sometimes it just seems like disagreements between people.

The intercom buzzed. Donna deCarlo's voice came onto his desk. "Robert, I've got that Motion for New Trial in the *Stanton* case prepared. You wanted me to let you know."

The *Stanton* case. Poor guy got killed in a tank for storing chemicals while he was cleaning it. Now I'm at the miserable stage of asking the judge for a New Trial. Stanton's husband had gone in alone, when company policy was to have two people; he didn't have his company phone with him; he hadn't notified anyone about where he was; and he hit his head and fell. Fell unconscious, that is, into a foot of water. And drowned.

The company had been so, so negligent. No warning buzzer. No tracking system. Scheduling Stanton so tightly that to keep up with his responsibilities, he had to go into the tank alone. But it didn't matter. The jury had found Stanton 75% negligent and the company only 25%.

In this state, a jury finding of negligence above 50% against the plaintiff meant that he could not recover anything.

So, Robert Herrick had gotten Ms. Stanton a judgment of exactly zero.

And now he was at the Motion for New Trial stage. With poor chances, because a Motion for New Trial always has poor chances.

And right before that, he'd tried a medical negligence case. The operating team had left a sponge inside his client and caused a roaring infection that nearly killed him. Okay, so he'd obtained a negligence verdict in that case. But the jury had awarded only ten thousand dollars.

A terrible loss. The costs before getting to trial had been over $250,000. Even worse, he had turned down an offer of settlement worth $100,000. His client would have been better off if he had settled without his lawyer trying the case.

Before that, a horrendous truck wreck. Same kind of result. The jury had found the trucking company at fault, but it had way, way lowballed the damages.

The last thing he needed right now was a challenge.

He stood up. He took a step toward the door, on the way to pick up that draft Motion for New Trial from Donna deCarlo.

He hesitated.

And he walked, instead, to the corner of his office, where he kept a bar. He had some good Scots whiskey stored there. A bottle of eighteen-year-old Talisker.

He got out two ice cubes. And hesitated again.

Then he poured four fingers of the amber liquid.

He would consider the Motion for New Trial tomorrow.

* * *

Around four o'clock, he went over to the desk again.

Slowly, he picked up the phone and dialed Tom Kennedy.

"Tom, would you please take over getting out the Motion for New Trial in the *Stanton* case? I just don't want to see anything about that case again. I've got to meet with Ms. Stanton, of course, and I'm determined to try to make sense of what happened, together with her. But I feel terrible. I want to never see the case again. And I just can't stand to work on it right now."

"I understand."

"Maybe it's my midlife crisis taking me over."

He was relieved that Tom laughed at that.

"You'll come back around. Meanwhile, I'll get the document from Donna."

He sat for a few minutes just looking out at the burning sky. Some wispy little clouds had formed, and the sun was well into its western journey.

He was aware that his stare was vacuous. Unthinking. And yet he was thinking—about how much he didn't want to work and how he might get back on track, if ever he could.

Nowadays, he didn't feel the excitement of growing his law firm. He remembered his first settlement of a case, and his first trial, which he unexpectedly won. He remembered hiring his first associate. He remembered when he had made that associate his first partner. He remembered the first business case he had taken on: a breach of contract suit against a supplier who had sold his client defective electronic equipment.

Dozens of new lawyers, legal assistants, and secretaries had gone through the firm, some to move on, some to make their own names for themselves.

But none of that mattered very much now.

What was he going to do next?

He reached out toward the picture of his first wife, Patricia, in the gold frame that sat on the corner of the desk. He realized, after starting to do it, that he reached for her image often when he faced a problem. Patricia had died twelve years earlier from ovarian cancer. But she was still with him in this picture. He had remarried years after her death, but he still reached for Patricia sometimes, just as he was doing now.

He stared at the telephone for a moment. And finally, he called his wife. His terrific wife now, who was as much an ally, as much a source of willpower.

"Hi, baby." He tried to sound upbeat. Cheerful. But he was aware that he probably wasn't succeeding. That Talisker wasn't helping.

"Robert?"

"I think I'm going to head home."

"Robert, you sound awful. What's wrong?"

"I had a new client with a big case today."

"Well, that sounds good."

"But it wasn't a good case and I turned it down."

"And there's more to it than that. I can hear it in your voice."

"My ship is becalmed. My locomotive doesn't have motive. My car is out of gas. My rowboat has lost its oars. My airplane. . . ."

"And you've been drinking. It's always a bad sign when you've been drinking in the middle of the day, my big guy."

"I don't have work that interests me now. Maybe it's time to retire. Just hang it up. Put myself out to pasture. Fade into the sunset."

She laughed. One of the things he liked about her was that she laughed a lot. "And I suppose you're thinking about shutting down the factory. Closing the store. Throwing your tools away."

"And hanging up my spurs. You catch on real quick, for a youngster."

"I'm worried about you, of course, you major-league dummy. I'd like it if you retired. You've got plenty of money, and you've accomplished everything you could have wanted."

At that, he thought about Ms. Stanton and her drowned husband.

She sighed. "Okay. Go home. You sound like you're still in good shape to drive—"

"Oh, sure. I stopped imbibing a couple of hours ago." That statement wasn't quite true. In fact, it just about doubled the time he'd had to absorb the alcohol.

"Okay. I can get away from here. I'll head home too. And minister to your needs."

"Good. I need some ministering."

4

The living room at the Herrick home on Willowick Drive was wide and imposing. Robert faced his wife, Maria Melendez, with both of them sitting on light-colored couches. "You've got another murder case?" he asked her. He wanted to change the subject. Away from his own doldrums.

"Yes, and this one is as much of a stomach turner as any I've ever seen. Ugly."

Maria was an assistant district attorney. She didn't look very much like a lawyer now, with her hair down and wearing cutoff blue jean shorts. But Robert stared at her, and for the thousandth time, he thought, "She's beautiful."

Maria Melendez had arrived in the United States from Castro's Cuba at age twelve. On a boat that wasn't much more than tied-together inner tubes. Her father had been the Director General of hospitals in Havana, but at some point, he had gotten crosswise of the Castro regime. As soon as he could bribe his way out of a Cuban jail, he had set off with his family for Florida, across that dangerous ninety miles of unpredictable waves.

Maria went to high school in Hialeah, and a few very different years later, she was a showgirl in Law Vegas. The newspaper clipping that Robert had salvaged showed her in a skimpy blue costume with what looked like hundreds of feathers, and the caption described her as "The Showgirl Who Turned Prosecutor."

She had had to correct his teasing about that, frequently. "No, Robert, we weren't 'exotic dancers.' It wasn't that kind of performance. We were a family show, even if we might have been the only one in the State of Nevada."

"So, what's the issue in your stomach turning case? The legal issue, I mean."

Maria had an unusual job. When a condemned murderer in a capital case was sentenced to death, it was her job to pursue the judgment through the courts, all through the seemingly endless loops of appeals and stays and habeas corpus hearings, until the sentence could be carried out. People always referred to the assistant district attorney in this position by an informal title. Inside and outside the office, she was called "The District Attorney's Official Killer."

Usually, Maria's responsibility was to fight tough, smart lawyers on the other side, up to the Supreme Court and back, to keep the sentence the judges and juries had imposed. But sometimes, her job required her to join with opponents in asking the courts or governor to reduce a given sentence to life imprisonment—or even to acquit a convicted killer.

There was no manual to tell a prosecutor when to choose one approach or the other.

"The issues are the usual issues," she told Robert, "which ignore the stomach-churning aspects of the case, of course. In other words, the issues have nothing to do with the horror of the crime, which is what usually happens. First, the defense lawyers claim that the jury wasn't instructed the way they would have wanted. Then, they argue that the defense at trial supposedly didn't develop or offer testimony that they could have presented, which the trial lawyers were right not to offer, because it would actually have been harmful to the defense, but these appellate lawyers don't have to be fair to the trial lawyers. And as always, there's the almost mandatory claim that the defense lawyers at trial were incompetent, which they certainly weren't."

She frowned. "Nobody could have defended this incredibly disgusting case successfully. The evidence was overwhelming, and so was the terror of the murders."

They both were silent. He looked again at her pale, clear Hispanic skin, the ringlets of her dusky red hair, and her dark, almost-black eyes, and didn't think about her case. Instead, for the thousandth-and-first time, he thought, "She's beautiful."

"Well, actually," she said firmly, "I'd rather leave that particular case at the office and talk about something else. It sounded like you were having some kind of meltdown this afternoon."

"No, not really."

"What's wrong?"

"Well, I'm just not happy being a trial lawyer right now. Nothing specific. But I'm like you. I don't want to dwell too heavily on it."

"All right. So you had this case today that you turned down. Tell me about that."

"Okay. You remember that case I mentioned about the covenant not to compete? And the president and general counsel were coming in to see me?"

"Yes. So that was the one?"

"Yes. Nova Aerospace against Dravos Corporation. The covenant not to compete in their contract was too broad to be enforceable."

"Okay. But there are ways around that problem. Maybe it was a good case?"

"Wait," he said. "Looks like they're doing a story about that very subject on the news. Let's turn up the TV."

On the screen, the news anchor flashed a toothpaste-ad smile. "Hello, friends, I'm Juan Moreno." Instantly, there was a scene behind him in what broadcasters call chroma key, showing a briar patch of electronic wiring. The background made the twists and turns of wire seem to wind around the anchor's shoulders.

"The American Manufacturing Association tells us that there has been an explosion of trade secret thefts in our area," John Moreno went on. "Especially concerning electronics."

"Yes, I'm sure there has been." Robert said it to the television.

". . . And especially, there are a lot of stolen secrets being sold to foreign countries," the television anchor went on. "According to the AMA, there have never been so many violations as there are now—violations of employment agreements by engineers who go to work for competitors. And when that happens, thefts of trade secrets are bound to happen too."

The scene shifted to an interview with an FBI agent who described a particular trade-secret case that the Government had just solved. The screen filled with pictures of men in pin-striped suits getting fitted with the plastic-wire tiebacks that are today's versions of handcuffs. And then it showed a series of electronic equipment parts.

"Well, Robert," Maria looked at him, "maybe there's a way that you can make something out of your case . . . the one that involves the covenant not to compete. Not with the covenant itself, but with trade secrets. Stolen ones, if there are any."

"The key to what you're saying, though, is *if there are any.*" He shook his head. "It's really rare that you can find out about stolen secrets."

He screwed his face into a frown. "And right now, I don't want to take anything on that's really difficult. Or anything that'll make me learn a whole new way of doing things. I just don't have the get-up-and-go. It's time for me to work slower and steadier."

She hesitated. "I understand. . . . The problem is, even if your competitor is stealing your trade secrets, it's hard to see that it's happening. And even if you know, it's hard to prove it. Violation of a covenant not to compete is different. It's an open thing, because everyone can see when an employee goes to work for someone else."

"Right. And a trade secret case is harder to spot. When the secret gets stolen, there aren't any alarm bells. The thief does it under cover. Without the FBI working for you, you probably wouldn't even find out about a stolen trade secret in the first place."

He screwed his face into a frown. "And right now, I don't want to take anything on that's really difficult."

"Maybe it's exactly the kind of case you need right now."

"So, should I get back to the people at Nova Aerospace? Well . . . no, because this trade secret idea isn't going to work either. It would take something new and different in the evidence department before they'd have a winning lawsuit.

"Maria, as usual, you want me to start thinking. But I don't want to think right now. I want to work slower and steadier."

She shook her head, said, "Uh-oh! Robert Herrick is thinking about whether he should start thinking?" And she laughed. But gently.

* * *

The skyscraper in Atlanta at 812 Peachtree Street looks like a box full of money, which is exactly what it is. The first seven floors are parking. The next twenty-six are wrapped in gold-colored opacity.

This is Dravos Corporation.

No one who comes to visit 812 Peachtree can enter the eighth-floor lobby without an appointment, which is always registered on the handwritten log kept by the secretary on duty. There is an anteroom maintained by armed guards, and that is where you stay until you are either cleared or sent away. Once inside, you have to travel in the custody of an escort at all times, and the escort alerts security about all movements, even from an office to the office next door.

People who have been to the home of Dravos Corporation give accounts of the guards throughout the building that make it sound like a depository full of gold. And in a way, that is a fair description. The building has one occupant, and one only. Dravos is one of the richest companies, per shareholder, in the world.

The building is in the heart of Atlanta. Known worldwide for its friendly people, southern hospitality, and welcoming openness. But these qualities do not exist at 812 Peachtree Street.

It is said that the first ten floors beyond the lobby are where inventions are born. New kinds of electronic devices, not just improving on earlier models, but new in their functions. Work goes on, now, on a military device that can detect human beings and separate their traces from animals for twenty miles in any direction. Testing is underway on a kind of airborne sonar that searches the surface for explosives. And there are a hundred other inventions in stages of development.

The top floor is management: executives and board members. Immediately below, several floors are full of administrative offices that watch the company's security, accounting, personnel services, and all of the other functions of a worldwide corporate power. And in the middle of the building, there is what Dravos euphemistically refers to as Media Services. Also called Publicity. Many people consider this the guts of the business.

This morning, the assembly room on Floor Sixteen was full. Dravos's Publicity Director walked briskly to the podium. He pointed to a floor-to-ceiling screen that said, "Dravos Corporation" in red letters, next to a logo with a gothic letter "D" in gold and blue.

"Our project today," the Director announced, "is to persuade the National Electronics Association to give its Lifetime Achievement Award, this year, to a man named deTravanian Wrenger. Our newest Vice President."

He clicked a remote, and the screen showed a picture next to the name, "deTravanian Wrenger." The photograph featured a black man with mocha-colored skin, wearing a huge pair of purple glasses with darkened, almost opaque yellow lenses, beneath a cranium that had a lump on the left side and scrawny hair on the right, all above a pointed jaw. DeTravanian Wrenger's jowls protruded into neckless shoulders, so that his face wore the appearance of a misshapen, upside-down cone. The left side of his face was decorated with a prominent plus-or-minus tattoo: "±."

The image on the screen showed the new Vice President sporting a purple lab coat that clashed with the different purple of his glasses and also clashed with the still-different purple of his big-collared shirt, which was dotted with abstract yellow spots.

"DeTravanian Wrenger was born somewhere in eastern Europe," the Director continued. "No one knows exactly where. His father was Bulgarian and his mother was from Cameroon. He was orphaned at age ten when members of the Russian Mafia killed his parents."

The Director paused and bowed his head, at that.

"But from those humble beginnings," he went on, "deTravanian Wrenger built an amazing life. He has a degree in electrical engineering from Harvard. And he has a Ph.D. from Stanford. He was a professor for a time at CalTech: the California Institute of Technology. His list of patents doesn't make for easy reading—the simplest item is a long chain of what they call amplifiers, or variations on them—but deTravanian Wrenger's inventions have been incorporated into unbelieveably many products. Smart phones, spacecraft, military equipment, medical devices, and all sorts of consumer items.

"We stole this genius away from Nova Aerospace Company. You know, a minor competitor with big pretensions and low budgets."

The Director pointed at the ± tattoo on the man's face. "Undoubtedly you've noticed this unusual mark, this plus-or-minus sign. DeTravanian Wrenger believes in adding the words plus-or-minus to everything, almost as a philosophy of life. He is fond of saying, *'Every statement you can offer is true if you add the words, "plus or minus" to it'*—and here, the Director grinned—*'including this statement by me, deTravanian Wrenger, about adding plus or minus to it.'*"

The audience slowly started spinning out the kind of weak laughter that signifies that the listener has no idea of the meaning, if any, of what he has just heard.

"And here's something of interest to all of us. Selfish interest, that is. This man has brought hundreds of millions of dollars to Dravos Corporation. When you got your bonus this past December, a big chunk of it came to you courtesy of deTravanian Wrenger."

A murmur of appreciation went up from the crowd.

"And deTravanian Wrenger has a moonlighting job. In addition to working for us, he is a professor at Emory University, right here in Atlanta. They say he is a favorite of the college students there. He teaches Physical Chemistry, which most of us don't know much about. But he knows a lot about it."

The Director grinned. "You all have information packages that were stacked into your laptops this morning. So, let's give a big Dravos Corporation effort to our task for today, which is to bring home that Lifetime Achievement Award for this great man.

"How are we going to do it? By contacting everyone who is anybody in this business. Here is the plan. . . ."

Twenty minutes later, the Sixteenth Floor emptied, and a gaggle of eager Dravos publicity specialists went to work.

* * *

Back at Robert Herrick's office, rain slammed against the floor-to-ceiling windows. The green of the bayou was barely visible. "Okay." Robert grinned at Tom Kennedy. "What are the cases like, that our referring lawyers want to send us? What kind of difficulties do they want to get us into?"

Donna deCarlo's voice on the intercom interrupted the response. "Robert, you're not going to like this. Your old friend Jimmy Coleman is calling." His longtime secretary had to stifle a laugh.

So did Tom Kennedy. "This lousy weather is a bad omen, and it's coming true."

Robert frowned and picked up the receiver. "Hello, Jimmy. I've got Tom Kennedy here with me and I'm putting on the speaker."

"Herrick, I heard a long-range rumor." As usual, Jimmy's voice grated like a bulldozer. "I heard you were taking on a lawsuit against my good client, Dravos Corporation. Bad idea, if it's true."

Robert could picture Jimmy on the other end of the line, sitting in his corner office in front of a priceless intarsiato Italian chest from the sixteenth century. Jimmy would have a baby blue or tan suit stretched across his flabby stomach. His eyes, usually so pale and dead that witnesses looked away when Jimmy cross-examined them, would be narrow slits. Jimmy Coleman carried a map of his life on his face, with burst blood vessels turning his nose red and mottled wrinkles splitting his temples from his nose.

"Well, Jimmy, I can't tell you very much. I have client confidences to protect about that."

"I'll take that as a Yes." Jimmy sounded like hailstones on concrete. "The talk on the street is true, and you're working up a lawsuit. But let me do you a favor. Let me tell you why getting into a war with Dravos would be a terrible idea for you."

Jimmy Coleman had been Robert's opponent in too many bitter lawsuits. He was a big name at the mega-firm of Booker and Bayne, where an army of associates could find precedent for groundless attacks, withholding of documents during discovery, and technical defects in almost anything.

"All right. Tell me." There usually was a strategic advantage in hearing as much as possible about the adversary's claims, by paying attention to simple intelligence through listening—as long as awareness of the source and the likelihood of exaggeration could be kept in mind. Besides, he thought, I don't want that lawsuit against Dravos anyway. Or anything too difficult.

"The covenant not to compete that you've got isn't worth a spit in the river. A claim based on that piece of garbage would be so obviously bogus that it would get you sanctioned with a big-ass fine. We'd see to it, for sure. And deTravanian Wrenger is a fine scientist. He's a finalist for the most prestigious honor of his profession, the Lifetime Achievement Award. Going after him would just get your clients buried."

"Jimmy, you've always got the talking part of the game down pat. As it happens, we're familiar with covenant-not-to-compete lawsuits in our shop. But I appreciate the call."

"Any time, Herrick. If you want a solid ass-kicking, you know how to get it, just by filing that lawsuit. Have a nice day." The sound on the telephone clicked into a dial tone.

Kennedy spoke first. "Well, everyone knows Jimmy Coleman comes from a background as a street fighter." And it was true; this caller had grown up as a gang member in Los Angeles. No one knew how such a primitive teenager had gotten into law school at UCLA, much less excelled there, and gone on to become a legendary figure in one of the biggest firms in the country.

Jimmy was the head of litigation at Booker and Bayne. The firm had been founded by Colonel Henry Anderson Booker in the 1800's. It was credited for building the city that grew around them. Now, the firm represented American Holdings, the Spinelli Corporation, and a hundred other billion-dollar companies, not to mention Dravos. And the lawyers still cherished Colonel Booker's motto: "Find out what the client wants and go get it for him."

The heir to the Colonel's reputation was Jimmy Coleman.

Robert smiled. "Well, at least we know that if there ever is a lawsuit against Dravos Corporation, there's something there that's important enough, and vulnerable enough, for them to send the big dog out beforehand to protect whatever it is."

"Sounds like a good lawsuit." Tom Kennedy grinned. "Unless you want to lay down and die, Robert."

"I just don't think we ought to take on that big a loser." Robert was beginning to show a little annoyance at Tom's insistence on needling him.

5

"Y"ou forgot my birthday, Robert."

"What?"

"Again. You forgot my birthday again."

"I . . . forgot your birthday?"

"Yes. Unbelievable as it may seem. Only it's not unbelievable, seeing as how this is, like, the third straight time."

"Maria, I thought it was tomorrow."

"No. And that was what you said last year."

"I . . . well, I throw myself on your mercy."

"That doesn't work in this case."

"I'll take off tomorrow and look all day. Or rather, I'll go out right now and get you something that I can hope you'll like."

"Robert, it's seven o'clock. Unless you're going to get this fabulous present you're dreaming about at the grocery store, it's probably not a prospect."

"Ahhhhhhhhhhh . . . okay."

"Tomorrow."

"Tomorrow. . . . I, I, I am so sorry."

She started laughing at him. "Robert, you have all those people who work for you, including Donna deCarlo, who schedules everything for you. Why can't Donna keep you in shape with stuff like this? I mean, unimportant things like your wife's birthday?"

"I just . . . I don't think that's part of her job. She has plenty to do. She doesn't just schedule things. She does a lot more. I don't think it's right to use an employee for my things that are not business."

"She scheduled that dinner with Max Lawson last week. I know, because I talked to her about it when you couldn't remember where it was going to be."

"Well, but that was business. Max is a referring lawyer. You know that. He sends us lots of business. Clients who come out of his commercial practice."

Now, she was laughing at him again. "So, all I've got to do is become a referring lawyer. Come to think of it, I am one. My friends have gotten in touch with you about several cases that your junior lawyers have taken on."

"Well, but. . . ."

"So, how about it? Donna deCarlo, I mean."

"All right. You're right, of course. I will tell Donna to calendar your birthday and to make me plan about it ten days before that." He hesitated. "And our anniversary, same thing."

"You realize that in spite of not having a personal secretary at the D.A.'s office, where I happen to work, I manage to keep track of these kinds of dates all by my lonesome self?"

And now he was laughing too. "Yes. I know. You're amazing. I'll tell you what. I'll get a reservation at Brennan's tomorrow night. After I hit all the stores."

"Brennan's? But you know we have to meet Max Lawson tomorrow night for dinner, don't you?"

"You're kidding. I must have forgotten."

"Yes."

He paused. "Yes . . . yes, meaning what?"

"Yes, I was kidding. There's nothing with Max Lawson. You can take me to Brennan's tomorrow night. We'll reschedule my birthday. You don't even have to tell Donna deCarlo it's rescheduled. Except, you'd better, because you need to make a reservation. Or rather, I'll call her because I can't trust you."

"After this conversation, I've got it pretty firm in my mind. I'll call Donna."

She stuck both arms up like a cheerleader. "All-l-l right!"

"I love you, my Maria."

"I love you too, but only because you're a lot better in bed than you are with birthdays."

* * *

The appellate section of the D.A.'s office featured the same worn blue carpet that covered the whole building. A secretarial desk faced the elevator, occupied by one of the section's most colorful personnel.

"Maria, these pictures. . . . I mean, these pictures. . . . Maria, you've got to get this motherfucker off the face of this natural world."

Wendy Bachman was known as "the cussing Mormon." She sat at the secretarial desk that faced the world, or so much of the world as ever walked into an appellate lawyer's office. At five feet zero, with blonde hair and blue eyes, Wendy looked impossibly young. She had a large print Bible and the Book of Mormon sitting to her right. And she earned her nickname by using a lot of four-letter words.

"I know," Maria answered. "The crime scene photographs in this case are pretty bad. Not the worst we've seen, but pretty bad. That's Billy Joe Armistead. He's the defendant."

"What the hell was this Billy Joe Armistead thinking?"

"How mad he was at his girlfriend. That's why this picture is out in the woods and shows this muddy hole with the bodies inside."

"Look at this little yellow dress on the little girl. Why is she in there?"

"The fight they had was about him abusing the little girl. He killed the mother with the closest object, which happened to be a table lamp, and then he wrapped her up with a rug."

"With the baby wrapped inside too? And then, this maggot Billy Joe, he takes them both out in the woods and throws the mom in the dirt, and the baby on top of her, before closing the grave?"

"Yes."

"Was the baby still alive?"

"The medical examiner thinks so. It's hard to be sure because the bodies are so badly decomposed. I mean, you look for dirt in the lungs, but it's hard to make that diagnosis when the lungs are half gone."

"Motherfucka. . . . Agh-h-h-! I bet the jury didn't take a long time in the sentencing hearing, before sentencing this bastard to death."

"Actually, they did. The defense lawyers put on evidence about how Billy Joe Armistead was abused as a kid. They put on character witnesses, if you can believe that, about how he was a good worker."

"And they probably showed the jury a picture of that gurney that they're gonna strap this piece of crap down on."

"I don't remember. Sometimes the defense lawyers do that, because the picture they use is disconcerting. The gurney looks like a cross, with the arms stuck out where they strap the prisoner's arms down and insert the intravenous tube. That picture has very little to do with anything, but it comes into evidence, and it works."

"And the weak-kneed jurors who don't give a damn about murder victims get creeped out by the picture of that gurney that looks like a cross."

"Yes."

Wendy put the pictures back in the file. She shivered.

Then: "Well, on another subject, how's . . . your wonderful guy Robert doing?"

"He's wonderful. And. . . ."

"And?"

"And he forgot my birthday again." Maria laughed and shook her head.

"He's a motherfucka too." Now, Wendy laughed.

"Wendy, where'd you get a mouth that talks like that?"

"Well, Maria, it's literally true. You're a mother, aren't you?"

Both Wendy and Maria laughed again, but in the back of Maria's mind was the thought that Wendy Bachman was getting to be a little too much.

* * *

Across town, Robert Herrick sat behind his long mahogany desk. There was soft rain on the greenhouse-style windows. It made the grassy banks of the bayou look fuzzy. The cars that you knew were there weren't visible on the maze of freeways down below, and only a moving blur could be seen.

He was trying to work, studying motions after verdict in the *Creuzot* case: a crane accident trial that had returned a big-but-barely-big-enough damage award. But instead of concentrating on the defendants' efforts to get a windfall escape from their defeat at the hands of the jury, he kept returning to thoughts about Maria. And once again, he wondered about Maria, the way he had so many times before.

We are so different, he reminded himself. For the hundredth time.

She has little soft stuffed animals everywhere. They drive me crazy.

She's a conservative Republican, and I'm a pragmatic middle-of-the-road Democrat, just like everyone ought to be.

She plays pranks on me. I hate it. She has friends in gangsta rap bands. I'd like to put them all in jail. She thinks I'm messy and I think she's a member of the excessive-neatness police. She likes the mountains—for skiing, no less—and I've had enough of snow as a kid to last me all of my life.

She likes to argue with me, and it makes me miserable. If she doesn't like something, she stamps her foot, and it's very effective. She would spend money like water if she could. She has more than a hundred pairs of shoes. I grew up with a single mom and I don't want to spend anything we don't have to.

She's punctual even when it doesn't matter. The only time I'm on time is when it really, really matters. In fact, I try to be the last one to get to every meeting, because then, everyone else spends the time waiting, wasting the time that is the lawyer's stock in trade, instead of me. It's an old lawyer trick, but she berates me for it.

She wants to watch the Hallmark Channel. Sappy, silly movies where girl hates boy at first, but she gradually changes her mind, and they live happily ever after. I would watch CNN instead, unless there's baseball or football on. At least there's some action there.

And right now, all the time, she's telling me I need to find myself. To get back to work. To find the fire in the belly once more. To take on some big cases with a little risk.

And I don't want to. I don't have to. I've accomplished a lot, including this big, wonderful law firm, and I ought to coast for a while. She tells me if I coast for a while, I'm going to coast forever.

Almost unconsciously, he pulled out the newspaper clipping that pictured Maria. She was in her costume as a showgirl in Las Vegas, which was how she had worked before going to law school. There she was, in her skimpy blue bodice, her blue shorts, her blue boots with stiletto heels, and lots of blue feathers. One more time, he read the caption: "The Showgirl Who Turned Prosecutor: Beautiful Maria Melendes."

He teased her about it sometimes. She always took it the right way. "No, Robert, it was a family show. Not that a guy like you would understand the difference."

And she really was beautiful, just as the caption said.

He thought: I can ask her advice on any case and get a useful answer. We always have a good time together, no matter what we do. Even watching the Hallmark Channel. She spends a lot on clothes, but they look good on her. I'm used to the stuffed animals, the pranks, and having to be on time. What the heck. I'm used to her. I'm stuck to her. I depend on her. I love her. She's loyal and hardworking and good to me.

And I've got to get back to these motions in the *Creuzot* case. A burst of wind slammed the windows as if to remind him.

But I'm not going to take on a lot of hard-to-win, pointless cases just to prove that I'm still a lawyer. I'm going to work steadier and slower.

I'm going to get to see my guys tonight. My homies. Guys I know almost too well. It's about time for that. My Viet Nam group.

* * *

Freddy Simkins lifted a bottle of Dos Equis and frowned. "Our guys was always talkin about fraggin the lieutenant. He was a jerk. Nobody ever got around to doin it, but the amount they talked it up was scary, 'cause there's always one or two off-brand types who might just get the lieutenant killed if everybody's encouraging it."

The Legends of Viet Nam met at the Stag's Head Tavern on the second Tuesday of every month. They knew calling themselves "Legends" was a little over the top, but it was fun.

Freddy was a perennial talker. That was the idea. These Viet Nam vets would understand, and you could leave the Stag's Head feeling a little less like you were still fighting the same battle.

"I was steering one of those swift boats." Dave Brznsky was tucking into a dark Modelo. "We had a whole different way of thinking. Nothing about fragging anybody."

"Fraggin, you roll a little tiny grenade under the guy's tent you don't like. Maybe, like our lieutenant. He was a jerk. And it was scary how much some guys talked about it."

"There was a lot more talk about fragging than action." Dan Sabich hugged a Corona. "The newspapers loved it. I guess it happened, maybe, somewhere. But it was the image of Viet Nam everywhere. That was what was scary, the misinformation."

"Viet Nam was scary like what they say is scary about being a police officer." Robert spoke up. "It was days of boredom punctuated by minutes of sheer terror."

"It was scary most a the time," Freddy insisted. "Because there's always guys who are crazy, and some of them, it's unfortunate they're armed. But it was just more scarier, some a the time."

"Scariest I saw, we were coming into a clearing in this gap between two ridges." Robert's eyes clouded. "A clearing—that's scary, yes, because the bad guys can see you, but you can't see them. Our point guy was called Cincinnati, a tough little guy, and he dives all of a sudden into the weeds and rocks because he heard something. Second guy gets hit. His face is all red and partly missing. Your ears got flattened from the noise of automatic fire, but you couldn't see the Cong at all because they're hiding behind pieces of jungle."

"But you got out," Freddy said.

"We called air cover, and here comes a Douglas B-66 Destroyer. In just a few minutes . . . , but it seemed like hours. They bomb the trees and bushes. There's a lot of orange fire and stuff cracking apart."

Freddy nodded. "That's the scariest part, callin for air cover."

"Yes, indeed. I'm at the back, hoping I got the coordinates right. Hoping they don't dump all that ordnance on us instead, by mistake. The thought tightens up your bowel just a little bit."

"Good thing, a tight bowel." Freddy grinned. "'Cause if some a the guys around this table didn't keep tight bowels theirselves, there wouldn't be too much a them left."

There was laughter and a lot of beer going down. "Now that's scary," Dave said, "but absolutely correct."

"Yeah, we got out." Robert lifted his own Corona. "Copters came right after the air cover. And it amazed me, but the guy with the injury to his face survived and nearly looked normal."

Freddy's voice took on a philosophical tone. "After comin back from Nam, nothin is normal, even if nothing is near as scary. Except maybe livin through life itself, livin with your ownself."

Suddenly, Robert realized he was thinking about the lawsuit he'd just turned down. Instead, I could have signed it up.

That would have been scary. But maybe not so, so scary. A for-real kind of scary was, like, that clearing between the ridges just south of the DMZ.

6

"When you pour coffee into a cup, does the cup get colder? Or hotter?"

Professor deTravanian Wrenger illustrated his point by filling a steaming cup, and then he lifted it high above the laboratory table in the lecture hall like a slapstick actor. "Ouch! Suddenly, this cup is too hot to hold!"

The students laughed. A good professor is a good comedian some of the time.

"Obviously, what happens is that the cup gets hotter." The man with the mocha-colored skin beamed, and the lumpy head with the plus-or-minus tattoo nodded vigorously. "And that's what we're going to study today."

He looked out at the huge lecture hall and its two hundred students. Here at Emory University, deTravanian Wrenger's Physical Chemistry course was filled, and a waiting list of students was fenced out. This professor had a following because of his sense of humor and his demonstrations. He could make abstract concepts easy.

"We all know that the coffee cup gets hotter, but it's not easy to explain why, scientifically. It involves something called *"The Second Law of Heat Transfer."*

He punched a button to show a PowerPoint slide that contained the words: *"The Second Law. Heat flows from a hot body into a cold one, and not vice versa."*

"Remember, my friends: Last class, we studied the First Law of Heat Transfer. The First Law is easy. Energy is conserved. The same amount of energy that you put into an experiment comes out of it. It may change its form, from potential energy in your car's gasoline to kinetic energy when the car moves forward, but the total energy stays the same. That's the First Law."

The professor waved his arms. "But the First Law doesn't explain why the coffee makes the cup hotter. The energy stays the same, yes. But why doesn't heat from the colder cup flow into the hot coffee, so that the cup would get colder and the coffee would get hotter?" He grinned. "We all know that's not what happens. But *why?*"

He waved his arms again. "Because of the Second Law!"

He changed the PowerPoint so that it had one word, in big print: "*WHY?*" And the next slide said, "*Because of the Second Law!*" And two seconds later, he changed the message again, to say: "*There's a concept called ENTROPY!!*"

The man with the strange tattoo pointed at the screen. "Here's a new word. 'Entropy.' The entropy of the cup of coffee increases. Entropy. Entropy is a measure of dispersal, disorganization, scattering. It's really undefinable, but those words are the best we can do to call up a mental image. Instead of just the coffee having its substance heated up and moving around more, it's the substance of the entire thing, the cup and the coffee, with the heat dispersed."

The PowerPoint changed. "*Energy is constant. But Entropy is always increasing.*"

The Professor turned to face his crowd of students. And he grinned again. "The Second Law says that the entropy, or disorganization, always increases whenever anything happens anywhere in the universe. And that is what we are going to study today. We're going to get to the bottom of this mystery of the coffee cup. By understanding the role of entropy, the Second Law, and the reason why the coffee cup gets hotter."

* * *

"These are the balloons we'll use to recover the Iranian missile." Admiral Ellison stood on the foredeck of the salvage ship *John Lethbridge*.

"We were lucky with the splashdown," he added. "I mean, the location where the first stage of the *Kharramshar* hit the water. We're near there now, ninety nautical miles south-southeast of the Gulf of Oman. The reason we're lucky is that this is shallow water. The first stage is on a continental shelf, and it's at a depth where divers can get to the missile."

He pointed to boxes holding floppy orange objects. "These balloons give us a simple way to float it up. Now, please look at the monitor. There's the missile, there."

He stretched out his arm. "This first stage must have come down nearly vertically, with the tail end first, because that's the heaviest part." The admiral pointed, again, at the image.

"Of course, this is only part of the mission. Then, we'll go after the second stage, and that will be a little harder, because it's in deeper water, out off the shelf and in the Arabian Sea."

Admiral Ellison pointed upward at the crane, which looked oversized for the ship. "The hardest part of all of this is that we want to keep our mission as secret as possible. And so as soon as the balloons are attached, our operations will all take place at night."

He grinned. "And it's just one step in trying to keep the Iranians from realizing their dream of a nuclear holocaust."

* * *

Every Tuesday night, Robert's clan gathered. The whole family. Even if he was in trial—or at least, he tried to do it even then.

He sat at the head of the table. Maria was to his left. Next to her, his daughter Pepper, whose given name was Cynthia but who was always called Pepper, by her insistence. Robert's mother, Rosalie, sat at the end of the table. On the other side, there was Pepper's husband, Jonathan, then Robert's grandson, Robert III or Little Robert, and Robert's son, also Robert, but called Robby to minimize confusion. But the names still left plenty of room for that.

"I learned how to do this when I was a cook in the army," Robert explained. "I can cook for a big group. Even something like *truite aux amandes*, the fish we're having tonight. Trout with almonds.

"I liked being a cook. It's safer. Later I was a platoon leader doing search-and-destroy missions." And everyone laughed.

"But I heard you're giving up on practicing law," said Rosalie in an accusing voice.

"Not giving it up. Just slowing down, I guess."

"Don't you do that without having something else just as demanding, to keep you busy. I'll never forget when your daddy retired. It almost killed the man, until he went back to work."

He smiled. "Yes, mama."

"And don't let me see you slacking off with your kids. I remember that soccer game where Robby did something good, and I never understood what it was, but I saw you run out and put him on your shoulders in the middle of the game. You've got to keep doing that."

He laughed, a little embarrassed. "Yes, mama."

"For instance, does Robert III play soccer? Little Robert?"

Robert looked over at Jonathan, who played football. "I don't know. Does he?"

"Well, see, that's what I mean. Be there with Little Robert too. You should know about him."

"Yes, mama." Sometimes she was like this: one shortcoming of his after the next, all unconnected. He laughed, because she was going to do the same thing all the way through dinner. He felt the way he sometimes did in court.

*   *   *

The twelfth floor at Dravos headquarters was even harder to get to than the rest of the building. It literally had bars across the hallway that led in from the elevator. "Secret clearance or above required," announced a yellow-and-black bordered sign. At the barred gate, an armed guard was stationed, wearing a dark gray uniform.

A light-skinned black man with a conical head, a short neck, and a "$\pm$" mark on his face stood talking to his laboratory assistant. "So, here's what I think, Romaine. I think the key to fewer failures in missile tests is a better feedback loop. The one we developed back at Nova Aerospace was good. It's a model. But here at Dravos, we can make a better one."

Romaine Cramshak looked at him. "Which device from Nova? Rollover? The microprocessor for the turn?"

"Rollover, but not only that. Feedback about the exact coordinates of rollover, yes—in all directions. Roll, pitch and yaw. But more than that, feedback about deviation from the ideal and more immediate instructions to propulsion and orientation to correct discrepancies."

"Which we will supply . . . how?"

"Miniaturization, Romaine. Some of the subroutines in the microcomputer are stock wiring. Off the shelf, so to speak. We'll need to take all those flowcharts and tighten them. And find places for fewer subroutines."

DeTravanian Wrenger preferred old-fashioned flowcharts, stacked and rolled, rather than computer images of his devices. The black laboratory table was spread with them now: long, wide paper, curling about its edges. Every sheet bristled with schematic diagrams that looked like overviews of city streets, compressed and crowded into hundreds of tiny communities.

"Here's one routine that we can cut down significantly." He tapped the paper. "Lots of pathways that don't take us anywhere helpful."

"And the diagram for this one has a different kind of marking and coloration," said the lab assistant. "So do some of the ones nearby. Why is this stuff different?"

"That's not important. Just treat it just like the other ones."

"Sorry."

"As I say, it ought to be possible to shorten this circuit layer by one-fourth, more or less. Plus or minus. Let's get to work."

* * *

"The Pentagon thinks the Chinese are still supplying missile parts to North Korea." The Chief of Staff took his horn-rimmed glasses off and looked straight at the big desk in the Oval Office.

"Well, that really isn't news, is it?" The President flashed his trademark grin, and his loose left hand raked his gray-speckled red hair. "When I met last with President Xi there in Beijing, he gave me a lot of promises, but all of them were said in sentences long enough to conceal a thousand Chinese alibis."

"No, it's not really news. Of course the Chinese did that." The Chief of Staff shook his head and loosened his tie. "But the Chinese trade with NoKo is becoming a big problem. And NoKo is sending stuff to Iran."

"Why any more so than usual?"

"They're essential parts, these electronic systems that the Chinese are supplying. They range from relatively simple timing devices to rollover programs. These rollover contraptions, that's an important component. And now Iran has the NoKo do-hickeys too. Some of the failures come from bad rollovers."

"I know." The President displayed that grin again, the smile that had helped get him elected, and his blue eyes crinkled. "That's what happens with our space program too."

"Even if the failure is a long way downrange, it can be precipitated by something hinky about the rollover."

"I know." The President loosened his tie, too, almost as though the Chief of Staff's action had suggested it. "And again, it happens with our space program too."

"Well, one of the best ways to put the uglatz on NoKo's missile program would be to find a way to stop this Chinese trade. And it'll also stop the Iranians."

"Tell me how. That's the real issue."

The Chief of Staff sighed. Loudly. He stood in the middle of the great seal centered in the carpet. "I know. Hard to do. It comes down to the usual kinds of proposals. Cut back more on Chinese trade. Find an excuse to do it. Garments, electronics, appliances, and all kind of other things, which get imported to every American port, from New York to San Francisco and from Los Angeles to Houston."

"We've been through this." The President shook his head, and his collar shifted under his blue suit. "Point one, we've already tried putting tariffs on everything we can. We've already had a trade war. If we expanded it, the Chinese would expand their tariffs too. They'd cut back on buying our computers and cars. We'd have major losses in those economic sectors and a civil war from the National Association of Manufacturers."

"Right. Unless we could find evidence of the Chinese dumping their products. Their pants and shirts and sneakers and TV's. Meaning, subsidizing them. We can almost always find evidence of that, if we look."

Silence. Then, the President looked up.

"So, we'd say we were doing it for one reason, even though we're doing it for another reason. But at the same time, we'd need to communicate to the Chinese why we were really doing it. That is, we'd need to let the Chinese know why, behind the scenes. We'd say something like, 'We're shocked—shocked!—to find out that there is dumping of Chinese goods going on.' And we'd say, 'We might be able to overlook it, or at least a little bit of it, if we could be certain that Chinese electronics would no longer find their way into North Korean and Iranian missiles.'"

"Trouble with that is, the Chinese can't even know for sure what all its sales to NoKo are. So, some obscure shop in Shanghai sends a fuel control to NoKo? President Xi wouldn't know it was happening. We wouldn't know about our own domestic companies doing that kind of thing, and neither can the Chinese."

"And for that same reason, if obscure Chinese companies continue selling end-of-the-world missile parts to the North Koreans without Xi's knowledge, we here in the good old USA wouldn't know it was happening, either."

"So, Mr. President, what do we do?"

"Ahhh—that's why I got myself elected to this powerless office, isn't it?" The President looked down at the desk. "We can't get a real agreement with the Chinese without shooting ourselves in the foot, because we'd set off a whole new trade war and hurt our own economy even worse than we already have. And that's only the beginning of the problem, because even if we got a real agreement, the Chinese couldn't live up to it. And it gets worse. If the Chinese didn't live up to what they'd agreed, we wouldn't know that they weren't living up to it."

"Yes. It's a problem, yes."

"Well, there is only one play in football that routinely goes for forty-plus yards, and that is the punt. Sometimes it's the right thing to do. We'd better punt. We'll wait for a better time to act."

"And that means. . . ."

"Yes. It means that we watch the North Koreans and Iranians working invisibly to get ready for building missiles once again. And ratcheting up the danger of destroying the world."

The President looked down at the desk again. "Well. . . . Call in the trade representative. Tell him we need ideas to put more tariffs on Chinese goods with the least amount of damage. And tell him to keep his mouth shut about the fact we're asking him this."

He paused. "In other words, all we probably can do is . . . next to nothing.

7

The Federal Bureau of Investigation's training ground is in Quantico, Virginia. Near there, the FBI concentrates its forensic laboratories. This is where you can find experts on everything from bullet fragments to DNA, from soil identification to voiceprinting, and from computer code to the putrefaction of dead bodies.

At the moment, this facility of the world's greatest law enforcement agency was concentrating its efforts on tiny sections of printed circuitry, chips, and connectors, all taken from the recovered *Kharramshar* missile.

The first stop had been at NASA's Thermochemical Test Facility in Houston. This cavernous building is capable of mimicking both the solar heat and the intense cold of deep space. For the Iranian missile, Thermochemical had been used essentially as a warehouse, set aside for examination of the *Kharramshar* wreckage: the two stages that the Navy had pulled out of the sea. The broken pieces of the first stage had been arranged in a straight line, followed by chunks of the second. Here and there, the steel shell gaped open, showing tubes, coils, and containers underneath. A major area of the first stage had been pulled back for study, as though split by a can opener. Photographs surrounded the gleaming metal, showing its earlier form and detailing the pieces that the analytic team had removed.

Now, at Quantico, the electronic contents of the first stage were laid out on a series of examination tables, with microscopes and probes nearby. Chains of printed circuits with chips, stitched together by connecting wires, dotted the table surfaces. Labeled signs signaled where each piece of electronics had come from.

A colonel in uniform stood next to a tall, gawky civilian in a white coat. "This assembly, taken out of the first stage, is what we would call the 'O-A-M-S of the *Kharramshar*,'" he explained. "It's formally known as the 'Orbital Attitude and Maneuvering System,' and we call it by one syllable: *OAMS*." The colonel pronounced it "*Ohms*." "It's the guidance system of the missile, and these electronics are its brain."

"Right," agreed his civilian counterpart. "And this section of it, I guess, is the assembly that does the rollover. The shift in direction soon after the missile lifts off."

"Possibly." The colonel pointed. "The out-wires correspond to the twelve maneuvering rockets on the sides of the craft. Are there twelve?"

"Sixteen, I think. It's a modified design, with more guidance rockets. For a bigger missile. But yes, I think these wires fire the guidance or maneuvering rockets. These maneuvering rockets are little ones, not for propulsion. They don't shoot the missile up into space. They just steer the missile. That's why it's called the 'Orbital Attitude and Maneuvering System.' Or *OAMS*, for short, because it controls the attitude, or orientation of the missile, and maneuvers it. America's aerospace industry likes to reduce everything to initials."

"And I'm guessing that each of the sixteen little guidance rockets has a quick ignition system. It has to ignite instantaneously, so that these microprocessors can tell the guidance system to shoot very short, timed pulses."

"And you know what? That part of the assembly looks awful damn familiar."

"Probably came from China."

"By way of North Korea. . . . Great. China to North Korea to Iran. All the wonderful civilizations of the globe."

"But I'm thinking . . . , it's probably a universal kind of design. It's a little bit like the rollover components in our systems."

"Well, yes, it would have to be. Wouldn't the firing of the guidance rockets be dictated by physical principles that are the same all over the globe?"

"Yes, I guess so. And that's why this rollover mechanism looks like the rollover used on Atlas missiles? From right here in the good old USA?"

The colonel laughed. "And so an Iranian-Korean-Chinese contraption would have an OAMS a whole lot like what we'd have, right here in America?"

"Look at these two flowcharts. And the out-wires that connect them. And this other pair, here."

"You're saying it's . . . like Atlas."

"Like Atlas. It looks a little bit like what you'd see on an Atlas missile from the good old USA."

"But this particular OAMS flow chart isn't quite like what you'd find on an Atlas missile."

"There are stylistic differences. Chinese chips. But there have to be similarities."

"I was sort of hoping you'd say that the Chinese must have stolen military secrets of the first order from us in America. And sold the plans for the Atlas to the North Koreans, or to the Iranians."

Both men laughed, the colonel and the civilian contractor.

"The Chinese . . . stole our Atlas designs and sold them to our bosom buddies, the Iranians?"

"Well, who designed the USA components? Let's get them to look at it. Maybe they'd get some help with designing new stuff by studying this one."

"Or maybe, in our imaginations, they can help us catch some slanty-eyed thieves." And they both laughed again. "Anyway, it was Nova Aerospace Company. Let's contact them."

*   *   *

"I got a call from those guys at that Nova Aerospace Company," Tom Kennedy said. "You know, the president is that guy named Mike Martin."

At that, Robert Herrick looked away momentarily from his partner, toward the window. Fog in heavy waves floated just outside the floor-to-ceiling glass. The green banks along Buffalo Bayou were barely visible today, and they couldn't be seen any farther than a few blocks away. Beneath Robert's big desk, the multicolored carpet still shone brightly.

"Those gentlemen are pretty persistent." Robert shook his head. "Mr. Martin thinks this former employee of theirs, deTravanian Wrenger, is violating their agreement by helping a competitor. They're right in a moral sense, but the law doesn't support the kind of claim they want to bring."

"I know. But they seem to think that things have changed."

"How so?"

"The FBI has come to them, to Nova Aerospace, with components recovered from an Iranian rocket. The design of the rollover microprocessor looks real familiar to them."

"Familiar? An Iranian rocket? What does 'familiar' mean?"

"That's just the problem. The electronics in these components have got to be pretty similar, because they perform similar functions. It's inevitable, even if no ideas get stolen. But the president, Martin, just talks right over that point when you raise it with him. He says that yes, functions are similar, right, and yada yada yada, but . . . the similarities of in this Iranian rocket and their own design aren't functional.

"In other words, he thinks the design would be different from this Iranian rocket, if the Iranians were designing a new system on their own. The details are too similar, he keeps saying. It's the details. They're too similar. He keeps talking about the flowchart and the loops that go through the same steps. He thinks the design is one of theirs, from Nova Aerospace. And he's convinced it got stolen."

"Loops?"

"Apparently, these things have what they call loops that form repeated calculations, containing decision points that depend on the numbers. And the hardware is different, because the Iranians use Chinese chips, but this Mr. Martin says that the decision loops are too much in the same places for the device to be anything but copied,"

"Okay. It still doesn't sound like a very good lawsuit to me, especially against the Iranians. How would we get a judgment against those good folks, over there in Iran? And if we got a judgment from the local ayatollah, how on earth would we enforce it?"

"I know. I told him you'd say that. But they want to meet with you. They say they think they can trace the parts. They'll bring diagrams and stuff."

"Diagrams? Great. What are we going to do with electronic wiring diagrams?"

"Yeah, I guess we won't understand the diagrams very well. They call them flowcharts. But these guys are insistent. And you know. . . . Well, couldn't electronic designs get stolen? I realize that these Nova guys are eager beavers, but maybe they're right."

"I just don't . . . want to do it."

"Can't hurt to listen. Might be something that would be good for us. Even for you."

He turned toward the window again. "Well, okay, Tom. Tell them to come on in. As long as there's even a far off possibility of something as dangerous as this, something like Iranians stealing plans for an American guided missile, we probably ought to listen."

Robert shook his head and laughed. "Nowadays, even my mama is after me and warning me against retiring or even slowing down. And so are you, Tom."

Suddenly, the intercom broke the silence with a too-loud, too-shrill, grating ring. Robert almost jumped as he flipped the switch.

Donna deCarlo's voice came into the room. "Robert, Maria is calling. Your lovely wife. And you'd better take this, no matter how busy you are. What she says is very simple. She says, 'Tell him it's Pepper again." That's what she said: "It's Pepper again. Your daughter."

"Go ahead, Robert." Tom Kennedy was familiar with the problems created by the Herrick daughter. "I'll go back to work. I hope it'll turn out to be better than it sounds.

*　　*　　*

Robert picked up the telephone, with his voice full of dread. "Maria? What's . . . what's going on?"

"It's Pepper. Your daughter. The one you always have to worry about. She's been arrested again."

"Not for drunk driving . . . ?" He groaned. "This will make the fourth time, and the last time—what was it? Two weeks in jail?"

"Something like that. But not drunk driving this time. Drunk in public—that's the charge."

"What kind of crime is that—'drunk in public?'"

"Well, there's good news and bad news. The good news is that there's no jail sentence that goes with it, usually. The bad news is that to be drunk in public, you have to be a lot more drunk than would qualify you for drunk driving. For drunk in public, you have to be so dead drunk that you become dangerous just by walking around."

"I'm . . . I'm just trying to understand. I'll leave the criminal law stuff to the criminal lawyer, namely you."

"Well, apparently she was pretty dangerous, in fact. She went to a McDonalds, and she got into an argument with the burger flippers over what she ordered, and she went behind the counters and was yelling all kinds of stuff about how it wasn't edible and might be poisonous. And when the police came, she yelled at them too. It sounds like she may have assaulted the officers in some minor way, you know, elbowing them and pushing, but these officers were sensible enough to realize that she was just drunk."

"They didn't charge her with resisting or whatever, you mean?"

"Aggravated assault on a police officer? No."

"Where is she?"

"In the city jail. Not yet transferred to the county."

"But you said there's no jail time for this, right?"

"Right. But if you're drunk in public, usually you do get arrested, and you get held until you're sober enough."

"All right. I'll head down there to the city lockup. Fortunately, because of Pepper, I'm familiar with where it is and how to pick her up."

8

DeTravanian Wrenger moved the computer mouse to draw a purple-colored electronic component marked "Do Loop" in place on a big schematic diagram containing the flowchart. He handed the finished product to his laboratory assistant. "Okay. That means that this part of that airborne laser assembly is basically done. I'm out of here."

He turned back for an instant and looked at his assistant. "You know, I'm glad we're here at Dravos. I was sick and tired of that Nova crowd. President had a running feud with me and threatened to fire me. Always criticizing what I did, who I met with, what I said about the company."

"Is that right?"

"I'd like to see them go out of business."

He punched his code at the hallway cage and called the elevator. It took him to the first floor, where he stepped out beside his purple Mercedes M-Class. The sign over his parking space was painted with a sign saying, "Reserved for Vice President DeTravanian Wrenger. Others Will Be Towed."

He turned on the pre-game show. "Our Atlanta Falcons are decimated by injuries as they take on a healthy Pittsburgh team tonight," said the voiceover. At that, the man with the "+" tattoo and the big purple glasses showed his badge to the two security guards who constantly watched the exit and eased his hundred thousand dollars' worth of automobile down the ramp.

He hadn't noticed the road crew across the street. If he had noticed, he might have seen that the workmen's clothes were not what anyone would wear to repair asphalt: spotless shirts tucked into smooth pants with creases. He might have seen that their tools were silent and that they weren't doing any work at all.

Suddenly, the workmen hoisted M-16's as if doing it together in response to a signal. The chattering sound that followed let the world know that their assault weapons had been illegally modified to fully automatic.

DeTravanian Wrenger's Mercedes floated forward through the cloud of bullets. The crashing sound of glass breaking mixed with the harder sound of bullets passing through the metal door frames. The big purple car glided over the grass curtilage and scraped into the side of the Dravos building, with a loud crash. The man himself flopped upward and back like a rag doll.

It took the security guards a second or two to comprehend what was happening. Then, they both pulled Glock handguns from their holsters and fired more than two dozen rounds. Luckily for them, they stood behind the shelter offered by the concrete pillars of the building. Unfortunately for the pretend-worker assassins, they were out in the open. One of them fled, circling the block. The other lay in the street and burbled out a trickle of blood.

By the time the security guards reached deTravanian Wrenger, he was unconscious.

So was the wounded assassin.

The ambulances were there inside of four minutes. It was an agonizing space of time for the security guards, who were trying throughout to stop the Vice President's bleeding. They manipulated the encounter with the paramedics so that deTravanian Wrenger was loaded first. Next stop, Phillips-Henderson Hospital.

* * *

The conversation with Pepper started out the way so many earlier conversations had started. And it developed the same way, Robert thought morosely.

"No," she said. "It wasn't my fault. The McDonalds guy shorted me my change, and not only that, he got my order wrong. He stood there bald-faced while he accused me of trying to steal."

"But Pepper, how did you get behind the counter? And what about the police officer who says you shoved him?"

"Well, he was pushing me. He started it. He had me pinned against the wall."

"He was in the process of arresting you and you pushed him?"

"I wasn't drunk. I wasn't. I wasn't. Daddy, you're treating me like a criminal. Don't be a lawyer with me because I'm not a criminal."

Being a lawyer is not an advantage when the trouble comes from your own daughter, he realized. In fact, it is a disadvantage. It furnished another way for her to deny the facts, by playing the you're-a-lawyer card.

These conversations always went around in circles. Robert was desperate to get Pepper into rehab, or at least into AA. Pepper was interested in maintaining her denials.

His face was crunched with pain. "Can't you see why I've been encouraging you for years to go to Alcoholics Anonymous? You had a drunk driving conviction that you hid from your family. Then you had another one, and another one, and finally you injured somebody in a wreck. Go and join AA, Pepper. Please."

"Well, I've been to a couple of meetings, but that was just to make you happy, Daddy. I'm not like those losers at AA. I'm not about to get up there and say 'Pepper's an alcoholic.' I'm not about to. Because it isn't true."

He couldn't think of anything more to say. In spite of her having said she wanted to make him happy, he could only look unhappy.

"Don't worry, Daddy."

That request was like asking him not to breathe.

"I'll work on it," Pepper said. "Will power. I just need to exercise some will power. Most of the time, I've been fine. I just have to watch how much I drink."

*   *   *

The FBI agent looked as though he didn't believe what deTravanian Wrenger was saying. In fact, he said so.

"Mr. Wrenger," he said, almost pleadingly. "Mr. Wrenger. You've got to have more information than you're giving me, about why you might have gotten shot."

"I don't have any idea why."

Wrenger's purple glasses stuck out of his thoroughly bandaged head. His shoulder was wrapped in white, and so were other parts of his body. The hospital bed didn't allow a full view of his injuries.

"I'm telling you everything I know. I have no idea who shot at me. Or who might have shot at me. Or who might be mad enough at me to shoot at me. I have no idea."

"Look, Mr. Wrenger. This kind of shooting isn't random. Someone went to a lot of trouble to hire people to kill you. And it's only because of luck and the miracles of today's medicine that they didn't succeed."

"You want to know what I think? I'm convinced that they got the wrong person. What I mean is, they must have been sent out to shoot at someone else."

"Well, let me tell you about the man we arrested for this. Maybe that will help. He was hurt bad too and got scraped up off the street. We found out his name is Hassan Malouf. Came to the United States from Iran. He got in on a student visa a little over five years ago. Now he's illegal, because he overstayed the visa. Lives in Washington, D.C."

"No. None of that rings a bell for me."

The physician assistant in the room spoke, now. "We have to end this. I'm sorry. Mr. Wrenger's just had a fragment from a bullet removed from his frontal lobe. A little further back and it would have been fatal, and he's not out of the woods yet. I told you, he can't be agitated."

"And I'm telling you, I don't know any more," the bandaged man said emphatically. Then he thought of something. "Could have been someone at Nova Aerospace. They hate me there."

"It seems improbable, Nova hiring Iranian citizens to go after you."

"Nova hates me. And it's mutual. I'd like to see that company buried."

"Well, we know a little about the guy who shot you already. This Hassan, we searched his D.C. apartment. All kinds of jihad propaganda and radical Islamist writings and anti-American posters, et cetera.

"But here's what might help you remember. There was a picture of you, Mr. Wrenger, in Hassan Malouf's apartment, in fact several pictures of you, good likenesses, good photographs, and there was even a piece of notebook paper that had the license number and description of your car. Now, surely some of that jogs your memory."

"No. I have no idea who these people are. Why don't you go interview old Hassan? He knows why he shot at me. I don't."

"We can't, as you put it, 'interview old Hassan.' The law is inconvenient. I'm sure the Iranians could make him talk in a hurry. But we can't. He can refuse to talk to us. He even gets those good old *Miranda* warnings that tell him exactly how and why he can clam up. And he's refusing to talk to us at all."

There was a pause. DeTravanian Wrenger looked blank. The FBI man looked irritated, frustrated.

*   *   *

"As we told you, we probably can't win a lawsuit based on your contract not to compete." Tom Kennedy sat behind the mahogany desk in his own office, across from Mike Martin and the other Nova Aerospace officers.

"Robert asked me to meet with you in his absence," Tom went on. "He's had a family emergency and can't be here."

"We appreciate it, and I hope Robert comes out okay." Mike Martin nodded.

"So, the covenant not to compete isn't a very good lawsuit." Tom smiled, "But there's a Second Law. And this law might fit your new information. It's the law of trade secrets. And if the facts turn out as you expect them to be, Mike, this Second Law might work."

"Okay," said Mike Martin. "And how does this Second Law work, the law of trade secrets?"

"Whenever there's a violation of the First Law we talked about— the law of covenants not to compete—there's a good chance there's going to be a secondary consequence. Namely, the misappropriation of trade secrets. That's why I call it the Second Law. A faithless employee who agrees that he won't work for a competitor, but then does just that, violates the covenant not to compete. But usually there's more to it than that."

He held up his hand. "Usually, there are trade secrets involved. Which the employee knows. And he knows he's not supposed to tell about those secrets. But in many cases, he does."

"Ah," said Mike Martin. He looked a little happier.

"And that way, a violation of the First Law—the noncompete—gets followed by violations of the Second Law, the misappropriation of trade secrets. In fact, it's hard for an employee to stick to his duty under the law. The employee is supposed to separate out trade secrets in his mind and not give them to his new company. But the two categories get confused in his mind, and he wants to succeed in the new job. And that leads to the information getting dispersed. It disorganizes his thinking about the trade secrets he's supposed to protect."

"That makes sense, even to an engineer like me." Mike nodded. "It's just like entropy in heat transfer."

"Maybe." Tom wasn't sure he understood. He paused and looked out the window as if recalling something from long before. Maybe . . . that strange course in basic physics. . . .

Then, he jerked back to the present. "Anyway. . . . Any kind of information that has business value and that you keep secret is a trade secret, and it's illegal for the employee or the new company to use it. A violation of this Second Law is called 'misappropriation of trade secrets.'"

The leaders of Nova Aerospace were all nodding and smiling at each other, and a couple of these longtime engineers high-fived, like teenagers, saying, "Second law. . . ." "Entropy. . . ."

Tom shook his head. "But don't get excited, my friends. It's a hard lawsuit. Hard to win. Robert wants you to know that he's still not sure it's a lawsuit worth attempting. In fact, I'd bet against us right now, because there are required elements of this trade secrets claim that we don't have much information about."

"Such as what?" Now, Mike Martin looked as if Tom had just pulled the rug out from under him.

"Such as the fact of misappropriation. Whether it even happened. We don't know for sure that this Iranian device is based on your roll-over mechanism. Your Orbital Attitude and Maneuvering control. We can try to prove that, but it's circumstantial.

"And also, here's something else that's not just a technicality. We don't know for sure how the Iranians got it. We strongly suspect it came from Wrenger and from Dravos Corporation. But proving that they misappropriated it—that's going to be the key to it all, and that's going to be hard to do."

"We're willing to try," said Mike Martin. "Not only do we want to get back what was stolen from us, but we'd also like to keep the Iranians from shooting missiles at Americans in the Middle East again."

9

Jimmy Coleman stepped into the forty-eighth floor office through the doorway marked in gold letters with the firm name. This was Booker and Bayne. It was home to him.

The carpet was thick and gold. The walls were blond wood, all from the same stand of white birch in Vermont, all matched in woven stripes. This was the top of the eight floors that Booker and Bayne occupied in its headquarters city. Which was one of many locations of the firm. They included offices in Atlanta, Austin, Beijing, Dallas, London, Los Angeles, Mexico City, and Washington. The associates learned to name all of the cities in alphabetical order.

As he strolled through the corridor, he heard the biting but to him soothing sounds of Booker and Bayne partners at work. From the office of Bailey Schauer, the oil and gas lawyer, he heard a loud yell: "If you don't pay the delay rental, we're going to foreclose! That silly claim of a title dispute won't even begin to support a suspension of your royalty payments."

It was a bluff, of course. But Bailey could put on an act that made it believable. Jimmy smiled. He loved the kinds of stab-your-brother-in-the-back disputes that came from the oil patch.

The next office belonged to Katherine Longo, who did patent litigation. From her door, Jimmy heard a calmer voice than Bailey's, but with the same dose of chill in it. "Yes, but your people got your letters by fraud. You didn't disclose the prior art from the folks at Tennahill, and their gizmo absolutely anticipated yours. If you try to enforce that patent, we'll have an antitrust counterclaim, and we'll win it going away."

Jimmy's smile broadened. Nobody called their opponents by worse names than the patent lawyers.

He walked past the big conference room, the one that posted the giant, shiny portrait of Colonel Henry Anderson Booker. The renowned founder of the firm. Colonel Booker had long since passed on to the great courtroom in the sky from which there is no appeal, but his presence was palpable still at the firm that carried his name. He had represented the city when it had developed the ship channel. He had led the financing effort for the first builders of River Oaks, the area's most opulent subdivision. And he had obtained the charter for the Humble Oil Corporation, which ultimately became Exxon.

With every new idea, every new development, every novel deal, Colonel Booker would ask, "Yes, but is it the right thing to do?" And then he would find a way to do it that worked, whether it seemed right or not.

Jimmy always felt a spring to his step when he saw Colonel Booker's image through the conference room glass.

"Hello, Lisa." He smiled at his six-foot-tall secretary, who towered over him. It was said that Jimmy liked her because he liked women taller than he was, and it was true; but Lisa also had other talents, such as the ability to turn out page after page of dictation without errors, a facility for charming clients even when she helped him dodge their calls, and a calm disposition whenever Jimmy explained his newest shady deal.

"Jimmy!" She bent down to give him a hug.

"Get me Jennifer Lowenstein. It's Robert Herrick again."

"Oh. I know how you love Robert Herrick. What's he messing with this time?"

"He's going after our good client The Dravos Corporation. He's nothing but a half-assed ambulance chaser who thinks he's discovered how to handle lawsuits about contract law and covenants not to compete."

* * *

"No, Pepper." Robert Herrick shook his head as he talked into the telephone. "You're not bothering us. Calling us is the right thing to do."

"I'm not really that drunk. I could drive . . . I mean, I could drive home jus' fine."

"No. You did the right thing. We'll come get you."

"Doesn't have to . . . Doesn't got to be both of you, come to get me."

"Well, yes, it does. Otherwise, what about your car? You can't leave it there at that bar, way out west of the city."

"Oh. I guess you'd . . . be right. Right, I mean."

"Maria and I will both come and I'll drive your car home while Maria drives you home."

"Oh. I guess thats's a good way. A good way to do it. A good way to spend your time."

Involuntarily, Robert sighed at that. "Okay, Sweetheart. Just stay where you are. Goodbye."

He stared at the phone. Then: "Okay, Maria, let's go be super-heroes."

* * *

Across town, Jimmy Coleman sat in his corner office, in front of his fourteenth-century Italian chest, made of honey-colored wood with green, brown, and red vines growing over it. Intarsiato style, with fine wooden inserts picturing the colors. His desk had been specially made to match.

Jennifer Lowenstein, his favorite associate, sat across from Jimmy, in a chair that also matched the priceless chest.

"Lisa!" he yelled through the open door. "Get me some more yella legal pads."

"I'll have to get some more of those requisition forms," she answered.

To Jennifer, Jimmy confided, "It's a pain in the ass. I can't go to the supply room and get a legal pad. This big firm, I've gotta 'requisition' it. And it practically took an Act of Congress to get yella ones. This firm is so environmental, they want white ones, so they're easier to recycle."

"Jimmy, a lot of us have wondered why you didn't go off on your own. Clients would follow you, and so would a bunch of associates and a few partners. Then, you'd have no big-firm problems."

"I learned early on in my life that it's hard to leave a gang."

"What do you mean?" Everyone in the firm knew vaguely about Jimmy's teen years, spent in a Los Angeles street gang. But usually, it was difficult to get him to talk about it.

"Well, my guys would do some bad stuff sometimes to folk who wanted to get out of our group and stay in the neighborhood. But it wasn't really that. The group was your group. Your people."

"Really?"

"Well, like, take drive-by shootings. We did that from time to time. Most of the time against brothers of the Deacons, whose territory smeared into ours. We find out the Deacons are poaching—you know, shaking down one of the businesses that were our businesses—we'll go leave a nine millimeter calling card.

"One time, I did it with my man Badbone. I don't remember his real name, but once he said, 'There's not a bad bone in my body,' which got him his name. It wasn't true. He actually didn't have good bone in his body. Anyway, we're in Badbone's '62 black Pontiac, with the shiny moon hub caps, which looked real slick but didn't run too good. Damn thing stalled right after we shot off a clip. We heard the bullets smacking bricks and breaking glass. People are yelling inside the building. They're running down the stairs, and we're about to be dead because that garbage car won't run."

Jimmy snorted. "Folks are running out the doors at us, and finally the thing started. Slowly. We got hit by a bunch of rocks, but Badbone was able to floor it. We got the hell out of there and started laughing like a pit crew that just put sugar in another guy's gas tank.

"Then, one time, a drive-by ended in a twelve-year-old girl getting shot in the head and killed. I wasn't part of that one, but my sister was about the same age. I told myself I wasn't going to do it anymore."

He paused. Jennifer was silent.

"I did, of course, do it again, and it might have been the next week." Jimmy's voice rasped even more than usual. "You gotta do it. It's your life. The meanness, recklessness—that's what gets you your rep. Your reputation. Everybody around you is doing stuff. And it's hard to get out of the gang."

"I still don't see why it's hard to get out."

"You're part of a fraternity. A club. A brotherhood. Like you were born into it. And in a way, you were stuck by what you did together. See, one time we caught this Deacon in our territory. I helped. A couple of us tackled the guy and kicked him all over. Then someone had the brilliant idea, let's lock him in a car trunk. This ten-year-old Chrysler was right there. A couple guys bent the trunk out of shape and dumped this bum inside it, then closed it again and made it lock."

Jennifer was hooked on listening, with a mixture of fascination and revulsion.

"It turned out uglier than anyone expected. Real ugly. They didn't have those inside-the-trunk escape latches back then. Nobody came to the car for over a week. When they did, that Deacon was dead, dead, dead, with all kinds of little animals crawling all over him. A couple of our guys went to juvie jail for a bunch of years. I didn't. Just lucky."

Jennifer's mouth was open. Jimmy looked out of the window. When he spoke again, he sounded faraway. Philosophical.

"The only way you got out of a gang was surviving while the other guys got too old or got killed, maimed, or put away. But if I saw one of my guys today, in spite of the fact I don't want to do that anymore, I'd do anything for him. We were bloods. Like I said, these guys were my people. I didn't have much family—no dad, not much from my mother.

"And you know, Jennifer, I feel the same way about this law firm. There are lots of disadvantages in a big firm. The problems are way bigger than having to requisition your legal pads. But I guess it's . . . loyalty, they call it. I'm stuck with the guys who joined this firm around the time I did. I'd do anything for them."

Silence. Then, she wanted to know: ". . . This firm is like . . . a gang?"

Jimmy laughed. Jennifer did too.

*   *   *

When the FBI finally traced the call that started it, agents found out that the guilty phone trail came from inside that Atlanta hospital. In fact, it came from the switchboard.

"He's in Room 650," said the operator. "There is a Mr. Wrenger in 650. I went to the sixth floor and looked, but they've got it restricted and I didn't get to the room. It's at the end of the hallway and the exit behind it is blocked off."

"They've got guards, right?" The voice at the other end of the line was flat.

"I saw two of them. With serious looking guns. Behind a guard station."

"What kind of guard station?"

"It covers the whole hallway. It has its own door. I couldn't tell what it's made of."

"Okay. Don't put the money in the bank. Put it someplace that's not easy to find."

"They already told me that."

But the FBI couldn't retrieve any of this conversation. By the time the agents got to it, the tape had been overwritten. Quantico tried to read the original, but there were too many earlier and later messages that interfered.

* * *

Jimmy Coleman sat in front of his priceless Italian chest, with red, brown, and green vines inlaid in it. Jennifer Lowenstein sat in a matching desk chair, straight up, almost sitting at attention. The floor-to-ceiling windows showed long shadows cast by buildings over freeways with cars streaming through them, looking tiny on the ground so far below.

Jimmy's voice grated like a chain dragging on asphalt. "Jennifer, you know our good client, The Dravos Corporation."

"Yes." Jennifer knew what these words meant. A "good client" was not one that gave to the poor, followed the law carefully, or maintained proper civic behavior. Instead, this phrase meant that the client got into shady business and regularly hired Booker and Bayne to get it out of trouble.

A good client also paid the bill right away without question, in amounts in the millions.

"Dravos is in the crosshairs of a lawsuit that is being cooked up by our friend Robert Herrick."

"Oh. He's a problem."

"Well, maybe not so much so in this case. We got a good dee-fense. But it may turn out to be a serious lawsuit, even if it's a long shot. If Herrick succeeds, Dravos could have some ex-po-o-o-sure."

Jimmy dragged out that word, because he liked the buzzing sound of it—ex-po-o-o-sure—and again, Jennifer knew what it meant.

Saying that Dravos had "some" ex-po-o-o-sure meant that Dravos was guilty as sin. For damages in the multiple millions. But it also meant that in this instance, it had built in some really smart ways to get out of trouble. If, on the other hand, Dravos hadn't done anything seriously wrong, Jimmy would say it differently, such as saying that Dravos had "just a little smidgeon of ex-po-o-o-sure."

"Some" ex-po-o-o-o-sure sounded really bad.

"It's one of those phony-baloney trade secret cases," Jimmy wheezed. "If you couldn't get a patent because your device isn't new, but your competitors have something like it, you claim that everybody in the industry has stolen your trade secrets."

Jennifer nodded. "Well, but it's hard to prove."

"That's right. It's not like proving patent infringement. You got to show not only that their device is like your device, but that they got the design by sneaking in and stealing yours. And that's hard to prove, yes."

Everybody in Booker and Bayne knew about Jimmy's background, even if they didn't know where the truth ended and the legend started. His gang had shaken down every storefront in their east Los Angeles territory for protection. Pakistani, Haitian, and Chinese shopowners knew that the police department couldn't keep up with vandalism and worse, much less stop it. Drive-by shootings were easy and untraceable. The hardest part of it was keeping out other gangs who tried to muscle in, and that meant real warfare.

That period in his life had a lot to do with Jimmy's methods today.

"Dravos does business on a huge international scale." Jimmy waved his hand. "They trade with the Chinese, the Saudis, and when they can do it, with the Iranians, with designs for electronics. What I understand is that Herrick claims we stole stuff from his client, which is called Nova Aerospace Corporation, and sold it to the Chinese, who then sold it to Iran. Or maybe straight to Iran."

"Wow. How's he going to connect all that up?"

"We don't know yet. But we need an expert witness who'll say that the device Herrick traces to the Iranians isn't like the device that Nova Aerospace invented. That the electronic pattern is different. And this expert has got to say it so that a jury will believe him. And Jennifer, that's what I want you to find for us."

"Yes sir." Jennifer smiled. It would be fun. "But Jimmy, don't we want to try to prove that Dravos never got the technology from Nova Aerospace in the first place?"

Everybody in Booker and Bayne wanted to work for Jimmy Coleman. In spite of his unconventional background, he was a wonderful teacher. And you could be sure of having all your billable hours paid and counted. Jennifer beamed at him.

But now, she saw the great man's face become clouded. "Proving that we didn't steal it, you mean? We'll do the best we can at that. But that's a point in our defense that we've still got to develop. Because that might be where Dravos has a dollop of ex-po-o-o-sure.'"

10

om Kennedy stepped into Robert's office and crossed over the huge oriental rug with its colorful squares, triangles, diamonds, and circles. Beneath the greenhouse-style windows, a hundred geraniums bloomed in red, pink and yellow. Rain splashed against the glass, so that visibility was interrupted by showers of water.

"Pretty dismal day." He shook his head.

"Well, I hope it's not an omen. I understand you've got a reading from our experts, saying that the Iranian bad guys' rocket design is so similar to Nova Aerospace's that it must have been stolen."

"Not exactly."

Robert looked up sharply. "What does that mean, 'Not exactly'?"

"We've got three different opinions from our experts. Three very different ones."

"That's not what I wanted to hear."

"You're telling me. First, McElvaney says it's probably not from the same design. Second, Eloff says it most likely was copied and, in his words, 'at least could have been.' Then, our third guy, Professor Eisner, says it's so similar that it must have been copied."

"So the rain was an omen, indeed. Pretty dismal day." Robert flopped his head down on his arms. "Oh, well. I didn't want this lawsuit anyway."

"Yes—but it coulda been worse."

"I'm not sure how. If it had all come back negative, we'd know to drop the case. If it had all come back positive, it would've been a good case, even if I still don't like it. This way, we're left with a muddled ball of conflicting doubt."

"Maybe not. We don't have to disclose McElvaney's negative opinion, of course. He's just going to be a consulting expert, and we won't call him to testify. Maybe the same with Eloff, depending on exactly where he finally lands. We just go with Professor Eisner."

"Tom, you've always liked this case, haven't you?"

"I don't like what I know about Dravos Corporation. And I don't like the Iranian missile program, either. Robert, I guess it sounds corny, but Dravos doesn't sound like truth, justice and the American way. And from what I see about Nova Aerospace, it's a fine company."

"Are we going to decide this by waving around the American flag, or are we going to be lawyers who evaluate our chances objectively?" Robert looked out at the rain. "See, here's what I'm thinking. If the experts we hired are this much in disagreement, Jimmy Coleman can easily hire a squadron of well-qualified electronics guys who'll say we have no case."

"I think our Professor Eisner is going to be a good witness. He looks the part, he can talk to normal people, and he knows the answers when you ask a question."

"Tom, you're the one who's always telling me we should represent more banks and insurance companies. Clients who can pay up front."

"Well, but we represent mostly people who're hurt or killed by careless big companies. Which is kind of what Nova Aerospace is, except that they're big, but they're a lot smaller than Dravos Corporation."

"Now you've got me deciding how good the case is by looking at which one is smaller. Not much better than waving the flag."

Robert laughed, and so did Tom.

"Oh, well. There are never any guarantees. Let's write it up."

"You coming around to believing in this lawsuit?"

"No. And I still feel like I've already done what a lawyer wants to do in my career. I'll only go along if you agree to do all the work."

"Okay, Boss, I can do that."

*   *   *

IN THE UNITED STATES DISTRICT COURT
FOR THE SOUTHERN DISTRICT OF TEXAS
HOUSTON DIVISION

NOVA AEROSPACE COMPANY,　)
Plaintiff　)
v.　)　NO. _____
THE DRAVOS CORPORATION,　)
Defendant　)

<u>PLAINTIFF NOVA'S ORIGINAL COMPLAINT</u>

Nova Aerospace Corporation appears before this court as Plaintiff, complaining of The Dravos Corporation, Defendant, and would respectfully show the Court and Jury as follows:

JURISDICTION AND VENUE

1. Plaintiff is a corporation incorporated in Delaware with its principal place of business in Texas. Defendant is a Georgia corporation with its principal place of business in Georgia. The matter in controversy exceeds the sum required by 28 U.S.C. 1332. The Court has jurisdiction by virtue of the diversity of citizenship.

2. Defendant has no agent and no place of business in this state. Therefore, Defendant will be served with process by service upon the secretary of state of this state.

3. Venue is proper because a substantial portion of the acts and omissions giving rise to the claim occurred in this District and Division.

THE FACTS

4. Plaintiff possessed certain trade secrets that were protected under the Uniform Trade Secrets Act (UTSA). These trade secrets included "information that derived independent economic value from not being generally known to other persons," and they were "the subject of efforts that were reasonable to maintain their secrecy." Specifically, the trade secrets concerned the guidance of missiles.

5. Defendant wrongfully acquired knowledge of these trade secrets by employing an employee of Plaintiff who had a duty to maintain the secrets and by making them available to others, including foreign nations. In addition to knowingly violating this duty of the employee, Defendant knowingly violated the same employee's contract of employment, which contained a contract and covenant not to compete with Plaintiff.

6. Under the trade secret law, Defendant "misappropriated" Plaintiff's trade secrets by this conduct, and by using and enabling others to use them.

7. Defendant acted through this employee to design or help others to design a competing device that contained features similar to the trade secrets that Defendant had wrongfully acquired from Plaintiff.

8. Defendant commercially exploited this device, which contained Plaintiff's trade secrets, by selling or sharing the device and its design internationally.

THE CLAIMS

9. Defendant is liable to Plaintiff for misappropriation of Plaintiff's trade secrets.

10. Defendant is further liable to Plaintiff under the law of unfair competition.

11. Defendant is further liable to Plaintiff for breach of a contract and covenant not to compete.

FOR THESE REASONS, Plaintiff prays that it recover its damages in the form of losses due to Defendant's conduct; that it recover restitution of income and profits derived by Defendant's wrongful conduct; that a constructive trust be placed upon the misappropriated secrets; that it recover its costs and attorney's fees; and that it obtain all other relief in law and equity to which it may show itself entitled.

*   *   *

"You've written it as a suit in federal court." Robert read the short document. "Instead of the state courts. I guess that's right."

"It looks as though Dravos removes everything it can from state courts to the federal courts." Tom shook his head. "If we filed in state court, they'd just remove it. We've got diversity of citizenship here, so they can take it to federal court, That causes delay and confusion, which is one reason Dravos does it."

"Sure."

"This way, we start out where we would end up."

"And I like it that your complaint is short. It says everything it has to, and since we aren't certain about all of the facts, it's good that it's short."

"When do we ever know everything with certainty?" Tom laughed. "In this case, according to the experts who disagree, we don't even know that our trade secret was taken."

"I still don't like this lawsuit."

"But it's a much better lawsuit than you thought. And I'll do all the behind-the-scenes unglamorous stuff. The heavy lifting. And Robert, you're a good American, and this is a suit for a good America."

"You're waving the flag again." He laughed. "Right. Anyway, we've got a lot of discovery to do. We're going to have to learn something about this lawsuit as we go along."

*　*　*

A thousand miles to the east, three men dressed like medical techs and armed with AK-47's wore protective vests under their clothing. They stuffed their helmets and assault rifles into medical bags and carefully put them onto a stretcher.

"We don't even know what these guards have got. I mean, what kind of weapons," said the tallest one.

"What's worse is that we don't know what they have for surveillance," the bald man said. "Is there a camera on the elevator that feeds to the guards? Will they see us all the way, including when we take the rigs out of the bags?"

"You know they'll be at alert when the elevator reaches the floor."

"Yeah. Great. We know that. Yeah."

"What gets me is, we don't know which one is deTravanian Wrenger's room." This third man was soft-spoken. "We know it's Room 650. But is that to the right, or to the left? At the end, or next to the end?"

"Yeah. This switchboard operator couldn't tell us squat."

"We've got this smoke grenade, which is supposed to cause confusion and panic. It's supposed to do that with the guards. But it might just be us who get confused and panicked when we get there and try to find our man."

"Oh, well. In other words, it's going to be a lot like every operation."

"You ready?"

"Ready as I'll ever be."

"Got your will up to date under the new tax law?"

"That's real funny."

"Lots to discover. This may be an operation we'll learn about as we go along."

11

The afternoon sun illuminated the priceless Italian chest in Jimmy Coleman's corner office. Its gold hardware gleamed, and the red, green and brown vines glowed.

"Here it is," Jimmy rasped. "Robert Herrick's planned lawsuit."

"Just what we expected, a demand letter with an advance copy of the petition." Jennifer Lowenstein sat at attention.

"No. It's not a state court petition. It's a federal complaint. In federal court."

"Herrick would rather be in state court like all plaintiffs, but he knows we would remove it to federal court anyway like all defendants do, so he filed it in federal court to start with."

"Right. And now we have a week or two before they file the actual lawsuit."

"Jimmy, you can try to see whether they'll settle it for something little."

"Something reasonable, we would settle it. But it's doubtful."

"Why's that? We settle most of them, like everyone else."

"Dravos is adamantly against this lawsuit. It'll disturb their business with China. We can't expect them to pay much more than the nuisance value of the lawsuit."

"And Robert Herrick's probably got stars in his eyes."

"Yes. And we'd better try to get his lawsuit in front of a judge who likes us."

"How are we going to do that?"

* * *

"Look at that!" The staff sergeant pointed at images on the screen showing two men in an elevator getting Kalashnikov assault rifles out of a medical bag and fingering the magazines.

He was no longer a staff sergeant, of course, having separated from the Army. But the men with him on this hospital protective assignment still went by rank. When he said, "Assume positions," they did. They were prone behind barriers called 10-brick walls, which weren't made of bricks but were rated at 10 of them in stopping bullets.

The guards held 6.8 millimeter Bushmasters. They punched the safeties and switched to automatic.

Within fifteen seconds, the elevator made a clunking sound. No one got out immediately. Someone inside threw out a percussion grenade, followed by a smoke bomb. Behind that, two men rushed out and hugged the opposite wall.

The percussive made a deafening sound. Then everything was quiet. The smoke spread, but the guards could still see what they needed to see.

A speaker near the intruders carried the staff sergeant's voice. "You have entered a prohibited area. Drop your weapons and lie face down on the ground. If you don't, you will be killed."

They didn't. They faced forward.

"Whites of their eyes," said the staff sergeant to his troops. Which was a corny way to say it, but it carried the message.

Within a few seconds, the assault force crept forward. And closer. And closer.

"Now," said the staff sergeant.

The air erupted with staccato blasts of Teflon-coated missiles, chattering and continuous. The kind of bullets designed to pierce armored clothing. The intruders got off a few rounds.

The guards stayed in position for a long five minutes. Nothing else happened.

"Okay," said the staff sergeant finally. "I guess the security guys at Dravos Corporation prepared us pretty well. This was a turkey shoot, with the turkeys in cages."

* * *

"We want to throw everything at them we can," Jimmy said in a hard-throated growl. The gold hardware on his Italian chest glittered in the morning sun, and its reflections sparkled on his matching desk, as if to emphasize his mood.

"Like, what are we going to throw at them?" Jennifer sat across from him.

"Well, we look into the things Herrick has to prove and write denials. Nova Aerospace screwed up, and that's our basic position. First, we deny that they worked hard enough to keep their design secret. Second, we deny that we 'misappropriated' it; we reverse-engineered it from stuff in the public domain. Third, it's not a valuable business secret. It's just a chain of known items."

Dutifully, Jennifer wrote it all down.

"Then, think about our affirmative defenses. Is there some sort of authority for a claim that they've waived their rights? Or what the law calls 'estoppel,' meaning they've done something, like having their people speak at conferences, where they've invited discovery of their secrets? Do they have what the law calls 'unclean hands'?"

Jennifer scribbled furiously.

"And of course, we'll file a counterclaim under the antitrust laws."

"We'll do what?"

"Make a claim against them. By the things that they've done, such as filing this phony trade secret suit, they've discouraged others from competing with them, including Dravos. Therefore, they've attempted to monopolize the manufacture of guidance devices for spacecraft, and that kind of attempted monopolization violates the antitrust laws. We have big damages from what we've lost in the industry."

"Can we do that? An antitrust claim?"

"It works if there's an unjustified patent suit. I don't know of a case where it's been used in a trade secret suit, but maybe it's the same thing. A wrongheaded trade secret lawsuit can scare off a competitor the same way a malicious patent claim can."

"Well . . . but what I mean is, can we really succeed in a claim like that, under the antitrust laws?"

"That's what I would like for Herrick and Nova Aerospace to wonder about. So, they've got a claim for damages from us, and they don't know for sure whether they can succeed at it? Our response is, we've got a claim against them, and if they lose, they'd wind up owing us millions instead of us owing them anything. We don't have to win our counterclaim for it to be a valuable weapon."

Jimmy's laugh sounded like a jackhammer. "It's like playing chicken. I'm guessing that Nova Aerospace might be the one to chicken out first. They're run by a bunch of white-shoe, prissy little Ivy League types who think they're above it all. And they just might chicken out first, because they're expecting smooth sailing. And then suddenly, they realize they've made a dangerous bet."

*   *   *

"All right. I'll tell you what I know," said deTravanian Wrenger. "But I don't know much."

The room was white. All white; deathly white. The walls were colorless, the window frame and blinds were plain, and there was a print of a painting on the wall showing what seemed to be a snow scene. The bed was white, of course, with white sheets and blankets, and the tables and chairs were hospital-white.

The man lying in the middle of it all had a white gown. His head was lumpy, and he had an odd plus-or-minus sign on his cheek. His all-over bandages were white.

"I know it won't do any good to keep quiet now," said deTravanian Wrenger. "I've got to tell you: I'm scared. I know they'll keep coming after me until they kill me. If I wasn't convinced before, I am now."

The strange man with the mocha skin and purple glasses did indeed look frightened. He had the covers pulled up all the way to his chin, and he trembled. There were extra lines on his face.

"We're here to prevent that from happening." The two agents stood out in contrast to the colorless room, in their black suits, dark ties, and shiny black FBI shoes. "We're investigating a foreign assault on an American citizen, namely you, but we need your help to be able to help you."

"To repeat, I can't tell you much."

"Well, tell us what you know."

"It's about the missile guidance system, of course. As soon as I moved here to Dravos Corporation, I got a series of contacts from various people who I gradually realized were from Iran. One of them who was most persistent called himself David Stern and identified himself as Israeli, but I heard one of his partners call him 'Amir.' That was only one of the signs that he wasn't on the level."

"And this was about the missile guidance system? The rollover mechanism?"

"They wanted it. They really wanted it. The rollover of a missile is one of the most delicate parts of its flight. They offered me a hundred thousand dollars, these two guys, Amir-David and the other one, who called himself Saul. They weren't from Israel."

"No. They weren't."

"If I told anyone, I'd be caught and taken away, they said. I didn't tell anyone. I should have. They were persistent. They offered more and more money, into the millions. Frankly, I was scared to cooperate with them. And I was scared not to cooperate. But I didn't."

"Well, we need to know what you know about this Amir-David character."

"I'm guessing he was five feet eight. Not tall, but very tough. Heavy black beard, black hair, black-looking eyes. Always wore a gray suit. A sharp-looking suit, fitted to him, and a pocket handkerchief. He had gold-rimmed glasses, but unusual gold rims, much thicker and more eye-catching than usual. You looked at his face, and all you saw was two thick gold circles stuck together."

"Okay. And they got it from you, the prototype for the rollover mechanism?"

"Not from me, no."

The two agents looked at each other and frowned. "How, then, do you claim they got it, Mr. Wrenger?"

"I don't know for sure. But they started romancing my assistant instead of me. They usually met me outside of my college classroom. I don't know where they met my assistant, but I saw them hanging around her. My assistant here at Dravos is named Romaine Cramshak. One day I came back to the lab late, after six. There was David-Amir and his partner, together with Romaine, right there in the lab, where nobody was supposed to be."

"That's a restricted space, right?"

"Yes. The whole floor is restricted. You had to have a badge. Those guys didn't, except for a normal visitor's badge. I reacted. In fact, I kind of blew up and told them to get the hell out of there."

"You think that's where the rollover got stolen?"

"I can't say for sure. But after they were out of there, Romaine told me, 'I was just showing them around.' And she said, 'They said they were friends of yours.' We never did that"—he screwed his face up, making his ± sign unrecognizable—"never. It was outrageous, her saying she was 'just showing them around.'"

"Any other indication of what happened to the rollover?"

"The plans had been moved and re-rolled. Big paper plans."

"Why didn't you report all of this?"

"For one thing, I wasn't sure about anything. About whether to accuse Romaine Cramshak. About whether she'd done anything wrong. Had I been the one to move and reroll the plans? I don't think so, but you know. . . . And also, there was the usual reason for staying quiet."

"What was that?"

"Mr. David-Amir met me again, after that. He made the point pretty clear. If I said anything to anyone, I'd be kidnapped and killed. And in fact, now they've tried to kill me, for real. Not once, but twice."

The man in the bed groaned. "Those people are capable of anything. Remember how the Saudis lured that journalist to their embassy and then killed him? And remember how the CIA said the Saudi Crown Prince ordered it?

"Well, that's the Saudis." Even behind the bandages, the pain on deTravanian Wrenger's face was evident. "From what I hear, the Iranians are the same, only worse."

12

Jimmy's filed his answer to our lawsuit. He's dumped in everything but the kitchen sink."

Robert sat at the big mahogany desk in his office across from Tom Kennedy. "Some of it I guessed." He shook his head. "Some of it I'd never have guessed."

"I know." Tom sounded philosophical. "What do you think of it?"

"Well, he denies we had a trade secret about missile guidance, which is ridiculous. He also denies it was worth anything if we did, which is about what I expected him to say."

Tom nodded. "And he denies that Dravos did anything to steal the nonexistent trade secret."

"Which again is what I expected. That's our weakest point. It's always the weakest point in a trade secret lawsuit. We don't know how they stole it."

"But then, Jimmy's affirmative defenses are even more outlandish."

"Yes. Nova Aerospace let its engineers give talks at industry meetings and seminars. About missile technology. Of course they did; everybody participates in industry conferences."

"Even us lawyers." Tom laughed. "And we discuss the updated statutes and court decisions. And we drink a lot. Probably more than the engineers."

"Well, Jimmy says that because of Nova's people speaking in conferences, Nova has waived its trade secret claim. We voluntarily gave it up. And also because of that, we're 'estopped' from asserting the claim, meaning we've done something to block us legally from using it. Then

Jimmy's put in this business of our having so-called 'unclean hands.' Which is a valid legal defense, even if it sounds strange, but Jimmy doesn't say how it applies here."

"And then, there's this antitrust counterclaim." Tom pointed at the document.

"You knew Jimmy was going to do that. He really waxes eloquent about the antitrust violation we supposedly committed. It deserves to be read aloud. 'Nova Aerospace has attempted to monopolize the industry in missile guidance systems by issuing unfounded threats, intimidation, and blackmail against competitors, including this Defendant. And the threats, intimidation, and blackmail include this lawsuit against the Defendant Dravos, which Nova Aerospace knows is innocent of its false charges.'"

"Jimmy's almost a poet, isn't he? You have to admit, he's got a lot of rhythm."

"Well, we don't have to reply to Jimmy's defenses, but we do have to reply to the counterclaim. Basically, we'll admit that we filed this lawsuit, but we deny that we are attempting to monopolize the industry, and we deny that we're making unfounded charges."

"I'm on it, boss. I'll have our reply ready tomorrow."

"Oh, and by the way. When we talk to Nova Aerospace, we don't want to sound too cavalier about Jimmy's answer or his counterclaim. You never know how something like this is going to turn out. That's what Jimmy's banking on, and he's hoping we'll get sloppy and ignore the counterclaim. He'd like that. Or, that we'll take it so seriously that we might get scared and fold."

"Jimmy would like that, too."

"So, Tom, we've got to let Nova Aerospace know that the counterclaim is serious, and we have to fight it. Which, unfortunately, is just what Jimmy wants them to be thinking about. He intends it as a threat. And as intimidation, and as blackmail, if I can be permitted to echo his own terminology."

*   *   *

Robert Herrick pointed his burgundy-colored Duesenberg south on Kirby Drive, past the columns in homes of the wealthiest in the city. He and Maria were on the way home after the symphony.

They passed Tiel Way. And glided past Lazy Lane, with its wooded, multi-acre mansions, all accessed by drives that were like country roads, right here in the middle of the city.

He grinned. "Don't you think I look a lot like James Bond when I drive this baby?"

They sailed past Pine Valley. Denman Road. And Brentwood Drive.

"Only if James Bond was sporting a really effective disguise," Maria kidded. "And only if he liked to throw money out of the window for antique cars."

The bulging, curved hood of the Duesenberg seemed to go on forever. Chrome-plated exhausts adorned the sides and trailed all the way back. Twelve cylinders purred in harmony. It was expensive to keep this car tuned, but when it was, the engine sounded so much better than six. They blended in a sound that was stronger and lower-pitched, and to Robert far more satisfying, than any of his twenty-four other cars, from the Testarossa to the '38 Packard.

He laughed. "Well, I guess I'm better looking than the real James Bond. But you're right about throwing around money. I've added onto the garage three times, and I'm about to have to add on again. That building costs a fortune. It's got better temperature and humidity controls than a wine cellar."

The Duesenberg turned right at Inwood Drive.

His 1931 Stutz had a fold-down windshield and a genuine rumble seat. The 1930 Bentley, actually, was the favorite or James Bond, agent .007, and Robert had one that was British racing green. His 1930 Cadillac had an incredible total of sixteen cylinders that warbled like a bird but got eight miles to the gallon. He usually wasn't ostentatious, and in fact he sometimes was reluctant to spend money for small luxuries because he didn't want to act like the rich and powerful people he disliked—and sued.

"But these beautiful old cars are something else," he said to Maria. "After my kids, I guess they're my biggest indulgence."

"That, and Mozart," she reminded him. "Like this concert with the title of 'Mostly Mozart' that we just heard. You give a lot of money to the Symphony so you can persuade them to do lots of Mozart."

"Well, you like it too, right? When they did the Haffner Symphony just now, you were so excited I expected you to get up and start dancing."

"Sure. Why not? They danced in the aisles at that Beach Boys concert. Same kind of thing."

"Ahhh, yes. The Haffner Symphony. In D major. Written near the end of Mozart's life, when everything he touched turned to gold."

They rode along in silence for a moment. Here was Willowick Drive. The home stretch.

She looked at him. "You're thinking again about how you would rather not have your latest lawsuit get answered by Jimmy Coleman, aren't you?"

"Yes. I'm not exactly worried yet, but you know—Jimmy knows how to make everything unpleasant. And he uses it as a strategy. It doesn't have to change the odds, at least according to my thinking, but it makes for a lot more stomach acid."

"I'll just have to do something." She smiled at him. "Something that's guaranteed to get your mind off of it."

"Uh oh," he said, and he smiled back.

* * *

In the bedroom, Maria was fast in unbuttoning her pretty pink blouse, one-two-three. She slipped it off, and in almost the same movement, she bent and unsnapped her bra. She dropped her short black skirt to the floor. Her pantyhose had a crossed pattern that flashed while she stepped out of them. Two long, slender legs framed a triangle of darker, shining hair.

Her fair Hispanic skin shone in the dim light. Her breasts arched away from her body, stirring and turning against her own movement, with icy hard nipples protruding from darker aureolas under her luminous face.

Somehow, he managed to get his own clothes off, without looking, because instead he was looking steadily at her. For the thousandth time, he was amazed by how beautiful she was.

Then she moved down, and he felt her breasts touch the insides of his legs. Her hair hung toward him, and her dark red lips paused above him.

She lifted her face and looked at him as she took him in completely.

He pulled her up to kiss her. She saw that look and was ready for what happened next.

He heard a sharp sigh, her intake of breath.

Quickly she felt herself giving to him. She knew he felt the same. He searched for the deepest part of her, and she tightened. Soon she sensed a longing nothingness, but without any concern; only a drive, a desire. Their shapes melted away, the world melted away, and she joined with him. Her eyes shone as she rose to meet him, and then she closed them, as the force within her grew to get as high as she could. Then she looked at him, his dark hair and blue eyes. He was beautiful. The muscles of his chest moved, and he was strong. It excited her to imagine, against all reason, that she couldn't get away even if she wanted to. I usually am careful, she told herself, but I'm going to be reckless, unthinking, and it was her desire that was driving everything, so that her last shiver of control disappeared.

She climbed, climbed, and still went higher. She was breathing a set of unmeasured sighs, of breath intake and out. Then, suddenly, all inhibitions were gone, and she was screaming. He could feel her legs thrash, tighten, and surround him.

And suddenly she relaxed.

"Come on, baby," she said to him. "I want you." And he began to lose control and shake, with his own inhibitions gone.

They lay with their arms around each other. "I love this woman," he said to himself.

She saw how serious he looked, and she laughed. "I love you," she said, "and being with you is better than Mozart."

13

Tom Kennedy stepped across the big oriental carpet in Robert's office. "Here's something that's just plain bizarre."

"What's that?"

"Jimmy's filed a Motion to Transfer. He wants to move our lawsuit to a different venue."

"To . . . Atlanta? Where Dravos has its offices? He's unlikely to get that kind of thing granted. Maybe he's filed this just to distract us."

"No." Tom's voice was flat. "Jimmy's asking to have us transferred to Galveston. Next division over."

"Ummm, yes. . . . I mean, yes, that's bizarre. What do you suppose his strategy is for making this kind of move?"

"Well, you know, there's a new federal judge in the Galveston Division. The new judge is . . . Dexter Medaxas."

"Ummm, Dexter Medaxas. . . . *Dexter Medaxas?* I haven't thought about that guy in just about forever. But now that you mention it, I remember reading about it, that Medaxas got appointed to that federal judge position."

"And you recall the history. Medaxas was a district judge. In state court."

"Yes. I know only too well. He was a crooked dunce of a judge. He hated us and all of our cases. It was always a battle in enemy territory, whenever he was on any lawsuit of ours. And then Medaxas quit. He had kids in college, and he said he had to go into private practice to earn some money."

"Yes." Tom frowned. "And he went to work for. . . ."

"For Booker and Bayne." Robert shook his head. "I remember."

"And it was Jimmy Coleman who hired him. Our favorite highly ethical lawyer. That fine Jimmy Coleman. And now, it's several years later, and lo and behold, Medaxas has shifted and he's shaken and he's slithered and made Jimmy Coleman proud. So, he's made enough money and wants to become a judge again, this time a federal judge, so he can screw things up even worse."

"Oh, well." Robert sounded unconcerned. "A Motion to Transfer Venue is a long shot in this case. Jimmy's not likely to get it granted."

"Jimmy makes a pretty good case for the transfer. This is pure Jimmy Coleman."

"What? Well, he's got an army of eager associates who can think up ways to stretch us out and then do the research to support it all with plausible-sounding arguments."

"Right. Which is what they've done here."

"Okay. So, how does Jimmy explain it?"

"Well, he points out that our plaintiff, Nova Aerospace, is located just south of the NASA Manned Spacecraft Center. The closest federal courthouse is. . . ."

"Ugh. Don't tell me. It's . . . Galveston." Robert spat out the word.

"The statute says that a transfer can be granted 'for the convenience of the parties and witnesses.' And Jimmy waxes eloquent in this Motion to Transfer about how convenient it will be for Nova Aerospace to appear in the Galveston courthouse, since it's closer, instead of the courthouse in the big city, with all that traffic congestion on the Freeway and the Pierce Elevated and Rusk Street. He practically draws a map of the streets in both cities, and he makes it sound like a mass of clogged traffic."

"Great. But . . . hey, I remember that the statute also says that it depends on where the claim arose. Our claim is for theft of trade secrets, and that didn't happen in Galveston."

"Ahhhh . . . But Jimmy says it did. He points out that Wrenger actually lived in the Galveston area. He had a home office in Galveston County, and he did a lot of the work to design stuff at his home, or so Jimmy says. The stolen secret was stolen from Wrenger, Jimmy says, if it was stolen.

"Besides, Jimmy points out that we also have a claim for breach of the employment contract—our claim based on the covenant not to compete. Good old deTravanian Wrenger moved from Galveston to

Atlanta to go to work for Dravos. So that claim arose in Galveston, according to Jimmy. And the trouble with all of these arguments is that, even if they don't fit what the statute was intended to do, they are—as you put it—pretty plausible."

"Oh, my aching cookies."

Tom laughed, at that. "Well, I'd better work on opposing this Motion to Transfer. Or else, we'd better start preparing for a trial in a minefield."

* * *

The National Security Advisor sat in front of the Presidential desk, on a curved couch in the Oval Office. "To sum it all up, the Iranians are going whacky again."

"I know. When it comes to misbehaving, the Iranians are the Big Enchilada." The President flashed his trademark campaign grin. "Seriously, it's time to get another answer from the Pentagon about what the options are."

The Advisor nodded. "The Iranians have abused us beyond all reason. It's built up over time, and a pretty short time. A month ago, the Iranians fed a cell of operatives, just plain terrorists, who went and shot mortar shells at the embassy in Baghdad. No damage, and private operatives, but CIA says the Iranian government funded them through a series of phony charities. And of course our consulate in Basra is vulnerable, being right by the Iran-Iraq border. It's scary being at that post. Now there's been another Iranian-sponsored mortar attack, this time in Basra, with actual damage to the building."

"Right. And what's worse, there's Iran's missile program. Their spacecraft are big enough to carry nuclear weapons." The President ran his hand through his bushy red hair, mottled with gray. "That's a violation of our treaty with Iran. And Iran's always on the edge of nuclear weapons."

"Which we're pretty confident they don't have, as of now. But how long would it take them to build them? Estimates center around a year or two."

"They've sent up another nuclear-capable missile since the one we recovered from the Arabian Sea."

"And now, Iran is going out into space." The Advisor laughed slightly at the absurdity of it. "Teheran has announced this new satellite program, with six planned units orbiting us. Which they say are for 'communications.' Sure. That will give them ways to build and test even more sophisticated missiles, not to mention guidance of those missiles worldwide. And snooping. The Iranian space program. 'Communications,' my ass."

"Tell the Pentagon to give us options for an operation to shake up the Iranians. Either operations against the Iranian missile capability or something else appropriate."

"And the only options we'll get back will either be meaningless or they'll be acts of war. Or, they'll be close enough to acts of war so we can't do them."

"Probably. But who knows? Maybe they'll come up with something in the show-of-force category that will work. And at the very least, the Iranians have ways to find out that the Pentagon is thinking about strategies to have the U.S. Air Force visit them. And maybe that will do some good."

The President shook his head. "The use of force short of war. Threats, troop movements, aircraft carrier relocations, bomber flyovers—not exactly a beautiful thing. I used to think the armed services were for fighting. Wrong. More often, they're for show."

The Advisor thought for an instant. "The theory of the use of force short of war is that it avoids war. And usually it does. But usually, it also avoids accomplishing anything."

* * *

The voice on the telephone from Galveston said, "Hello. This is Dexter Medaxas. Your newest colleague on the bench."

"Congratulations," said the Chief Judge heartily, in the big city. "I'm glad you made it. I thought it was unfair the way those senators treated you with all those questions involving underage girls. Unsubstantiated allegations. But you hung in there and got confirmed, and it's great to hear from you."

"Thanks. But those Senate hearings are water under the bridge. I wanted to start thinking about the future. To start doing a little planning with you about the court docket here in Galveston."

"Right. There's not a lot on the docket down there. We stopped assigning cases to your predecessor, Judge Spevak—God rest his soul—when he got into his final illness. Now, we need to assign cases back to your docket. And build you up some business. You've been a judge before, so you know basically what to do. We can give you a full bucket of work."

"Certainly. I'm ready to go," said newly-robed Dexter Medaxas. "So have at it. I've been setting things up all week, and I'll start hearings Monday."

"Good. We'll send you everything we stopped sending to Galveston. The ones that belong there but couldn't go there. Plus some cases from this division that look like they can travel well."

"It's a strange feeling, being here in Galveston. Smaller city. Seems inbred."

"Absolutely. You'll find the natives to be pretty protective of their people. One of the problems you'll have is the BOI's—people 'Born on the Island.' You're an outsider unless you're BOI. You have to have gone to good old Ball High School, which is the only one there. You have to know all about George Mitchell, the local hero, and you have to have walked the seawall as a kid."

"I've run into the BOI's. It's weird."

"They're not just an annoyance, you know. They create unique problems. The jurors are going to side with the blue collar members of their community, or at least the plaintiffs and defendants that are like them. But the real problem is the lawyers. They'll cross party boundaries, and the plaintiff's lawyers who are BOI will cooperate with the defense lawyers who are BOI so they can gang up on outside lawyers. You will get halfway through a trial and find out you're facing a mistrial because the BOI's have hidden their illegal agreements."

"I'll watch for that. Thanks."

The Chief Judge laughed. "Along with about a hundred other oddities in that community."

"Ahhhhh—I've got . . . another thing I want to mention to you." Dexter Medaxas's voice was conspiratorial, all of a sudden. "There's one case in particular you can transfer here. It's called *Nova Aerospace Company v. Dravos Corporation*. You might send that one, along with all the others you're sending.

Now, Judge Medaxas sounded insistent. "The reason I say you should send *Nova Aerospace v. Dravos* is that I know there's a Motion to Transfer that case here. Plus, Nova Aerospace—that's the plaintiff—

is closer to this courthouse than to yours, even though the lawsuit is filed with your courthouse. And the claim arose here."

"Makes sense."

"I understand that *Nova v. Dravos* is the kind of complex case that will consume a lot of time. And I'd like to help out. If it's part of a routine transfer to adjust the dockets, you won't even have to rule on the Motion to Transfer. You can just send it."

"Good. You certainly can help out, that way. Again, congratulations. We're glad to have you."

*   *   *

Romaine Cramshak was nervous. She fidgeted and shifted her feet, then shifted them again. The FBI agents were not surprised. Many people are nervous when talking to law enforcement, whether there is a reason to be nervous or not.

"You were deTravanian Wrenger's lab assistant back at Nova Aerospace?"

"Y-yes."

"And you came with him to Dravos Corporation?"

"Yes."

The FBI agent was gentle. No reason not to be, yet. "It speaks well of you, that a man with his talents would rely on you enough to bring you with him."

"Thank you."

"He's been shot and still is in the hospital. Do you have any information about who it was that shot him or why?"

"Well, I heard it was two people and I heard the name of one of them because he got shot too, but I don't remember that person's name."

"Do you have any information about why he was shot or who might have wanted to shoot him?"

"Gosh, no. It was a complete surprise to me and to everyone I know. Who would have a grudge against Mr. Wrenger?"

"That's what we want to find out. Search your memory, please."

"I . . . really don't know anything more about it. Maybe Nova Aerospace. He left Nova under bad conditions. But no, I doubt that. I also heard that someone tried to attack him in the hospital."

"On another subject, do you have any information about how the plans for the rollover mechanism could have gotten out to other people?"

"They *did?* No! Those plans are secret and protected all the time."

"Do you have any information about how those plans could have gotten into the hands of a hostile foreign power?"

Romaine Cramshak's eyes opened wide. "They got into the hands of . . . who?"

"Do you have any idea how the plans could have gotten into the hands of anyone from China, North Korea, or Iran? Or any foreign people?"

"Gosh, no! I can't imagine. That couldn't have happened."

* * *

"It doesn't make any sense," said the FBI agent who had questioned Romaine Cranshaft.

"Of course it doesn't," answered his partner.

"Why would deTravanian Wrenger clam up after being shot if he knows nothing, including not knowing who shot him?"

"Or what the reason was, about why he got shot?"

"I'm trying to be open-minded and give Mr. Wrenger the benefit of the doubt. But it's hard to do. I can't think of any reason he wouldn't at first tell us who it was. Not wanting to get involved? He obviously knows he's involved. Thinking he's safer this way? Unlikely."

"Not unless he knows exactly who it is who's trying to kill him."

"Or . . . is Wrenger telling the truth, and Ms. Cramshak knows something? If that's so, she's a really good liar.

14

Grey clouds hid the sky outside Robert Herrick's floor-to-ceiling windows. The green along Buffalo Bayou glistened with wetness, and the horizon was too blurred to see.

Across from Robert sat the President of Nova Aerospace, Mike Martin. "So, we're finally going to be getting into something real, about our lawsuit against Dravos."

"Yes. We're finally taking depositions."

"I've never seen a deposition. I have a vague idea that you ask questions of the other side's witnesses. But what's a deposition like?"

"It's to find out what the other side knows. What their witnesses are going to say at trial. It's really just a type of investigation, only the other side's people are required to show up and answer questions, just like a police officer questioning witnesses."

"You can make them tell you how they stole our trade secret, then?"

"No. We can't 'make' them say anything in particular. We can ask them questions in front of a court reporter, who takes down the answers. That way, we can get them to tell us the story that they want to tell. It may be true, or it may not be true, or it may be that a given witness doesn't know. If they don't confess to what we've claimed in our lawsuit, it will be up to us to prove it."

"Which we do—how?"

"Well, by the similarities in the rollover device that your firm made, and the rollover device that turned up in the Iranian missile, plus inferences from the fact that deTravanian Wrenger went to work for Dravos. And that Dravos does work internationally."

"Which is all circumstantial."

"Indeed, yes."

"Will it be enough? Will the judge be persuaded? And the jury?"

Robert smiled. And shrugged. "I always said, it's a hard lawsuit."

And Mike Martin's questions reminded him that he wanted to take things easier. Why am I doing this?

* * *

Atlanta, Georgia. A conference room in the usual law firm of Dravos Corporation. The conference room was borrowed for the deposition of deTravanian Wrenger. It showed wealth in the tapestries on the wall, in the marble-and-walnut table, in the matching walnut chairs, in the swirl-painted walls, and even in the carved baseboards.

"Do you want to make the usual agreements?" asked the court reporter. She was a dark-haired, pretty Latina lady, about thirty, and she looked first at Jimmy Coleman at her left and then at Robert Herrick at her right.

"As usual, all objections can be stated at trial," Jimmy's voice grated. "Formalities in setting up the deposition are waived. The witness can sign in front of any notary. I agree."

"I agree," Robert responded.

The court reporter turned to her immediate left, where Wrenger sat. "Raise your right hand, please."

The witness, a black man with a misshapen head, purple glasses, and an odd plus-or-minus tattoo on his cheek, obeyed.

"Do you swear or affirm that your testimony will be the truth, the whole truth, and nothing but the truth, so help you God?"

"I do," answered Wrenger.

Sounds like his first lie, Robert Herrick thought to himself.

He looked at the witness's eyes. "Please state your name for the record here—and for the court and jury." The question was worded to establish a solemn atmosphere, to the extent a question can do that.

The witness stared back. "DeTravanian Wrenger."

"And how are you employed, Mr. Wrenger?"

"Vice president, Dravos Corporation. Research and development."

"You know what a deposition is?"

"The lawyers have explained it to me."

"And so, you know that the same requirement of truthfulness applies as if we were in a courtroom, and the same penalties of perjury apply?"

The witness smiled as if the question were a silly one. "Of course I know that."

That's a true statement, thought Robert Herrick. But it didn't mean that the rest of the witness's statements were going to be true.

Now, Robert shifted to asking about the witness's background. His upbringing, his education, his experience. His interests, hobbies, and employment. DeTravanian Wrenger was born in eastern Europe. Mother from Bulgaria, father from Cameroon, both killed when he was ten. A degree in electrical engineering from Harvard, Ph.D. from Stanford, professor at CalTech. Too many patents to know the exact number. Same with publications.

Interests? "At the present time, inventing new electronic devices." And what interests for fun? "Chess, watching soccer, and studying the Riemann Hypothesis."

The Riemann Hypothesis? Should I ask, what on earth is that? Robert hesitated for an instant.

Then: "What's that, the Riemann Hypothesis?"

The witness brightened, and instantly, he became a professor. A teacher. "The hypothesis is that all non-trivial zeroes of the zeta function have real part one-half. You know, that means they lie on the one-half or point-five vertical line on the complex plane. It's the biggest unsolved puzzle in number theory."

Now the man with the strange $\pm$ sign on his cheek was smiling, wound up, and talkative. "The hypothesis was first proposed by Bernhard Riemann more than a hundred and fifty years ago. Riemann was studying the distribution of prime numbers, and he offered this tantalizing suggestion, but over the century and a half, nobody's been able to prove it. There have been dozens of claimed proofs, all falsified, and several proofs that it is not true, also falsified, and at least one proof that it can't be proved, and that also has been falsified."

Everybody at the conference table was dumfounded and fascinated, both at the same time. Bewildered and shell-shocked. The witness went on.

"Various kinds of calculus have been proposed as tools for potential solutions to the Riemann Hypothesis, but nobody knows what will work. It's probable that analysis will be needed, too. You know, analysis, meaning algebra. Some have suggested that matrices might be useful. In particular, Hermitian matrices—"

"Thank you, Mr. Wrenger," Robert said finally. "We all understand. But we've got limited time, and I need to ask you some other questions."

"Yes, of course," said Wrenger enthusiastically.

Everyone else who had just heard about the Riemann Hypothesis looked the way a prizefighter looks after the fifteenth round.

Sometimes it works, Robert thought. You start a deposition with subjects that the witness knows well. And if you're lucky, you find something that he likes to talk about. Now you've got him talking. Good. The hope is that he talks a lot about the important issues in the lawsuit too.

But Jimmy Coleman intervened. "It's time to take a break. The court reporter needs one. And after learning how to solve the Riemann Hypothesis, I do too."

*   *   *

Two hours later, Robert had Mr. Wrenger's answers to questions about how the rollover trade secret got stolen, if it did.

"I don't believe it got stolen. And if it did, I don't know how."

Did the witness have any theories or suspicions? Here, Wrenger answered by talking about Romaine Cramshak, his assistant, the strange visitor she "showed around," and the plans that had been opened up. But it amounted only to suspicion.

It sounded fishy to Robert. But the witness couldn't give any more details. Or wouldn't.

"It's true, isn't it, that you have a grudge against Nova Aerospace? And you'd like to hurt them?"

"I don't like Nova. They treated me badly. But I wouldn't do anything illegal to hurt them."

"You've deposited a lot of money since you came to Dravos. Where did it come from?"

"From Nova, what they owed me, and from Dravos. Bonuses."

"Not from Iran? Or some other foreign country?"

The witness's forehead wrinkled. "No. Definitely, no."

We weren't able to pin down the source of that money, Robert thought unhappily.

"Have you ever been in contact with anyone from China or North Korea?"

"A Chinese company was interested in a smartphone application. But we didn't do any business."

"Have you ever been in contact with anyone from Iran?"

"That I knew was from Iran?"

"Yes."

"No."

Robert paused for an instant. Then: "Have you ever been in contact with anyone you suspected was from Iran or representing Iranian interests?"

The witness hesitated, thinking. Maybe he was trying to remember. Maybe he was calculating whether he could get away with a false denial. Travel records can be obtained. So can emails.

Finally: "I got a series of emails from a man named Amir Massad. He was interested in rocket technology."

"Did you meet with him?"

"Yes. He came all the way from Teheran to my laboratory in Atlanta, at Dravos Corporation."

But the witness was adamant. Nothing concerning any rollover mechanism was talked about. Nothing concerning any Orbital Attitude and Maneuvering System, or OAMS. Nothing concerning any *Kharramshar* missile.

"I can see that you're fishing around for something about stolen trade secrets," said deTravanian Wrenger finally. "Forget it. It didn't happen. I don't think any trade secret got stolen, and if any secret did get stolen, I don't know anything about it."

He smiled. And he crinkled the ± sign on his cheek when he smiled.

Robert recognized the pattern. There are some people who can't lie without smiling. So, every time they lie, they smile. It wasn't possible, usually, to get them to admit it. But sometimes you could disprove the lie.

And, he told himself, sometimes you couldn't.

15

Assistant District Attorney Maria Melendes stood and faced the three judges in front of her. But they weren't real judges.

She always practiced her argument beforehand in a moot court, with lawyers playing the parts of judges. These three lawyers would ask her every sensitive question they could think of and tell her what they thought worked in her argument and what they thought didn't.

In a week, she would face the real judges of the United States Court of Appeals to argue for affirmance of Billy Joe Armistead's death sentence. This was that awful case in which the defendant had dug a grave for his murdered girlfriend and had thrown her baby on top of her before burying both of them.

Maria looked up from her notes.

". . . The defendant's first argument, then, is that his trial lawyers were incompetent. Nothing could be farther off base.

"The defendant's new lawyers are accusing the trial lawyers of incompetence because they didn't call a particular alibi witnesses for this defendant named Clarence Banacek. Actually, those trial lawyers did the right thing. This Banacek had a long criminal record, which the jury would have heard. His memory of the date was only, as he put it, approximate. Cross examination would have admitted more crimes by Billy Joe Armistead. He would have been worse off with this witness."

She shifted slightly to signal that the explanation of the law was coming. "The leading Supreme Court case about the standard for performance of a criminal lawyer is *Strickland v. Washington*. The Court said that the Constitution requires a trial lawyer to make what it called 'independent decisions.' There is a range of possible strategic pathways, and if the lawyer follows a path that is within that range, there's no incompetence. And, quote, 'the benchmark for judging any claim of ineffectiveness' must be whether the lawyer's conduct undermined the adversarial process so badly that the trial cannot be relied on as having produced a just result."

After reading those words, she looked up at the three "judges."

"This case is far from meeting that standard. In fact, no lawyer could have kept Billy Joe Armistead from looking like anything other than a prime candidate for the ultimate punishment. They did the best they could by putting family members on the witness stand to tell vividly about Billy Joe's abusive childhood, and they even persuaded the judge to admit in evidence a picture of the death chamber, over objections that it was irrelevant. These lawyers weren't incompetent at all."

Now, she faced a barrage of questions from the three pretend-judges. "When does a lawyer have to offer character evidence, then?" "Under the *Strickland* standard, only if the character testimony is so good that it's unreasonable *not* to offer it." "What if the defendant insists on calling character witnesses even if his attorney doesn't want to?" "That didn't happen here, and this isn't one of the decisions where the lawyer has to forfeit making an independent decision."

And then, the three lawyers offered their critiques. From one: "I think you're doing the right thing by keeping this part of the argument short. The defense argument is weak. Save your time for other things." And from another pretend-judge: "You might mention what some courts say: You need almost a 'mockery of justice' to show incompetence of counsel."

Maria made one-word notes of these suggestions. Then she picked up where she had left off: "Next, let me address the second argument that the defense makes here. . . ."

Two hours later, the moot court ended. Maria would get only fifteen minutes in the real argument. "Let's head over to the bar, guys," she said to her judges. "After anything that has anything to do with this nightmare of a case, I always need a stiff drink or two."

* * *

But she didn't get to the bar the way she had expected.

Her phone rang. Robert was calling, and he sounded despondent. "It's Pepper again."

"Oh, no."

Pepper Herrick was Robert's oldest child, and she had been a favorite of Maria's since she'd been a baby.

But recently Pepper had been arrested for driving while intoxicated. And pled guilty, while hiding the whole thing. And arrested again. And pled guilty again, this time with help from her father. And then arrested again for the same crime, driving while intoxicated, in a case where a man was injured, fortunately only slightly. She had gone to jail in that case, after her lawyer got her a good plea bargain deal, and had served her sentence on weekends.

With weekend service and a sympathetic supervisor, Pepper had managed to keep her job. But then, she got arrested for drunk-in-public. Not as bad as drunk driving, and it only meant a traffic-court fine, but her boss was becoming impatient.

"Oh, yes," said Robert. "Pepper called me, sounding good and drunk. She kept the agreement we had. She called, instead of driving."

"I'll go with you to get her." It always took both of them, because someone had to drive Pepper's car.

"No," he said gently. "No. Her friend is there, and sober. I spoke to her, too. She went there with Pepper. She'll drive Pepper's car and then I'll take her home."

Maria sighed. "It makes it all so complicated."

"Yes. And I could spend the afternoon more productively by doing something about my *Nova Aerospace v. Dravos* case. But I know what you've been doing this afternoon. You deserve some R 'n R time."

"But. . . ."

"Maria, I insist. You've overworked yourself these days. I'll get Pepper. Besides, I want to talk to her."

Now Maria had another reason for going to the bar with her colleagues. She really found herself shaken by this Billy Joe case, even though she'd seen a lot of violent crimes. And she realized there was an irony to her going to the bar with Pepper's drinking in her mind as part of the motivation.

*　*　*

Being a lawyer gives you absolutely no help when it comes to family matters, Robert thought. If anything, it makes some of the issues harder. Your kids or your wife or your friends or your neighbors know who you are, and they discount what you say. It's lawyer talk.

Especially with Pepper.

He hugged her when she trundled out of the Tom Foolery Saloon, where she'd been with her friend. "You did the right thing by calling me," he told her softly. "I know it's not your first instinct, to call. But it should be. Always call."

"I hate it. I don't like to call you when you're working."

"Either I will come or Maria will come. If it's truly impossible for us—if we have a live witness on the witness stand—I'll get a taxi. I'll send one."

"Or rather, an Uber." Pepper was always technologically up to date.

Then, silence. He didn't want to embarrass her with her friend in the car.

But finally, he was bursting to say it, and he did. "Pepper, we just desperately want to do what we've been discussing for so long. Isn't it clear to you?"

She had adamantly refused to go to Alcoholics Anonymous. And now, having been told so many times to do it, she lost her temper.

"Daddy, I've told you a million times, I don't have anything in common with those losers at AA. Please believe it. Please believe it. There's nothing about any of this that I can't do on my own. I have willpower. I am tougher than you think. And smarter. And I can do it, without your nagging."

Friend or no friend, embarrassment or not, it was too much.

"Pepper, listen to me. Do not—do not—talk to your father that way. I am taking you and your friend home because you've had too much to drink. And even aside from that, it is a terrible thing for you that you talk that way to your father."

"I could have driven home just fine."

She was disheveled and slurring her words. Four arrests and a trip to jail, an injured man, thousands of dollars to repair two cars, and she still didn't get it.

Silently, he counted to ten.

"Tomorrow, you will realize that you had no business driving. Tomorrow, in fact, you'll feel the effects of drinking too much. Tomorrow, you will regret talking to your father this way, or at least I hope you will regret it.

"And tomorrow, please think about solving this repeated, repeated problem. Or at least doing what you can to solve it."

They were silent for the rest of the ride home.

* * *

At the office, next morning, he looked out the window. Dreary fog. Oppressive gray in every direction. Tiny cars on tiny freeways limping along, slipping, stopping, in sheets of mist.

He couldn't make himself concentrate. He had the occasional thoughts and made notes, but with wide spaces of down time.

He got out the picture of Maria in the newspapers. As usual, it amused him and at the same time made him proud of her. He reached out and touched the picture of his first wife, Patricia, sitting in a gold frame on the corner of his desk. Twelve years now she'd been gone, but unconsciously, he reached toward it whenever his mind clouded.

He found himself rearranging the pens and blotter and trinkets on his desk. A pair of scissors with an inscription of gratitude given by a client: moved a few inches to center it. Then moved again, to the side. An inkwell from the Exchange Club for a job well done as President one year—useless because few of us use inkwells any more, but beautiful, in marble and brass: moved to a corner. A stack of files, which he lifted one at a time. And changed their order.

He looked at the legal pad on which he had been writing. It had only a few scratched lines.

"We have almost nothing to show rollover got stolen. Professor Eisner, good witness—says Iranian microprocessor too similar to Nova's for coincidence. But debatable.

"Jimmy's witnesses? Will say devices not similar at all. But bigger problem? Only evidence Dravos stole it is that Wrenger or his assistant or both left it sitting out while someone visited."

He hesitated. Then, he wrote: "Loser case. Looking at a Jimmy C win in middle of trial, by a Judgment as a Matter of Law.

"Meaning, insufficient evidence. Judge won't even let the jury deliberate."

He shuffled to the corner of his office. He swung down the cover to the bar he kept there, pinching his finger in the process. He shook it and swore a little. And he poured four fingers of good eighteen-year Talisker over a pair of ice cubes. Ironic, he said to himself. It's not just this case. It's my daughter's drinking, too, that's driving me to drink.

16

Across town, Jimmy Coleman sat in front of his Italian chest at his desk that matched it. Jennifer Lowenstein was taking notes across from him.

"Get that deposition of Professor Eisner—you know, Herrick's big expert—summarized as quickly as possible. It's a good one."

"You think that deposition's helpful to us? Of Herrick's expert, who says that the Iranian rollover OAMS device is so similar to ours?"

"Yes." Jimmy's rasp was smoother, more syrupy, contented.

"But this Professor Eisner—he stuck to his conclusions. He didn't backtrack at all. At the end of the deposition, he was still saying that it must have been copied."

"You wanted us to prove in this deposition that he's not credible?"

"Well . . . yes."

Jimmy smiled. Jennifer thought to herself, as she had many times before, that every associate in the firm wanted to work for Jimmy. All of your hours would be billed and paid for, which is a big deal in a law firm. The year-end reports would show that you'd been a positive money-maker for the firm.

And in spite of that gruff exterior, Jimmy was a wonderful teacher.

"Jennifer, it's unusual to destroy a witness in one deposition alone." Jimmy's growl sounded as smooth as honey, now. "It happens occasionally, but not normally. In a deposition, you're searching. You're finding out things. You can only ask questions. You can't take the guy by the neck and 'make him say' this or that."

"So, what makes it a good deposition?"

"You take just a little off of his credibility. You find things that make him seem a little less than truthful, or a little less than sure. You find out things that help your side. Not necessarily things that make the witness completely unbelievable."

"Did that happen here?"

"Sure. This Professor Eisner, Herrick's big witness, said that his opinion was 'debatable.' He might just be cautious in saying that. He might be modest. And he might be truthful and honest. But if a so-called expert witness says that his opinion is 'debatable,' he's going to have a problem in front of a jury."

Jimmy showed his teeth. "At trial, I'll ask this guy, 'So! The opposite opinion can be true?' and 'So! You might be completely wrong, because that's what 'debatable' means?' And that gives me an opening to make him look ridiculous, honest or not."

"Oh." Jennifer was quiet. "You have ammunition now. With this deposition, you can go for the jugular, I guess."

She was thinking about Jimmy's gang story—the one about the dead teenager in the car trunk.

* * *

Robert was thinking exactly what Jimmy was thinking. It's an important case. A big case. And I'm going to lose it.

What can I do? Is there anything? Should I just settle this miserable case for whatever tiny amount Jimmy will pay? Settle it for what lawyers call the 'nuisance value' of the lawsuit? Meaning, settle for what a defendant will pay just to avoid the cost of the lawsuit, not even worrying about the outcome?

That might be less than a few hundred thousand dollars, he thought. Settle for the nuisance value, when the damage to Nova Aerospace was probably in the multiple millions, probably hundreds of millions, the lost value of its trade secret . . . ?

He started making notes. "What Can We Do?" . . .

In scratchy letters, then: "Romaine Cramshak—Wrenger Ass'tnt. See what turns up, her deposition.

"Try to find this mysterious Iranian visitor—name is Amir, but called himself David—will that even be possible? Or worth the expense of trying to find out?

"Find another expert? More persuasive? Definite?

"Anything else?"

He looked again at the list. And found himself breathing raggedly. A lawsuit boxed in, after you've filed it—boxed in by defects in the evidence—it's more than frustrating. For a lawyer, it's personal defeat. He pictured himself: like a spider caught by a child and put into a jar. The spider tries to get out. But can't.

He keeps trying. But he can't.

And it's that much worse, knowing that Jimmy's the one who's put me into the jar.

*   *   *

Again, the ornate conference room in Atlanta, Georgia. Again, with a court reporter, a witness, and Robert on one side, Jimmy on the other, of the huge conference table.

This was the deposition of Romaine Cramshak.

The witness had wispy gray hair and a round, wrinkled face. She wore a too-big brown jacket and skirt and a blue-and-white blouse that clashed with it. She held her hands clasped together, near her neck. Her skin was mottled and sere.

She fidgeted. Looked down at her skirt.

Ms. Cramshak was nervous.

The court reporter had her raise her hand and swear to tell the truth. Her name? "Romaine, R-O-M-A-I-N-E, Cramshak, C-R-A-M-S-H-A-K."

Born in Romania. Family came to the United States when she was fourteen. Graduated from Penn State University. Majored in electrical engineering.

Jimmy looked sleepy throughout these preliminaries. His suit was sharkskin, an electric powder blue color, with a texture that seized onlookers' eyes, and the green striped shirt over his belly protruded from the front of his coat, which stretched across him like a tent pulled tautly against its poles. He wore an ornate black-and–white striped tie with gold in it. Too loud and not very becoming, especially on Jimmy, but that was Jimmy. And however conservatively or not he dressed, he would be able to represent his client to the fullest and eager to push the envelope.

Robert wore a grey coat, black slacks, and a red-and-gray tie over a white buttondown shirt. More conservative than the big-firm lawyer, however counterintuitive that might seem.

After a half hour of questions about Romaine Cramshak's personal history, education, publications, activities, military service (that too), criminal record (none), and family—after the part of the deposition that lawyers call "Getting to Know You, Getting to Know All About You"—Robert was ready to start asking the questions that mattered.

His first few questions were designed to rattle the witness just a little. A nervous witness sometimes makes mistakes and admits the truth of something that was intended to remain concealed by evasions.

"Ms. Cramshak, you know, don't you, that Nova's lawsuit is about a theft of trade secrets?"

"I know that there's a lawsuit that says that. . . . Yes."

"And a theft of trade secrets, of course, can be a crime?"

Jimmy didn't object. No objection would have been proper, but Robert was surprised that Jimmy didn't make one, however improper, to coach the witness. So . . . Romaine Cramshak answered, after hesitating.

"I . . . don't know. I'm not a lawyer."

It wasn't important to press for an answer to that.

"You've seen the diagrams of the rollover device that was recovered from an Iranian missile as part of its Orbital Attitude and Maneuvering system, haven't you?"

"I've seen it or seen something that said it was from an Iranian craft."

"The Iranian device is very similar to the device you and deTravanian Wrenger developed at Nova Aerospace, isn't it?"

"I think so. I guess so."

Bingo.

Sometimes a nervous witness responds more truthfully to a key question.

"It has all the key features in the same places, doesn't it?"

"Yes."

"And the same functions in the different steps of the flowchart?"

"Yes."

"And Do Loops in the same places?"

"Yes."

"Were you surprised by all the similarities?"

"Yes. Some similarities would be expected because the function of the rollover device is similar in every spacecraft, though."

"But these similarities are more extensive than function would call for, aren't they?"

It wasn't a question, the way Robert said it.

"Yes."

"The Iranian device must have been designed by someone who knew the design of the device made at Nova Aerospace? You'd have to say so."

"I. . . . I guess. . . . Right."

At this point, very deliberately, Robert told himself to stop asking questions about this subject. Too many questions can give the witness an opportunity to backtrack. Pushing too hard at anything can backfire.

For example, Napoleon won everything. Then he invaded Russia. Bad mistake. The German Wehrmacht had success with blitzkrieg after blitzkrieg. Then came the German attack upon Russia. Major losses. The early theorists about combat called it exceeding the "culminating point" of victory. You lose from doing that.

Lawyers call it the "one question too many." You lose from doing that, too.

So now, Robert changed the subject.

"There came a time when you and Mr. Wrenger had a visitor from Iran at Nova Aerospace. A person named Amir, I believe?"

"Yes. I don't recall the exact name, but that sounds right."

"From Iran?"

"Yes."

"And how did it happen that you met this Mr. Amir?"

"He came to our lab. Knocked on the door. Introduced himself and asked for deTravanian Wrenger."

"What happened then?" Sometimes, the best question just asks the witness to keep going, to keep telling the story.

"DeTravanian came up and knew Mr. Amir. They shook hands. One of them, I can't remember who, said that it's been a long time since I saw you, and the other one laughed and said, right, last week."

"Kind of like they were old friends?"

"Yes, but I don't think they were, really. They were just making a joke. It wasn't very funny, but both of them laughed."

"Then what happened?"

"I excused myself and went away."

"And let me guess." Robert's voice was as confident as he was incredulous. "When you got back, the design papers for the Nova rollover device were on the lab table, spread out."

"Yes, and both of them were looking at the designs together. How did you know about this, Mr. Herrick?"

"Let me understand. DeTravanian Wrenger and this Amir were both looking at the plans for the Nova rollover device spread out on the laboratory table and talking about the device?"

"Yes."

"Did you hear anything?"

"No, not really."

Robert asked only a couple more questions about the meeting with Amir Massad. Then he changed to another subject. How much money would Ms. Cramshak think a device like the Nova Aerospace or the Iranian one be worth, in current dollars, if someone wanted to buy it?

Her answer: "Probably millions. But I'm not a financial person."

In the cab back to the airport, Robert and Tom Kennedy marveled at what had just happened.

"Jimmy must have told her to tell the truth. Of course. We all say that to our clients, so that if the witness is asked, she can say, 'I was told to tell the truth.'"

"The problem is—for Jimmy—that this Ms. Cramshak followed that instruction."

"Maybe. Maybe. But of course, it doesn't get us a lawsuit win."

"Why do you say that?"

"First of all, we have two different stories. Wrenger's testimony is completely different. He says he found the plans unrolled and doesn't know anything about how they got that way. He didn't show Amir anything, according to him. And anyway, it's a circumstantial case at best."

"Okay. That's first. What's second?"

"It's Jimmy Coleman who's on the other side. I just suspect Jimmy's got something up his sleeve that makes us lose."

17

Maria Melendes sat alone at a table by the window. The restaurant was Emeril's, one of the best in New Orleans—and therefore one of the best in the world. Tomorrow she would argue the case for affirming the judgment against Billy Joe Armistead. The court of appeals meets in New Orleans, and she had arrived here early this morning. She was as ready as she would ever be. Traditionally, she took the evening before to have dinner in this strange, magnificent city.

"Do you want a menu, Ms. Melendes? I reckon you pretty familiar with it from the times you been here."

She laughed. "Yes, thank you, Ralph. I might want to look for something different."

A pause. Then: "What's this? 'Sugar Cane Lacquered Duck.' It's . . . lacquered?"

Ralph laughed. "Yes ma'am. The juice from sugar cane is spread all over it. It isn't really like lacquer. It doesn't harden, but it's shiny like lacquer."

"Is it any good?"

Ralph showed a kind of mock offense. Then laughed. "This is Emeril's."

"I'm curious enough to go for it."

She had a glass of chardonnay, a Buena Vista, and tried to think about nothing, or as close to nothing as she could. It occurred to her that she was going to exceed her allotment from the office, by far. She would pay personally, and gladly. She wondered what Robert was doing. She missed her time in Las Vegas. The pictures from Billy Joe's case, the pictures of the grave, kept coming back to her.

Finally, the lacquered duck arrived. She was able to stop thinking.

* * *

The next morning, three hundred and fifty miles to the west, a group of lawyers gathered in a big room with folding chairs. Big cases can involve dozens of lawyers, and this one—*Nova Aerospace v. Dravos*—had the attention of a number of Robert's associates.

"Welcome to our Demonstration Center," said a man in a dark gray suit. "My name's Derek Zender, and I'm a vice president of Data Analytics Corporation, which is your host right now and your partner for analyzing the mountain of documents produced in this case."

"Thank you, Derek." Robert Herrick stood and faced the group. "My friends, these folks at Data Analytics are our team for winnowing down the documents produced during discovery in our *Nova Aerospace* case."

He spread his arms. "Lawyers, here's what we're up against in this case. The defendant, Dravos Corporation, has produced literally millions of documents during discovery. Our client, Nova, has produced millions more. Nobody could study all of them individually. And that's why we have Data Analytics. We've hired them to search the documents electronically."

"And that's what we do for a living," said Derek Zender. "We search documents in big cases to identify the relevant ones. We've developed algorithms that look for key search terms. We know how to generate effective search terms. And we have proprietary software to do it with."

He pointed toward a screen, which featured the words "Data Analytics Corporation" above a red, blue, and gold logo made up of the letters "DAC" in modified script. The lights dimmed gradually.

"We start by figuring out the search terms we want to look for. The choice of search terms is a crucial step. It's part art and part science. For example, in this case you can't use search terms like 'microprocessor' or 'connection,' because they'd be in nearly every document. You'd still have millions or hundreds of thousands to read one by one."

The screen changed. "And also, the search terms can't all be rare words, or phrases that don't appear much, because you'd miss a lot of important documents."

"This is the key," Robert said. "The search terms. Derek and his colleagues will be working with you lawyers to generate the search terms. What we want him to do, of course, is to isolate documents that will help us at trial or in questioning witnesses. Documents that show how deTravanian Wrenger and Dravos handled our rollover design. We also want him to identify documents that can be used to hurt our side—the ones that Jimmy Coleman will claim are damaging to Nova Aerospace—so that we can answer him at trial."

"That's the basic idea," The man in the gray suit changed the screen again. "We've done a little experimenting, but next we'll need help from you lawyers. For example, we found that looking for sentences containing the phrase "Do Loop" produced way too many documents. To get it right, we need to pick you lawyer's brains."

The screen changed again. "As I say, we experimented, and we discovered that a search term seeking the word 'decision' and the phrase 'Do Loop,' or certain other combinations of words, all together in the same paragraph, could produce a workable quantity of documents. And we thought we might be statistically likely to have unearthed the important ones. But to determine that, we need you lawyers."

Another screen change. "But that's just one example. Here are a few others." And Derek Zender took them through a dozen other word combinations that might make good search terms. "But we need your help to generate more and better search terms. And to tell us whether the documents we're finding are helpful to you."

Finally, the screen showed the firm name and logo again. And the lights in the room brightened.

"All right, Derek," said Robert." Looks like you've made a start toward getting this pile of documents analyzed. And flagging the useful ones for us, at the same time he's eliminating the other ones."

He smiled. "And that's the good news. But the bad news is, my buckaroos, when Derek identifies the important documents, we have to evaluate them the old-fashioned way."

"What's that?" asked a new associate. "What's the old fashioned way?"

Robert laughed sympathetically. "There will still be a huge number of documents. And we'll have to do something very painful. Specifically . . . we'll have to read them all."

*   *   *

The judges' bench in the courtroom was long and high. The ceiling was distant, with too-bright lights. The walls were white, still, and nondescript except for a few photographs and paintings of deceased eminences.

This was the United States Court of Appeals for the Fifth Circuit. For most supplicants, this was the end of the line. A prisoner looking at fifty years had to depend on a long-shot win here. A severely injured plaintiff could only hope for victory here against a determined, outraged corporation that insisted its people had done nothing wrong.

Everybody's heard of the Supreme Court, but most would be wise to forget about it. That Court gets many thousands of what are called "petitions for certiorari" every year—each one begging the justices to consider this case and making as much noise as possible—but the Supreme Court agrees to hear only a few, on the order of a hundred. If the lightning doesn't strike, and it usually doesn't, the Fifth Circuit is the last stop.

Maria Melendes sat at one of the simple counsel tables: brown-stained wood, with a broad rectangular top and four simple legs. The court's docket was printed in front of her. The first case, styled Henderson v. Pedernales Transit Company, was about a collision between an eighteen-wheeler and a Volkswagen Jetta, with two deaths. The second case, *Wade v. Mississippi*, was about a convicted bank robber whose sixty-year sentence had been affirmed on appeal and who now was seeking release through a petition for habeas corpus.

The third case was Maria's. *Billy Joe Armistead v. the State of Texas*. The inmate condemned to death for killing his girlfriend and throwing her baby, still alive, into the grave before filling it.

Suddenly there were three loud knocks on the door behind the judges' bench. This signal is traditional, but it always sets the lawyers' teeth on edge. A law clerk wearing a dark gray suit stepped out and pronounced the traditional introduction.

"Hear ye, hear ye, hear ye: The United States Court of Appeals for the Fifth Circuit is now open pursuant to law. All ye that have business before this court, draw nigh and ye shall be heard. God save the United States and this honorable court!"

Three judges in black robes walked in a stately manner to take their places behind the bench. A man, a woman, and a man. The one in the middle, the woman, was the Chief Judge. "Be seated, please," she said pleasantly.

The Chief Judge made a short speech about the ground rules. "We've read the briefs and we are familiar with the facts." This was a message to the attorneys: Keep it short.

The first case, *Henderson v. Pedernales Transit Company*, went by as a blur for Maria because she was reading and re-reading her notes. The defendant claimed that the trial judge had excluded an expert witness that he should have allowed the jury to hear. There was a lot of discussion of the Supreme Court's "*Daubert* decision," which is familiar to every lawyer, and of later cases related to that one. The judges sounded inclined to reverse the plaintiff's judgment and spoke harshly to the lawyer who argued in favor of it. The Fifth Circuit is known for some panels that will treat a plaintiff's lawyer like a criminal; it depended on which three judges you got.

A half hour later the judges heard from lawyers arguing *Wade v. Mississippi*. The defendant's argument was that his confession should have been suppressed. There was discussion about a range of post-*Miranda v. Arizona* cases.

Suddenly, the Chief Judge called out, "*Billy Joe Armistead.*" Maria's case.

A lawyer in gray pinstripes shuffled to the podium. The defense lawyer would speak first. Maria's role would be limited to taking notes.

"May it please the court: I am Travis Tennenbaum, and I represent the defendant, Billy Joe Armistead, who is under a sentence of death."

"Mr. Tennenbaum," said the Chief Judge.

The defendant's lawyer looked up at the court.

"I want to start with point one in our brief. The jury should have been instructed to consider every type of mitigating evidence that was admitted. And there was a lot of mitigating evidence, from the fact that the defendant was abused as a child to his model behavior behind bars. The trial lawyer requested a jury charge in those words. All the judge had to do was to adopt the language he was given by the trial lawyer."

The chief Judge frowned. "Are you saying that the trial judge has to say to the jury whatever the defense lawyer wants him to say?"

"No, of course not, your honor. But the trial judge has the duty to listen to the defendant's proposed charges and cover the substance of what is required by law."

"You're saying that that wasn't done here? But the trial judge used a standard instruction that told the jury to balance the mitigating evidence against the aggravating evidence."

"That's not the same as telling the jury it has to consider *all* the mitigating evidence. And that's what the Supreme Court has said the jury has to be told."

"Your argument is that telling the jury to balance 'the mitigating evidence' is not good enough to alert the jury to its duty to balance *all* the mitigating evidence?"

"Exactly, your honor. The Supreme Court has said 'all' the mitigating evidence. Hinting isn't enough. Suggesting isn't enough. The jury should be told it directly: '*all*' the mitigating evidence."

Lawyer Tennenbaum shifted behind the podium. "Now, with the rest of the time I have, I want to turn to issue number two. Trial counsel was incompetent. For many reasons. To begin with, there was an alibi witness, a good alibi witness, and the trial lawyer didn't call him as a witness. The alibi witness, whose name was Clarence Banacek, would have told the jury that Billy Joe Armistead was with him at about the same time as the murders here, on a fishing trip."

The judges asked a barrage of questions about the alibi witness. Wasn't the decision not to call this supposed alibi witness a strategic decision? If it was, there was no incompetency. The witness had a horrendous criminal record. He had given inconsistent stories. He had only been able to say "approximately" which day the alleged fishing trip happened. "Wouldn't that testimony have just made this defendant look worse?" It was not only a strategic decision to omit this so-called witness; it was a sensible decision.

And right after that, the red light between the podium and the bench flashed. "I see I'm out of time." And Travis Tennenbaum sat down.

"Ms. Melendes." The Chief Judge's voice was flat.

Maria made a point of stepping sharply to the podium. Her right hand held a single manila folder. On the inside right flap were her argument notes. The left contained references to case decisions she might need.

She had developed these habits as a means of appearing—and being—well organized. In her left hand, she held photocopies of essential decisions, but she had never, in all her arguments, referred to these. They were more like a security blanket.

This single manila folder was everything.

"May it please the court. I disagree fundamentally with Mr. Tennebaum's theory that the trial judge has to adopt instructions provided by the defense lawyer. Or, for that matter, by the prosecutor, or any lawyer. Lawyers are partisans. The law is the law, and what lawyers might prefer to have the judge say is not the law.

"Counsel's argument comes down to one word: *all*. Instead of telling the jury to consider 'the' mitigating evidence, the judge should have told them to consider "all" the mitigating evidence. But what's the *difference?* Where is the prejudice to the defendant?"

The judges were silent. Inscrutable. Which is what they should have been. But it's unnerving, for a lawyer in front of them.

"Counsel would have this court undo the result of a six-week trial because of that word. And at the retrial, what is to stop the defense lawyer from requesting a charge that says, 'Consider *absolutely all* of the mitigating evidence,' and then appearing here to say that not adopting *that* instruction was reversible error?"

She shook her head. The standard advice that all appellate lawyers get is to stand still and avoid movement. But sometimes movement is effective. Now, Maria caught herself and stood immobile.

"That's not the law. The instructions are required to be correct and complete. These were. And there's not a requirement of any 'magic words,' like Mr. Tennenbaum's arguing."

Suddenly, way too soon, the red light went on. Maria stopped because she had to. She stepped to her chair and sat down heavily.

A memory of the pictures in this case flooded her mind again. The mounds of dirt, dug up in a patch of briars, where the defendant had led the detectives. The partly skeletonized body of the woman who was unfortunate enough to have been Billy Joe Armistead's girlfriend. And the smaller body, barely recognizable as a child, incomplete, riddled with bites and missing parts, smeared with dirt, in a tiny pink dress.

But here—in the majestic simplicity of a federal appeals court hearing a petition for habeas corpus—none of that mattered.

18

The search for evidence in Robert Herrick's office had reached epic proportions for a firm of this size. Two lawyers worked with the first team of investigators, trying to find something that would tell whether deTravanian Wrenger, or Romaine Cramshak, or both were involved in transferring Nova Aerospace's design to China, or North Korea, or Iran.

Or whether someone else had done it.

Or whether no one had done it, and Nova's case was meritless. That is the way it can be, with circumstantial evidence.

Another team focused on Hassan Malouf. He was the assassin who had shot Wrenger, whose accomplice had gotten away, and who refused to talk to the FBI. The team included a former FBI agent and an information technology specialist, as well as an attorney. "We can't tell you much, but we'll tell you what we can," FBI agents had said. Malouf had had an Iranian passport in his possession, which correctly identified him by name. A search of his hotel room had produced evidence of his membership in the Quds Force: a part of Iran's Revolutionary Guards that carried out unconventional warfare and intelligence activities.

The assassin also had information about Wrenger: photographs, a biography, acquaintances, contacts, computer passwords, and identification leads, down to the address and room number where he worked. The biography identified Wrenger as an electrical engineer who had invented guidance for missiles. But it stopped there. Tantalizingly, it did not show any connection of Wrenger's work with anyone else.

Another team tracked down the shadowy Iranian figure who had met with Wrenger and visited his laboratory. Amir Massad. The man who Romaine Cramshak had said might have looked at the plans for Nova's rollover device. The man who deTravanian Wrenger had said was in the laboratory with Romaine Cramshak "showing him around." The investigators went through dozens of Amir Massads who lived in Iran, then dozens more, and some who lived in the United States. There were a few with educations or experience that might equip them to search for electronic designs. But all of those were in Iran. Efforts to contact and interview them met with nothing but refusals, some of them accompanied by anti-American slogans.

One of these "Amir Massads" had visited the United States around the time deTravanian Wrenger had said he met with the man.

"Tom," said Robert Herrick to Kennedy, "can we try to question this Mr. Massad in Iran?"

"Sure, we can try. You can try questioning the Pope or the premier of Kazakhstan. We'll try. But Iran? We'll try, but. . . . Don't count on it."

"We've done this before. In Qatar. We used an unusual process called 'letters rogatory' to petition the Qatari courts. We didn't think it would work, and we didn't get all we wanted, but we got something that was useful."

"We can try."

"Let's try."

"Okay. I will go and study the Iranian court system. If they have a court system. We may be at the mercy of the local ayatollah."

*   *   *

Mike Martin, the president of Nova Aerospace, sat across the big mahogany desk from Robert Herrick. The day was full of sunshine. It streamed through the floor-to-ceiling windows like a bank of floodlights, shining the carpet into brilliant shapes of color. The flowers added another dimension of multiple shades, happy shades.

But the mood in the office was somber. Serious.

"The lawyers for Dravos have filed what is called a 'Motion for Summary Judgment,'" Robert said. "It was filed yesterday."

"Yes. I got a copy. But you'll have to remind me—what's a Motion for Summary Judgment?"

"It means he's asking the judge to throw our case out without a trial because it's absolutely clear we can't win. That's what Jimmy's motion means."

"But that's . . . not true! We have evidence and arguments to make."

"I know." Robert sighed. "But that's Jimmy's argument. He's gotten all of our evidence during the discovery period of this case, and his position is that we don't have enough factual information to let a jury even decide whether we're right."

Mike Martin's face was screwed into a mask of disbelief. "It's ridiculous."

"This is the way lawsuits work, and we've got to take it seriously. We've got to fight against it with everything we've got. Because we could lose this motion. And have our case thrown out."

Robert waved his hand to emphasize the point. "Especially with this judge. I've told you about him. The judge practiced with Jimmy Coleman, remember? And was his partner."

"It gets worse and worse."

"I know. I feel the same way. I told you it was a difficult case to begin with, and on top of that, we're playing on an uneven field."

* * *

The Secret Service officer didn't know how to tell the Chief Judge what he knew he needed to tell him.

He knocked on the nondescript door to chambers and entered a surprisingly elegant foyer. "Officer, how can I help you?" asked the judge's secretary, who recognized him.

"Is . . . the Chief Judge in?"

"Of course. He's meeting with his law clerks."

The officer hesitated. Then he said, "It's important."

The judge's secretary knocked and went into chambers. Less than a minute later, she re-emerged, along with two law clerks.

The Secret Service officer went in. Federal judges usually have large, well-appointed offices. They meet frequently with attorneys in planning meetings called "pretrial conferences," and they need plenty of room. They also need settings that convey power and solemnity.

The Chief Judge's chamber was huge, featuring photographs of his honor with the last six presidents, and as an eagle scout, a law firm managing partner, and with his five kids and wife.

Exactly twelve minutes later, the officer exited chambers, leaving a stunned look on the Chief Judge's face.

After a few minutes of silence, the Chief Judge called for his law clerks to return, with a different agenda. "We need to reassign the entire Galveston docket. Some of the cases can be brought back here, to the big city, to this division. Most of them will have to be covered by judges who will work temporarily in Galveston."

*　*　*

Robert Herrick's office felt every bout of thunder, every bucketful of rain pounding on the windows, and every flash of lightning outside. It was not a nice afternoon.

"Tom, I think we ought to file a Motion to Dismiss this phony antitrust counterclaim that Jimmy's filed." Robert looked past the bright oriental carpet and into the storm outside.

"It's a silly claim," Tom Kennedy agreed.

"Not only silly, but legally without any foundation. You don't have an antitrust claim against someone who's sued you in a single lawsuit, if the lawsuit has any basis at all. Our lawsuit might or might not survive a Motion for Summary Judgment, but there's evidence to argue for it."

"What effect will our Motion to Dismiss have in a hearing on Jimmy Coleman's Motion for Summary Judgment? In other words, the two dueling motions, considered together?"

"It's a psychological thing. Judges instinctively try to avoid making decisions. They have to make too many of them, and making decisions is hard work. Giving a judge a chance to split the baby gives him a kind of 'out.' It's not supposed to work this way, of course, but if a judge can decide so as to give half to one side and half to the other, within the law, that becomes an attractive option. It's the nearest thing to letting the judge avoid making a decision."

Tom smiled. "Yeah, I understand. I've even heard judges say things like, 'I sustained an objection against your opponent, so now I'm going to sustain this one against you.' As though the two were connected, even if they had nothing to do with each other."

"Right. Splitting the baby. So, we hope that if Judge Medaxas has the chance to avoid making a real decision, he might. He can deny our

Motion to Dismiss the antitrust claim against us, and then equalize everything by denying Jimmy's Motion for Summary Judgment. That way, we might avoid having our whole case thrown out."

"Well, but that's not going to work here. Our judge is Judge Medaxas, and he loves Jimmy Coleman."

"Right. All we can do is try."

And both of them thought about old cases: lost causes that magically had become winnable, just because of hope, effort, and perseverance, in the face of seemingly inevitable defeat.

There was a knock on the door. "Come in." It was a member of the investigative team, the group that was trying to find more evidence to show that Dravos Corporation could have, would have, or might have misappropriated Nova Aerospace's trade secret.

"Robert," the young attorney announced, "here's some good news. Judge Medaxas is off the case. The Chief Judge has transferred us back to the mainland. We've been assigned to Judge Shanice Leeds instead. She's new."

There was a short silence, followed by cheerful expressions from everyone.

"Yes, Shanice Leeds is new," said Tom Kennedy, "And I bet she never was a partner with Jimmy Coleman."

"I know the lady from her time as a lawyer," said Robert. "No, she wasn't Coleman's partner, and she has every reason to know Jimmy's style from her law practice. Shanice Leeds? I suspect she'll stick to calling the balls and strikes according to the law, rather than trying the case against us, the way Dexter Medaxas would have."

He still didn't want this case. Tom looked at him. Tom knew it.

*   *   *

The shadows lengthened on the spreading lawn in front of the Herrick household on Willowick Drive. The last flicker of sunlight crept through the plantation shutters surrounding Robert and Maria in their living room.

They sat on tan leather couches over a light brown carpet, bordered by darker brown wide-plank flooring, with grasscloth on the walls. Flowers and abstract paintings supplied color. It was a time for unwinding, with only light conversation about the day that was completed.

"Let's see what's going on in the world," Maria said. She flicked on the television.

"Good evening, friends." The news anchor favored viewers with a toothpaste-ad smile. "I'm Juan Moreno, and this is a Channel Five News Alert."

Suddenly a picture of the Federal Building appeared behind him in what broadcasters call chroma-key, so that it seemed to rest right on his shoulders. The edifice was unmistakably federal in architecture, with boxy, square windows across a boxy, square frame, mostly colored off-white.

"The Federal Bureau of Investigation has arrested a federal judge on charges of possessing child pornography," Juan Moreno announced breathlessly. "This morning, a team of officers entered the courtroom of Judge Dexter Medaxas and led him away in handcuffs."

Now, the screen showed an unusual perp walk, featuring a middle-aged man in a gray suit and dark red tie accompanied by too many armed officers to count, walking out of a nondescript lobby through steel and glass doors.

"The information we have is limited at this time," the news anchor continued. "We go to Channel Five Reporter Reba Abrams, who is standing by at the courthouse."

"That's right, Juan," said a woman in a heavy beige raincoat, trying to fend off the rain. "Judge Medaxas was arrested right in the courtroom over which he presided. We will report only what we have been able to confirm, which is that more than two hundred images were found on Judge Medaxas's home computer, showing young children in compromising positions.

"Ironically, the judge was taken before a magistrate judge in the same building, although he usually would outrank the very magistrate judge who gave him *Miranda*-style warnings and asked him whether he had an attorney. The judge answered that he didn't, but he would certainly 'engage counsel,' as he put it. And the magistrate judge determined that the judge was not a major flight risk, so he set bail at five thousand dollars."

"What will happen next, Reba?" Juan Moreno wanted to know.

"Arraignment, in front of a full-fledged federal judge, or possibly another magistrate judge, at a date still to be determined. Judge Medaxas will hear the law explained and have the opportunity to plead guilty or not guilty. This is Reba Abrams, Channel Five News; back to you, Juan."

The news anchor went on to another story. Robert clicked the remote to turn off the television. He had a shell-shocked expression on his face, but it was a look that was not altogether one of unhappiness.

19

Being new, Judge Shanice Leeds inherited one of the smaller courtrooms, on the eighth floor of the Federal Building. The Chief Judge's courtroom was huge by comparison. If you took away the bench, bar, and chairs, you could play a pretty good game of touch football in there. Judge Leeds's courtroom was like a handball court.

At least twenty-five lawyers crowded at counsel tables. The spectator section was filled. Jimmy Coleman's entourage all wore the Booker and Bayne uniform, both men and women: black suits, white shirts, and red or blue ties. Jimmy himself sported a brown suit with orange pinstripes that almost fit him, but not quite, and a peach-colored shirt and orange tie. Robert Herrick wore gray pinstripes with a red-and-blue tie, alongside Tom Kennedy, with his trademark brown suit with tan shirt and brown tie. Tom was the one who wore the same colors every day and gave the impression of someone too busy to take time selecting clothes in the morning.

At exactly nine o'clock, as scheduled, Judge Leeds entered the back door of the courtroom, accompanied by her law clerk's announcement: "Order in the court. Everyone rise, please."

The judge was a tall black woman with short hair and bright, piercing eyes. Her robe, in fact, was a little too short for her. She was known to have gone to Texas A&M University on a basketball scholarship, where she was a standout forward and near the top of her class academically. "It's hard to do both," Robert had said, when he had first heard about that.

"Be seated, please," said Judge Leeds.

She turned right to business, but she was disarmingly informal. "Mr. Coleman, I see you brought the whole firm with you. You've got a Motion for Summary Judgment. I've read your brief, but tell me in your words why I should grant your motion."

"Of course, your honor. The plaintiff has no legally sufficient evidence. The reason I say that is, we have received all of Nova Aerospace's evidence, and it consists of two kinds of information: first, so-called expert comparisons of the device made by Nova to a device in an Iranian missile, and second, testimony showing that Dravos employees met with a visitor from Iran who could have seen the plans for the Nova device at Dravos's headquarters."

"Well, but there's more of a connection than that, isn't there?"

"I don't think so, judge." Jimmy's rasp was softened into a kind of purring sound, now. "All it shows is that there was some opportunity for the Iranian visitor to see the plans, not that he ever did see them. The evidence just doesn't allow an onlooker to see proof that Dravos stole trade secrets by the greater weight of evidence, because there's an equally obvious explanation, and that's that nothing happened with Nova's trade secret."

"Mr. Herrick?" The judge turned to Robert's side of the courtroom.

"You're right, judge; there *is* more of a connection than Mr. Coleman admits. The so-called employees that he mentioned are not just ordinary employees. One was deTravanian Wrenger, who designed the device at Nova, and the other was his lab assistant. Their depositions tell inconsistent stories. At least one of them is misstating things. Wrenger says the lab assistant showed the Iranian around and opened up the plans while he was there.

"And it's all too much of a coincidence. Soon after that, the device shows up, virtually identical, in an Iranian rocket. The jury will have plenty of evidence, and it all fits together."

"It's all circumstantial."

"But circumstantial evidence is valid proof. Our expert says that it's impossible to imagine that the two devices were invented separately, because they're too similar, down to the details. That's the smoking gun. The device was copied, and it was copied right after Iranian agents visited Dravos to get at the plans."

"You'll really have a steep hill to climb, persuading a jury with evidence that indirect."

"Well, judge, I'll have to wear my best law suit that day, I guess. Nova Aerospace deserves its day in court, to have the jury decide."

The judge smiled slightly. Jimmy waved his arms.

"Judge, there's no evidence that this mysterious Iranian guy even looked at the plans. Only that they were there." Jimmy's voice sounded like a monsoon in a bamboo forest.

"Well, in this hearing, the issue isn't who's got the better story." Judge Leeds smiled again. "You've got to show that Mr. Herrick has no legally sufficient evidence, before you can get a summary judgment. Mr. Herrick may have a heavy burden in front of the jury, but in this hearing, you're the one with the steep hill to climb."

The judge looked down to make notes. "I'll issue an order on this Motion, probably within a day or so. Thank you, gentlemen. I've got three other motions to hear, now, before we bring the jury in for the case I'm in the middle of trying today."

Then, Judge Leeds hesitated. "Just a minute. Mr. Coleman, Mr. Herrick, this is a case that you can settle. It ought to be settled. I'm going to issue an order requiring you to meet with a mediator. Be ready. Thank you again, gentlemen."

Mike Martin spoke up just outside the courtroom. "Sounds like the judge is on our side." He wore a toothy grin.

"Careful," Robert said, a great deal less cheerfully. "Sometimes, the judge's words signal that she's with you. But sometimes not. Sometimes, a judge will give a harder time to the side she's going to favor with her ruling, just to test that side's argument. And it makes her appear more impartial than she may, in reality, be.

"And she didn't announce her decision. We can certainly still lose this motion and have a summary judgment against us. I surely don't want that, but it can happen."

*　*　*

"Those judges didn't sit on their asses very long." Wendy Bachman, the Cussing Mormon, seemed satisfied with the result.

"Yes. Billy Joe Armistead's sentence is officially affirmed." Maria was relieved. "The arguments his lawyers raised weren't very persuasive. Of course, they couldn't do any better. These were all the arguments they had. But even when you think the other side's arguments aren't any good, you can still lose, and it's good to get a result like this."

"There's an old saying. You can't make chicken salad out of chicken poop."

"Wendy, you have a way with words. But I think I've heard that one before, somewhere."

"So, when is the main event? I mean, the passing of this sorry bastard from the earth?"

"We don't put it quite that way, as attorneys, Wendy. I'd have said it a little more delicately. But to answer your question, the case has to go back to the original state trial court for the setting of an execution date. But meanwhile, there's an indefinite delay. Billy Joe's lawyers are entitled to try to have the Supreme Court take the case. And that can take forever. Or it can be a short time."

"More of that due process stuff. I suppose we've gotta have it, but sometimes due process is a pain in the ass."

* * *

"All right." Tom Kennedy wore his always-uniform: brown suit and tie, tan shirt. "The judge has done what we expected. Denied Jimmy's Motion for Summary Judgment. And also denied our Motion to Dismiss the antitrust counterclaim."

"Now all we've got to do is prove our case at trial." Robert looked out the window at a foggy day. "Which doesn't sound easy to me, especially since the judge says we have an uphill battle."

"And especially since he's right about that."

The fog was thick as molasses and gray as the smoke in a barbecue pit. It seemed to curl around the windows. It barely let you look straight down, at the freeways and tiny cars, and you couldn't see the Bayou at all.

"We're getting too many days like this," Robert said. "Sort of the same fog I get when I try to see how we can persuade this jury."

"Well, before we take that step, we go to mediation. The judge's order also says we've got to go try to settle our case with Jimmy while having a mediator to help us."

"If I know Jimmy, the mediator won't be much help."

Robert looked as though he had been hoping the judge would grant the defendant's Motion for Summary Judgment, throw the case out, and end everyone's misery.

*　*　*

Two hours later, Tom was back. And excited.

"Robert, the investigating team that was chasing this Amir Massad has come up with something! In fact, it looks like they've struck pay dirt."

"Who? Amir who? Who's that?" He was tired, and he'd been sleeping in his chair.

"Come on, Robert. Amir Massad is the mystery Iranian. He's the one who met with deTravanian Wrenger, and he also met with Romaine Cramshak in Wrenger's lab at Dravos."

"Yeah?"

"And remember, the investigative team asked him written questions. The judge sent the questions—Judge Medaxas sent them, before he got removed. We were amazed he let us do this. So, the questions get sent to a court in Iran. And if everything went right, we hoped the questions would get answered by the witness we're chasing, in this instance Amir Massad."

"Okay. I'm remembering."

The whole process is called *'letters rogatory.'* It's allowed for in the rules, even though it's unusual. But the name of the process doesn't matter."

"No. It doesn't."

"So! Now we have answers from this guy, Amir Massad. Under some sort of oath taken in Arabic."

"All right. You got me up to my neck in suspense. What's this Amir dude got to say?"

"That at Dravos, they left the plan spread out on the desk. For the microprocessor—the device—the rollover mechanism—you know, the flow chart that's the key to all of it—and Wrenger's assistant, who would have been Romaine Cramshak, left him alone with it and said something like, quote, "don't look at this.'"

Robert was sitting straight up. "Oh, yeah?"

"Yes. And so this Amir Massad says that then, he photographed every page, all by himself."

"Wow."

"Why do you suppose Amir Massad gave up this information? It surprises me."

"It surprises me, too. But then again, the Iranians have a history of making public statements that embarrass or frustrate the United States. They like to brag about putting one over on Uncle Sam." Robert paused. "And there's another possible reason why old Amir told the truth."

"What's that?"

"Sometimes people just up and tell the truth when you don't expect them to. Maybe the local ayatollah presiding over this Iranian court put the fear of Allah in Amir and made him try to summon up some honesty. I think the Koran and Mohammed's writings both favor telling the truth. And maybe, just maybe, old Amir took that advice."

"Well, anyway, we've got Jimmy by the short hairs now. Don't you think?"

"Well, . . . no. This is helpful, but no."

"Why not?" Tom was astounded.

"Theft of trade secrets is an intentional tort. We've got to prove that Cramshak or Wrenger or Dravos acted intentionally to steal the trade secret. This looks like they were only negligent. It's helpful, but. . . ."

"Well, from this, a jury can decide that they acted intentionally together with Iran to steal the secret."

"Yes. Or they could decide the opposite. This is one more piece of the puzzle, but we don't have Jimmy by the short hairs. Or any hairs. Everyone else tells a different story, including both Wrenger and Cramshak. We've got the same difficult burden of proof we've always had, and this testimony from Amir is just one more pebble to paste into the mosaic."

20

The mediator was tall and wiry, with gray hair circling a wrinkled bald head. He had librarian glasses with a red string around his neck. His suit was gray, his shirt was gray, his tie was gray, and the red string stood out like a thoroughfare marked on a city map.

He was giving the standard mediator speech. "Mediation is just assisted settlement. You, the parties, are in the driver's seat. I have no power except to urge you to settle. And this case can be settled. . . ."

Robert and Jimmy sat quietly. They both hoped that their clients were listening.

Finally, the mediator finished. It was Robert's turn: an opening statement. It wouldn't impress Jimmy, but the Dravos executives probably didn't know the story he could tell.

"Cramshak and Wrenger give contradictory stories, which is a bad beginning for Dravos." He spoke deliberately, raising his voice slightly on the last phrase. "Because either way, it's very bad for Dravos. It shows that Wrenger and Cramshak, working for Dravos, intentionally gave the plans for Nova's rollover microprocessor to the government of Iran."

The Dravos executives looked up sharply.

"The two devices are nearly identical in their flowcharts. If there's a trial, Professor Eisner has more than a hundred examples of loops, decisions, and other features that are so similar that they had to have been copied."

Now, the damages. "This secret was worth many hundred millions of dollars. Our witnesses will fill in the details for the jury about this.

And don't blame us if we wave the flag. It's a betrayal of the United States of America."

"Your settlement figure, Mr. Herrick?" The mediator was quick to get to the bottom line.

"Three hundred million dollars. At trial, we won't be saying that. We'll be valuing it according to the testimony, at a higher figure. But we'll settle for that."

The mediator turned to the other side of the table. "Mr. Coleman?"

"We respect your organization, Mr. Martin." The pudgy man's voice sounded like steel dragging on concrete. "And we respect you. But not this lawsuit. We intend to vigorously defend our excellent reputation at trial. And we're convinced that your actions violate the antitrust laws. You will end up owing us millions, instead."

Jimmy pointed his finger at Mike Martin. "You've never admitted it, but the two devices are totally different. The pathways that the electrons take are no more similar than the orbit of Halley's Comet is to the way that Mars turns.

"And the expert you've got—your Dr. Eisner—makes a poor witness. He admits that his opinions are debatable. At trial, he'll be destroyed by cross examination. I'll ask him, 'That means, the opposite is just as possibly true?'"

Jimmy went on to blast Nova's damages witnesses as "incredible" and "world class exaggerators." Then he got to the point. "We deny that we are at fault. We are convinced that you, Nova, are at fault in bringing this lawsuit in violation of the antitrust laws."

Jimmy cocked his head to signal a new subject. "But every lawsuit has a nuisance value. The 'nuisance value,' Mr. Martin, is the cost of defending the suit. Speaking generously, the nuisance value here might be a million dollars. And that's our settlement proposal: one million dollars."

The mediator smiled. A big smile. He was enthusiastic. For a mediator, being enthusiastic is strategic.

"Splendid!" he exulted, and spread his arms wide. "We're going to get this thing settled. Now, let me caucus first with the defendant."

* * *

Two hours later, the mediator had met, or "caucused," with both sides twice. Jimmy at first had moved his settlement offer upward, to two million. The mediator had urged the plaintiffs to make what he called a "proportional" move, to $200 million, but Robert declined: Instead, "$275 million." Then the mediator got Jimmy to up his offer to $5 million. Robert and Mike reciprocated by coming down to $260 million.

"Splendid! Wonderful!" pronounced the mediator. "We're gonna get this thing done."

* * *

Three o'clock. The negotiations were beginning their seventh hour. Jimmy was at $40 million. "That's now what we think is the nuisance value," he grated.

The plaintiffs were at $200 million.

"All right," said the mediator after the next caucus. "Jimmy's moved to $50 million. Give me your reciprocal offer. Offer Jimmy $100 million. Then we're off by only a factor of two."

"One hundred ninety million."

"Splendid! I'll take it to them. We'll get this case settled yet."

* * *

Eleven o'clock. Then, ten minutes after eleven.

Jimmy and the defendants were at $60 million.

"Mike, let's settle this case." Robert was forceful. "I'm not saying we should take the sixty million. But we ought to get close enough so that we can persuade Jimmy to split the difference between our last offers. That's a time-honored negotiating method."

Mike thought for a minute. "I've always believed in this case. Dravos is just a plain bad actor. They'll do something else to hurt us if we fold."

"It's not folding. It's a lot of millions. And remember, the case is a difficult one. I'd like to see you take those millions to the bank, rather than see you win a big goose egg."

Mike Martin hesitated. "A hundred eighty million is a nice round number. Let's do that."

"Make it one hundred," the mediator said quickly. "Listen to your lawyer. He's right. One hundred million, and I think Jimmy will reciprocate."

"Let's say something close to a hundred million, at least." Robert pleaded.

"A hundred . . . seventy . . . million." Mike had to push himself to say it.

"Wonderful! We'll get it settled." The mediator was still upbeat.

* * *

Jimmy's next offer was sixty-one million. Up from sixty million.

Less than a two-percent increase. It meant, "We've reached the end of what we're willing to do."

The mediator sat down in the plaintiffs' caucus room and shook his head. "As soon as I stepped into the room, Jimmy said, 'Don't be asking us for any more money.'"

He smiled. "I told them, 'I'm not asking. I'm begging!'"

As tired as they were, Robert and Mike laughed.

"That's when they went to sixty-one million. And they said again, 'That's it.' I worked on them. But Jimmy said, 'Tell Herrick to think about the nuisance value. We're not budging until they get a lot closer.'"

"One hundred million, Mike?" Robert asked.

Mike was silent.

"Mike, it's just not as good a case as you might be thinking." Robert was feeling desperate. Desperate for getting out of this mediation.

Desperate for getting out of this case.

"All right." Mike sounded disappointed. "One hundred million."

* * *

At two o'clock in the morning, the mediator gathered everyone together. And declared an impasse.

The defendant was stuck at $61 million. And the plaintiff, Mike Martin, was holding firm at $100 million.

The mediator wasn't enthusiastic anymore. He made the usual mediator's speech. "Both parties, keep your offers open. . . . Both parties, keep your dealings respectful. . . . You can settle this case. . . ."

The lawyers slammed their briefcases shut. And headed for the door.

But before they got out of the building, Jimmy had the last word. "Thanks for refusin our last offer, Herrick, and makin it so we can have the fun of tryin this piece a shit case of yours. And wipin your ass all over the courtroom."

So much for keeping the dealings respectful, Robert thought miserably.

21

Two days until trial. Feverish work by both sides.

Studying motions, already drafted, to be filed on the day of trial. Considering arguments in support of them. And outlining opposition arguments to motions the other side was expected to file.

Reconsidering preparations for jury selection. What do we say to the jury panel? What do we suppose the other side will do? Will the judge let us say what we want to say? What do we do to stop the other side from saying what they shouldn't be allowed to say?

One more time through the jury analysis. What kind of jurors do we want? What kind do we want to eliminate, since we don't get to choose but only to eliminate potential jurors? What kinds will the other side want?

Opening statements. Studying notes, already written out. Predicting what the other side will say, so we can anticipate and neutralize it.

Witness preparation. Going over the questions we want to ask with each witness. Preparing them for cross examination by doing a mock cross with each one.

And on and on. All the way to analyzing the court's charge, the instructions and questions for the jury, all prepared in model form before trial.

* * *

Robert was a carefully controlled bundle of pent-up nerves. He always was, at this point. Unfortunately, right now, so was Maria. As she approached every Wednesday, these days, she watched for the

128

Supreme Court's ruling on Billy Joe Armistead's case. If they were going to reject this one, they'd probably do it promptly. It seemed improbable that the Justices would want to use this case to set a new standard for the performance of criminal defense lawyers, as Billy Joe's appellate lawyers were asking. Or that they would listen to Billy Joe's team and invent new rules about what the jury had to be told in the instructions.

But as time passed, the possibility grew that the Supreme Court might agree to hear Billy Joe's case.

Their irritation showed. "Robert, you left the back door unlocked."

"I was planning on going back out to the car to get my pile of stuff to study, and I guess I forgot. Sorry."

"You know it's dangerous. People follow you home from the grocery store these days and rob you."

"I know. I said I was sorry."

"They'll see me at the grocery store, or the drug store, or the gas station, and see my purse, and figure we have money. It's happened right down the street from us. People who want to rob you notice things like purses."

"I know. *I said I was sorry!*"

"Sorry won't do it when we have a home invasion and they slit our throats. You've got to remember these things."

"Maria, *go out and buy yourself a cheaper purse* and get off my back! I've got to go to trial in two days, and I don't need this."

Finally, silence.

And he knew that he was irritable enough so that if she opened a jar in the refrigerator when there was already another one of that particular thing open, he'd blow up. Or if she put the TV on too loud. Or if she left her bra on the bed, which for some reason, was something she did. And it drove him nuts every time. If it happened now, there probably would be an all-out war.

*　*　*

The next morning. One day to go.

Tom Kennedy was trying to imitate a rational, calm exterior. "Robert, do you want to do a dry run?"

"Yeah. Here goes."

He stood up. Contrary to television portrayals of trials, lawyers stand when they address either the judge or the jury.

"Ladies and gentlemen, thank you for being here. You are performing a service that only free people can perform. And in this case, it's more than just a minor duty. It's a patriotic duty. A patriotic duty! Because this case involves conduct by the defendant that endangers national security."

A focus group had told them that the patriotic theme was a winner in this case. "So, Tom, I'll return to that idea later."

"Good start."

"Have any of you served your country? I don't mean just in the armed services. Worked as a teacher, a V.A. doctor or nurse, or a government agency, or any kind of service?—*And Tom, I expect a lot of hands here to be raised, and I'll say*—Thank you for your service, and you know how important this kind of case is.—*I'll talk to a couple of those people individually. . . .*"

"You can't keep making speeches," Tom reminded him. "You've got to direct more questions to the jury panel."

". . . This case involves what the law calls a theft of trade secrets. The evidence will show that Nova Aerospace Company, my client, invented an important component for guiding American missiles. We also expect the evidence to show that employees of the defendant, Dravos Corporation, knew about that component because they hired our employees, and they gave the secret to Iran. To the government of Iran. And Iran used Nova's invention, right away, in their own missiles, and they're using it to this day. Mr. So-and-so, do you think you can serve on a jury where the issues are that weighty?"

The focus group had also told them they should play the Iran card early and often.

"Three minutes, Robert. You'd better introduce your client."

"Okay. I'll tell Mike to stand up, right here, and I'll tell them about him and Nova."

* * *

Across town, Jimmy Coleman had his team gathered in the main conference room.

He waved his arms. "Consider who we want as jurors and who we don't. What does the report on that telephone survey tell us, again?"

Jennifer Lowenstein had practically memorized the report. "First of all, young people are good for us. They tend to be uninvolved in world politics and often think that there's too much conflict—we should just get along. Likewise, older people are good for us. They've made their peace with the world and don't want to engage with it nearly so much."

"But with important exceptions, right? Some young people are news junkies. As for older people, they're bad for us if they are former military."

"Right. So we want to find those things out, but otherwise, we strike people who are between about twenty-five and fifty. And here's another curious thing. Some kinds of people believe that trade secrets aren't very important."

Jimmy grinned. "People who make hard decisions in their daily lives are bad for us. They know the value of information. So, we don't want a business manager, or a loan officer, or a geologist, because those guys collect all kinds of information, secret information, and make a controlled gamble: 'drill that oil well here.'"

Jennifer smiled too. "And instead, we want people-pleasers. Folks whose daily lives consist of persuading other people by being nice to them. The ideal juror for us is a shoe salesman. He doesn't know about keeping secrets, and he doesn't make decisions like sticking a defendant with millions in damages. Or, we'd like a beautician, or a waiter or waitress."

"I love this stuff," Jimmy confided. His voice rattled like rain in a cornfield. "It sounds like voodoo. But if it's scientific, and our telephone survey is, then it darn sure works."

"I love it too." Jennifer's eyes flashed. "Robert Herrick won't know what hit him."

* * *

Jimmy always set up an unusual ritual the night before trial.

Tonight, he looked like a Buddha sitting on the floor with his legs crossed, stripped to his shorts, while his trophy wife, Barbara, rubbed palm oil on his shoulders. She was in battle dress, with a T-shirt that featured a helicopter, a blazing sun, and the legend: "Soldier of Fortune: The Magazine of Professional Adventurers." Barbara Coleman was two inches taller than her husband, and with her jewelry and tights, she looked like an Amazon warrior preparing for a beach vacation. Or maybe, the first woman four-star general, undercover.

While she rubbed oil on him, she chanted. "Tomorrow is going to be a great day for Jimmy. Tomorrow is going to be a great day for Jimmy." She repeated the mantra again and again, with only slight variations. "Tomorrow, Jimmy will win a big one."

This was the was the pudgy man always prepared for trial. The whole scene, down to his wife's military bearing, was always the same.

And the oil, the chant, and his big beautiful wife were having the desired effect. Jimmy tilted his colorless eyes and smiled.

"Thank you, my Wonderful One."

"Oh, you're welcome. I like this ceremony. But do your partners and associates know that you prepare for trial this way? I might just tell them."

He recoiled in mock terror. "You wouldn't do that?"

"Just keep buying me stuff with diamonds."

"No problem."

He waited for a minute while she chanted. And then, in his frog's voice, he said to her, "Now, maybe we change to the other goal. The other message. About how badly Herrick's going to lose."

She continued rubbing, but promptly switched to an angrier tone. "Tomorrow is going to be a terrible day for Herrick. Tomorrow, Herrick is going to get his tail kicked. . . ."

Jimmy shuttered his eyes again. And he flashed an even bigger smile than before. To him, this was better than honey sauce on barbecue.

". . . Herrick is going to get poured out of the courtroom, and he'll become a grease blob in the street. Tomorrow is going to be a disaster for Robert Herrick. . . ."

He was easing into the right frame of mind. His opponent wasn't even entitled to be in the same courtroom with him. His opponent was a slug. A worm. His opponent was trash, and Jimmy was ready to stomp all over the guy.

". . . Herrick is gonna to lose his ass, big time. Herrick is going to be sorry he ever got into this lousy case of his. . . ."

And finally, Jimmy was ready.

22

"All right, Mr. Bailiff. Bring them in!"

And an excited buzz went up from a gallery crammed with spectators.

The morning of trial had finally arrived. The judge had ordered twice the usual number of potential jurors, because of the possibility that there might be a large number of disqualifications.

"Walk into this set of seats, please." The bailiff pointed to the front row of benches. Dutifully, ten potential jurors filed in and sat down.

"These seats next, please." And the next ten shuffled into the second row.

They kept coming until all sixty-four were in place.

Now, a law clerk banged the knocker on the outside of the back door. ". . . Order in the court. Everyone rise, please." And all of the jurors, including those who had just sat down, stood up again, along with all of the attorneys, the parties, and the spectators.

Judge Shanice Leeds walked through the door and ascended to the bench. "Be seated, please."

The judge looked out over the six-plus-rows holding the jury panel. So did Jimmy. So did Robert.

He marveled, as he always did, at the mixture he saw. Men and women, old and young, black and white, well-dressed and shabby, rich and poor, wearing T-shirts and expensive suits. A few politicians have referred to their "rainbow coalitions." A jury panel always fit that description.

But he didn't have time to wonder. The Judge was beginning to address the panel. "Ladies and gentlemen, the case on trial today is

133

called *Nova Aerospace Company versus Dravos Corporation*. This is a civil case that will be tried before a jury. . . ."

Robert was scanning the juror information forms that all of them had filled out, looking for the characteristics that trial lawyers always looked for. The first juror, Number 1, was a young black man. A waiter. A bad profession for the plaintiffs here, his jury pollsters had said.

Juror 2, a plumber. Probably bad for the plaintiff. Juror 3, a flight attendant. This was not looking good.

He read all the way down to Number 7 before he found one he liked. A fifty-year old grocery manager. Good. This woman probably understood keeping information secret and could make a decision.

But it wasn't a favorable panel, as he looked at it.

The judge was telling the jurors, now, what they should and shouldn't do. ". . . Do not speak to the parties or the attorneys, except for casual greetings. Do not accept or give them any favors, such as rides or refreshments. . . ."

Tom had started looking at the last half of the jury panel. He was at Number 48. Robert's quick glances had taken him through Number 25.

The good news was that there were eight potential jurors in that group who were good for the plaintiff, according to the surveys.

The bad news was—that meant that the other seventeen weren't very good.

Now, the judge was telling the jury panel, "The length of this trial, after we get a jury, will be between two and three weeks."

A dissatisfied rumble went up.

". . . Let me remind you that jury service is not optional. You are expected to do your duty as citizens. Only if there is real and serious hardship will the length of the trial be any excuse for anyone on this panel."

With that, the judge lined up those who claimed a "real and serious hardship."

The first man who wanted to get out of serving was a country club manager. And he had responsibility for all operations of the club. "Isn't there a second in command?"

"Yes, your honor. My assistant manager."

Excuse denied.

The next woman explained, "I have birds, and my husband never can take care of them properly."

Excuse denied.

All in all, Judge Leeds considered the pleas of twenty-eight members of the jury panel. She excused fifteen, including a college student who would lose a semester that was half over if he served and a doctor with an operating schedule three days a week. Robert tried to get the judge to keep most of these people. The types of potential jurors he wanted were those most likely to have real and serious hardships.

So now, the jury panel was even worse than it had been.

The judge was winding down her remarks. ". . . The attorneys have the right to ask you questions about your jury service. Listen to their questions and give full and honest answers. The attorneys will now proceed with their examinations. Mr. Herrick?"

He stood. He still had a churning stomach, because he always did at the start of trial. But it settled when he started talking.

"Thank you, Judge Leeds. And good morning, ladies and gentlemen."

They answered with "Good morning!" in steady unison. That was a favorable sign.

"The judge told you that my name is Robert Herrick, and it is. He also told you that I represent Nova Aerospace Corporation, and I do."

Somehow, that line always came across to jurors as humorous. Just a little laugh. Good.

"I know you've been herded around, and you're told that you'll be here two to three weeks, and you have to sit on these benches. I think they order special, extra-hard benches for courtrooms everywhere."

Again, not very funny, but any kind of lightheartedness works with jurors who are leery of attorneys anyway. This line got him a slightly more audible laugh.

"My official client is Nova Aerospace, but my real client is Mike Martin, who's sitting next to me here. Mike, stand up, please."

Robert pointed to him. "Mike is the president of Nova Aerospace. It's his company. It wasn't faceless corporations or concrete buildings that did the dealings in this case. It was people. Now, Mike will be one of the witnesses you'll hear from in this case.

"I need to ask all of you. Is there anything about Mike, or anything you've heard about his company, that might make you hesitate to do justice for Mike, if that's what's called for? Anything that might make us start this race ten yards back? If so, please raise your hand.

"I didn't see any hands, and I didn't expect to. Thank you, Mike; please sit back down."

Robert stepped to the side a little, to signal a new subject.

"This case involves what is called the law of misappropriation of trade secrets. Misappropriation is just a big word for stealing trade secrets.

"How many of you have worked at companies that had trade secrets? Valuable trade secrets?"

A forest of hands went up. Good.

Robert turned to the lowest-numbered juror who had held his hand up. "Mr. Speit, please tell us what the trade secrets were about, in your case. But hey—don't tell us any of those trade secrets themselves!"

Laughter and a little applause. Good.

"I work for Exxon," the man said. "We have tons of trade secrets. For example, about drilling prospects. I mean, where to drill and how good the prospects are. And that's just an example."

"I'm familiar with the kind of trade secrets that are all over the oil industry. And let me ask you: Did Exxon value these secrets about drilling prospects, and work to keep them secret?"

"Oh, my! You'd better believe it. If someone tried to steal them, it was treated worse than if it was a murder."

"I take it that you could imagine high damages for misappropriation of trade secrets."

"Of course."

"Thank you, Mr. Speit. . . ."

Robert's jury examination lasted two hours. He "knew" the jury panel now, and he had a grip on a slate of potential jurors to strike. Of course, his "knowledge" was guesswork.

I wish I really knew, he thought to himself.

* * *

Now, it was Jimmy's turn.

"Circumstantial evidence!" He thundered. "Mr. Herrick doesn't say this, but if you think about what he's saying, circumstantial evidence is all he's got."

The chubby defense lawyer turned to the first juror. Juror Number 1. "Mr. Amburn, it's proper to be careful with circumstantial evidence. If you were to listen to Mr. Herrick's bag of hints, indirections, and circumstantial evidence, and you didn't quite believe it, could you render a verdict against the plaintiff? And for the defendant?"

"Of course."

"Thank you, Mr. Amburn. Now, let me ask the same question of everybody on this panel. If you heard circumstantial evidence and you didn't quite believe it, is there anyone who'd be unable to say no to the plaintiff, and yes to the defendant?

Silence.

"I didn't see any hands and I didn't expect to. Now, let me turn to another issue. Mr. Herrick refers to my client as *Dravos*. That's correct, but it's misleading, because it creates a picture of an unthinking, unfeeling big firm. The reality is, it's Sarah Townsend's company, and she's here with me. Please stand up, Sarah."

Sarah turned out to be a beautiful, elegant lady with long blonde hair. She wore a feminine pink suit and matching two-inch pumps.

"Is there anyone who will hesitate to listen to and believe Sarah, or her company, just because of appearances? . . . I didn't think so. Thank you all. By the way, Sarah is the Vice President for Government Affairs of Dravos Corporation, and she's here because it's her job. This isn't just Dravos. It's Sarah's company."

Jimmy took two and a half hours to joke and cajole with the jury panel. His grating voice had a sugary layer over it.

At the end, Tom Kennedy summed it up. "This guy is a quick-change artist. Jimmy Coleman would love to slit your throat with an underhanded stiletto, but in front of the jury panel he's a plush, lovable teddy bear."

23

People usually think a jury has to consist of exactly twelve people. Not so. The Supreme Court has said it can number as few as six.

Surprisingly, the federal courts don't have a rule about how many there have to be. It's up to the judge. Federal judges usually want to shorten the process. They are disposition-minded, because they have to be, unless they want a huge backlog. They prefer six. But if there are only six, and one juror gets disqualified during trial, everything has to start over. So they tend to take on a couple more jurors.

Judge Shanice Leeds decided on eight jurors for this trial.

At the end of the jury examinations, more than half the panel had been eliminated for one reason or another. Exactly twenty-three potential jurors remained.

Each side would have three "peremptory challenges," as they are called. Three "strikes," which can be used to eliminate three potential jurors who seemed unfavorable to that side.

The strikes are guided by attorneys' bald hunches. Based upon peoples' gross characteristics—on stereotypes, frankly. On judgments about broad classes of people, supplemented in this case by each party's jury surveys, which evaluated whether young or old people were "better for us" or "worse for us," or whether rich or poor, or decision-makers or people-pleasers, or Catholics or Baptists.

Peremptory challenges are precious. Good predictions can win a case, and bad ones can lose it.

"We've got to strike Number 1," said Tom. "Young, a waiter, a people-pleaser. And he seemed to respond to Jimmy."

"Agreed," said Robert, and he drew a line through the man's name. "Next, Number 2. She's not favorable to us. But she's a follower type. She won't influence the jury, and she'll go along with the majority."

"So we don't strike her."

Mike Martin looked on with a puzzled expression on his face. "You guys are kind of like poker players."

"Maybe more like Russian Roulette," Tom answered.

That made Mike even more skeptical. "I liked the first guy, Mr. Amburn. He was clear and responsive. He knew what he thought, and he had no problem expressing it. I wouldn't necessarily remove him."

Robert shook his head. "But that's exactly why we need to get rid of him. The research—the survey—makes it obvious that he is in a category that is against us. His expressiveness translates into persuading other jurors to be against us."

Mike looked even more puzzled. "Well, okay. It's all weird. But I'm used to following my lawyer's advice. It just—it just seems like a chancy way to decide about who decides this case that is so important to us."

"Tell me about it. But that's our system."

Ten minutes later, they had drawn lines through three of the first fourteen potential jurors. Fourteen, because eight would remain on the jury, and a total of six would be struck by the two sides. They gave the jury list, with the crossed-out names, to the clerk.

A minute later, they saw Jimmy filing his list, with three different names crossed out.

Tom laughed. "I bet Jimmy didn't keep that guy from Exxon. The one who knows the value of a trade secret."

*   *   *

"The clerk will call the names," Judge Leeds announced. When your name is called, please take your place in the jury box."

A moment later, eight citizens sat in jury chairs. They remained standing and swore that they would "a true verdict render, according to the law and the evidence."

Robert stared at them. Four women and four men. Two of them were black, two white-Hispanic, and four white non-Hispanic. A taxi driver, a waitress, an employee at a carwash, a postman, an automobile mechanic, a flight attendant, a school secretary—and a bank president.

True to prediction, Jimmy had removed the guy from Exxon.

"Only one juror whose job consists of making decisions," Tom whispered. "Seven people-pleasers, and only one decision-making bank president. It's a terrible jury for us."

Robert swallowed hard. For the hundredth time, he wondered why he'd gotten talked into taking this case.

Tom was right. It wasn't a good jury. Usually, at trial, there is one side that would benefit from a hard and logical look at the law, comparing it to the evidence. That's us, he thought. But this was not a jury for hard decisions. The other side wants a jury that will view the evidence in a lighter, more pleasant, and human way. A jury that would be reluctant to convict someone of a theft of trade secrets; a jury that would respect deTravanian Wrenger and Romaine Cramshak. And be sympathetic to them.

This was a jury for Jimmy Coleman.

"All we can hope for is that the bank president will be the presiding juror," Robert whispered. "And that everyone else will be a follower."

*   *   *

The opening statements went by in a blur. Robert had prepared his opening statement carefully in advance. Maybe too carefully. He had a hard time conjuring up any emotion. "It was too dull and dry," he thought, and too analytical.

Jimmy was full of fire. His gravelly voice practically shouted the words: "You will see that the program in the Iranian device is completely different from the one Mr. Herrick accuses us of copying!" It couldn't have been stolen, he thundered.

He repeated this mantra four times, throughout his statement.

"In a minute, I will sit down." Now, his voice was a whisper, but rough and urgent. "Mr. Herrick will call witnesses to accuse my client Dravos of wrongs that *it did not do*."

He pointed forcefully at Robert, across the courtroom. "But at the end of this case, you will see that this case is about nothing but greed on the part of Mr. Herrick and Nova Aerospace Company. They have lost no money. Dravos has gained no money. But out of greed, they want a *windfall* to be paid to them by Dravos, for nothing!"

Jimmy sat down, heavily. All of the jurors' eyes followed him into his chair.

Robert thought to himself that one of the abilities that skillful trial lawyers have in abundance is the ability to project absolute disgust at their opponents. At that, Jimmy was one of the best.

And for the hundred-and-first time, he wondered what had motivated him to take on this loser of a case.

*   *   *

It was Friday evening. The judge recessed the trial until Monday. She gave the jurors the instructions she had repeated several times already. Don't watch television accounts of this trial. Or read about it in the newspapers. Don't discuss it with any other person, including your wife or husband.

"I'm going to play baseball tonight," Robert said to Tom.

"Do you think that's a good idea?" Tom was surprised. "We've got a lot of preparation to do."

"Playing ball sometimes is the only thing that keeps me sane. My guys keep me sane. I'll turn into a crispy wreck if I don't get a break from this."

*   *   *

Jose Davila grinned when he saw Robert coming into the Cardinals dugout. "Hey there, Mr. World Series!"

Robert, wearing his red team jersey, grinned back. "Hello, Biggest Bust."

Jose was a police officer. It was said that he had collared the guy with the biggest score of meth in the city, one year. And so his nickname with the Cardinals became "Biggest Bust." And when these gentlemen had learned that Robert, too many years earlier, had pitched in the College World Series—"He pitched in the College World Series!? Wow!"—the words went from a tone of respect to the name he normally went by here. Mr. World Series.

"Robert, take it easy," said Don Basset, the catcher and the captain. "I'm going to go for about three innings with Cardon pitching. Then, you get the rest of the game."

Robert hated to sit. He'd much rather start. But in a baseball game, we're all good soldiers. He sat.

The opponent was the menacingly-named Colt .45's. Navy blue jerseys, a big team, with about twenty players. That meant they had some good players, just by having a bigger selection. They also had some not-so-good ones, but they didn't have to play them as much.

The first three innings crept by in slow motion. The Cardinals were behind the Colt .45's, three to two. Basset pointed to him. "Okay, Robert. You ready? Need a kick in the balls or anything to get you going?"

He felt clumsy when he started warming up. He got to a speed somewhere above eighty with his fast ball, then tried a curve. His wrist didn't snap the way it was supposed to, and the ball trailed over to the left and hit the fence.

Next try was better.

Now, four pitches from the mound. Not great, but good enough, I hope.

Basset gave him the signal from behind the plate. One finger. Fast ball. Good. I can throw that one.

It was too high. Ball one. The umpire hardly moved.

Two fingers. A curve. Bad wrist action. The ball actually passed behind the Colt .45 batter and bounced to the backstop.

Third pitch. One finger. Basset, my catcher, doesn't trust the curve. Probably right. Basset's set up squarely in the middle of the plate. He really doesn't trust either pitch.

Nice speed. A little movement. Low, around the knees. The umpire shouted a word that sounded like "Hike!" or "Sike!" Umpires must work at being inarticulate. But all right; good. Strike one.

One finger. Basset really doesn't trust the curve, or the change-up either.

Robert was thinking too much. "Don't aim. Fire!" Basset yelled.

He grooved the ball. Middle of the plate, waist high: a mistake pitch. The .45 hitter swung and knocked a hard line drive into the hole between third base and shortstop, Fortunately, it was centered enough and hard enough so that the left fielder got the ball back in quickly enough to hold the batter to a single.

Robert looked straight down at the ground for a second. I've got to stop thinking. I've got to stop aiming, and fire.

He got the next two Colt 45's out, using curves as his strikeout pitch. Then, the fourth batter hit a double to right center, and the earlier Colt .45 scored all the way from first base.

Now, Robert felt it. Heat. A kind of competitive anger that wasn't really anger but felt like it.

Determination, maybe you'd call it,

Next: Three fast balls, well placed, with the Colt .45 batter swinging and missing all three.

He relaxed. The Cardinals were behind four to two, but he knew what to do. Just stop thinking, stop aiming, and fire.

He held the line for the rest of the game. No more scoring by the Colt .45s.

Senior Baseball League games don't go for nine innings. They last for a measured time, usually less than three hours. This game ended after the seventh inning, with the Cardinals ahead six to four.

"Good job, World Series." Basset patted him on the back. "In fact, nice comeback. After that first inning, I thought I was going to have to call 9-1-1 for you."

I just need to stop thinking, stop aiming, and fire, he told himself.

Maybe that'll work when I'm trying my lawsuit too.

24

Gentlemen, you're not going to believe this." Judge Leeds had a puzzled look on her face. "Nothing ever moves in a straight line. Trials are always bumpy."

Jimmy Coleman and Robert Herrick bellied up to the bench, with their seconds-in-command close by.

The judge lifted both hands in a kind of surrender gesture. "The bailiff has just told me that one of our jurors is not a citizen. Mr. Hernandez. The guy who works at the car wash. He is illegal. A citizen of Mexico."

"A wetback working at a car wash?" Jimmy thought it was hilarious. "Now, isn't that some kinda poetic justice!"

The judge frowned at that. "Anyway, Mr. Hernandez isn't eligible to be a juror. One of the other jurors talked to him and told my bailiff."

"What do we do about it?" several lawyers asked at once.

"Well, he can't serve."

"But we can both waive the error." Jimmy's voice sounded like a lawnmower. "Speaking for Dravos, we'll agree to let Mr. Hernandez serve as a juror here."

But for Robert, getting the man off the jury would mean one less juror who might be against his case. He shook his head. "We can't agree to that."

The judge stared at them. "I'm not sure that you can legally agree to let him serve, even if you did agree. We might try the whole case, then, and have the court of appeals tell us we've got to do it all over again."

144

The judge looked up at an imaginary sky and pretended to be a farmer. "Oh, Lord, send rain! Our crops are wilting."

Then: "Mr. Bailiff, thanks for letting me know. Please get the jury together. I'll excuse Mr. Hernandez and explain it to all of the others.

"So, we're down to one alternate. I hope no one else turns out to be ineligible."

*　*　*

With a jury of seven sitting in the box, Judge Leeds turned to Robert.

"Call your first witness, please."

"Nova Aerospace calls Mike Martin. Nova's President."

Mike didn't have far to walk, because he was sitting next to Robert at counsel table. He stood, raised his right hand, and swore to "tell the truth, the whole truth, and nothing but the truth, so help me God."

"State your name for the jury, please."

"Michael Alan Martin."

"And I believe that the name people call you by is Mike?"

The witness smiled and turned toward the jury. "Call me Mike."

He was smooth under pressure. He was going to be a good witness.

Robert took Mike through his background. Born in Rochester, New York. A degree in information technology from the University of Pennsylvania. Married to Patricia Martin for twenty-seven years. Two children. Liked riding horses and woodworking; had a table saw in his garage. A series of executive positions in electronics firms led him and friends to found Nova Aerospace fifteen years ago. "Nova's customers include NASA, Apple, Exxon, and many other fine American companies."

Great. The jury likes this guy, Robert thought.

Mike told the jurors how Nova Aerospace had come to design parts of the Orbital Attitude and Maneuvering System for NASA. "That means the system that orients or steers the spacecraft out in space. Not propulsion rockets. Steering rockets."

"You don't have a steering wheel or brakes or tires out in space, right?"

"No." That amused the jurors. "It all has to be done with pulses from a rocket engine."

"And the OAMS includes the rollover mechanism, right? Tell us what the rollover mechanism is and why it is a key part of the spacecraft."

Mike had had a lot of practice explaining things like this to ordinary folks, Robert thought. Great.

"And did there come a time when the FBI contacted you about a rollover mechanism in a foreign nation's spacecraft? Specifically, one from Iran?"

"Yes." And here, Mike explained that NASA thought the Iranian rocket had been copied from the American design. The one made by Nova Aerospace, under Mike's leadership.

"And did you conclude that the design of the Iranian device had, in fact, been copied from your own device, designed by Nova Aerospace?"

"Yes."

"How many strange similarities did you find between the two devices?

"Hundreds. Here, I will give you twenty-five typical examples, and after that, we'll summarize the rest. In fact, the entire flow chart was copied."

Robert flicked on the PowerPoint. The first slide said, "Twenty-five examples." Then, he tapped the control again, and the slide said, "First Do Loop: Identical to Nova's, with exactly the same repetitions."

"Mike, Please tell us about this Do Loop. First, what is a '*Do Loop?*'"

"A Do Loop is a repeated series of calculations. Very simple. An electronic device like the microprocessor in this device can do thousands of calculations in a tiny fraction of a second. So, we often have repetitive series of calculations done in a Do Loop."

"And was the first Do Loop in the Iranian device similar to the one in the Nova device, your device?"

"Not just similar. More than similar. It was identical. It had the same series of calculations, and it had the calculations done 99 times. For this calculation, that would mean that the result is accurate to twelve decimal points. And that was exactly the same in both devices."

"What would be an example of twelve decimal points?"

"Well, for example, the smallest number that would have twelve decimal points would have a period or dot followed by eleven zeroes and then a one. Or, one ten-million-billionth. So, the result of the calculation would have a decimal point down to one ten-million-billionth."

"Pretty small. Teeny-weeny, as we would say out in the country."

"A tiny tiny teeny-weeny."

The jurors liked that.

Robert took the witness through the twenty-five examples. Then:

"And there were hundreds of other examples you saw that were similar?

"Yes."

"And in fact, Mike, did you find that the whole sequence of the steps, laid out in the two flowcharts, was identical?"

"Yes."

"Now, Mike, as you know, we will have a separate presentation for the damages or restitution in this case. That will be later. But I want to ask you, just for now, would the commercial value of this device, if sold, be high or low?"

"High. Hundreds of millions of dollars."

"Thank you, Mike. Your honor, I pass the witness."

The judge said, "We will be in recess until one thirty this afternoon." And the jury filed out. Good. They'll have Mike's testimony in mind during lunch.

But that optimistic thought was quickly replaced by a less pleasant one. After that, Jimmy Coleman was going to cross-examine Mike Martin. And Robert had a nagging suspicion that Jimmy had something up his sleeve—something that would destroy the careful case he had built with Mike's testimony.

*　　*　　*

One-thirty three p.m. The jury was back in the box.

"Mr. Coleman," said the judge, "you may cross-examine."

"Thank you, your honor!" Jimmy's scraping voice was enthusiastic. He turned toward Mike Martin.

"Mr. Witness," he said with sudden distaste, as though he was not willing to dignify Mike by calling him by his name. "You told this jury that the Iranian device was identical to your device, from Nova Aerospace."

"Yes. It is."

"And you told these jurors that the two were so similar that the Iranian device must have been copied from yours."

"Yes. And it must have."

"But you bent the truth a little, didn't you?"

Mike stared at him. Then: "No. I didn't 'bend the truth,' as you put it."

"I guess, instead of bending the truth a little, you bent the truth a lot, didn't you?"

"Mr. Coleman." Mike's face was red. "I did not bend the truth at all. The answer to your question is, No."

"Well, let's see about that. First thing, the chips used in the Iranian device are not the same as your chips, are they?"

"No. They're Chinese chips. The Iranians use Chinese chips. They have a hard time getting American chips. They can only get them on the black market."

"And being as how they're Chinese chips, they're different, aren't they?"

"Yes. But the programming is the same."

"Well, let's see about that, too. The first command in the program is entirely different from yours. Isn't it?"

"I have to admit, I don't speak Chinese. I don't speak Iranian, or I guess Persian is what they speak in Iran, and I don't speak that either. It is entirely different, the language."

Jimmy's rasp sounded angry, disgusted, and patient, all at the same time. "I didn't ask you about foreign languages. I asked you about microprocessor commands. Let me ask again, slowly. The first command in the Iranian program is completely different from the first command in your device, isn't it?"

"The command itself, yes."

"And the second command to the Iranian microprocessor is different from your second command too, isn't it?

"Yes. But the program is the same. The key is the flowchart. And it's the same."

"Fact is, Mr. Martin, every single command in the Iranian device is different from every single command in yours, isn't it?" Jimmy was doing his best impression of an adult talking to a first-grader.

"Yes. But again, the program is the same."

"You've been trying to pull the wool over these jurors' eyes, haven't you?"

"No, Mr. Coleman, I have not tried to pull the wool over anyone's eyes. No."

"And in your direct testimony to this jury, you just conveniently didn't mention that these so-called identical programs had different commands, from top to bottom."

"It didn't come up. And it's beside the point, because the thing that counts is the programs. The flowchart. The steps that the computer follows. The inputs, the outputs, and the calculations. And those are the same."

"Except that they're all different, and you didn't tell us that."

"Look, Mr. Coleman. I need to explain it to you. The King James Bible is in English. But it's copied from the Greek. And every word is different, but it's copied. This is the same thing."

Immediately, Jimmy was on his feet. "I object to the witness's nonresponsive answer, Judge, and ask for an instruction to disregard."

The judge's response sounded almost automatic. "Ladies and gentlemen of the jury, that was a non-responsive answer. The witness has to confine himself to answering the question. Mr. Martin didn't do that. You will disregard his last answer and will not consider it for any purpose."

"Let me ask you the last question again, Mr. Witness. The commands in the two programs are all different, and you didn't tell us that."

Mike spoke through clenched teeth. "Yes."

"I've got no more use for this witness." Jimmy was even better than Mike at sounding disgusted.

The judge spoke quickly. "Let's take a short recess—fifteen minutes—for the court reporter to change the paper in her machine."

* * *

Robert's stomach was bubbling. But he had to settle Mike Martin down.

"I meant to point out that the commands are different, of course. Different hardware, different commands. They have to be different. Mike, I should have asked you about that. I had that on my outline, but I just flat screwed up and left it out.

"But Mike, you're doing fine. You're doing fine. On re-direct, we'll clear it all up. Above all, keep your temper and don't let Coleman get to you. And I'm going to keep you on the witness stand a little longer. Mike, that Bible reference that you used was a good explanation of it. When I ask you, you can repeat that."

But I really did screw up, he thought, by failing to point out that the superficial aspects—the commands themselves—are different, even if that's not the point. Juries hate to think that someone's fooling them. I made a terrible mistake by letting Jimmy Coleman tell them that.

It's only the first witness, he said to himself. I can come back from it. But that thought was replaced by another one. This is the first witness, . . . and I'm already losing.

* * *

Evening. After a disastrous day in court, Robert sat in a student's seat with a foldout desktop. In his pin-striped suit and dotted navy tie, he looked strange in the middle of a classroom full of nineteen-to-twenty-two year olds.

As Professor Ray Marikeh stepped into the well in front, a hundred pairs of eyes in a semi-circle looked down at him.

"Today is Iran day," he announced, and he nodded at Robert. "We have a guest who is a major donor to this University. Thank you, sir." And all heads turned in Robert's direction. "Mr. Herrick, this is Political Science 3326: Government and Politics in the Middle East. And today we study the Islamic Republic of Iran.

"The modern era begins in 1953. A coup overturns the elected government of Iran, and with the cooperation of the United States CIA, the military installs a new Shah, Mohammed Reza Pahlavi. It's great for the U.S.: an ally in the Middle East, a reliable source of oil, and a buffer against Saudi Arabia, which is populated by Sunni Muslims as opposed to Iran's Shiites. But the Shah is autocratic and expensive, with a series of elegant, luxurious wives. Most of the country hates him. In 1979, the people revolt.

"There are immediate changes. The Ayatollah Ruhollah Khomeini is the real government, and he installs a strict religious regime in this previously secular society. The United States is the 'Great Satan,' and the Iranians' hatred now suddenly has a religious basis. Even if you don't know much about Americans, Allah is commanding you treat them as enemies. Rioters storm the United States embassy, stand on its walls to burn the flag, take 52 Americans hostage, and hold them for more than a year.

"In the forty years since the hostage crisis, there have been several attempts at better relations. None of them has produced any real breakthrough. Today, Iran is implacably hostile to the United States, with a hatred fueled by history, by religion, by American support for Israel, and by American economic sanctions on Iran.

"This sentiment is so strong that the mullahs often boast about victories over the United States, including inconsequential or nonexistent victories. Perversely, they tend to brag about military or aerospace triumphs, real or imagined, even when they compromise secrecy."

Robert sat bolt upright. This is why I came here, he thought.

Professor Marikeh would be an excellent witness to explain why Amir Massad, the Iranian spy, blew open a military secret when he testified truthfully about stealing the American rollover device.

25

Mike Martin sat down again in the witness chair.

Judge Leeds's eyebrows went up expectantly. She knows what's going on, Robert thought. She sees through what Jimmy's doing. I hope some of the jurors do too.

"Mr. Herrick, your re-direct examination?"

"Thank you, your honor."

He turned toward Mike. "Mr. Martin, you have just answered Mr. Coleman's questions. He accused you of 'bending the truth.' Did you do that?"

Mike was forcing himself to be relaxed and pleasant. Good.

Nova's President faced the jurors and actually smiled. "Of course not."

"Did you 'pull the wool over the jurors' eyes,' as Mr. Coleman accused you of doing?"

"Of course not."

"Now, what is it that's copied here? Is it the individual commands, or is it the program? The flowchart?"

"It's the program. The flowchart."

"Please explain what you mean. In layperson's terms, please, so even I can understand it."

"What is copied here is the steps in the program. The inputs, the outputs, the calculations, and the decision points. We call a diagram of those steps a 'flowchart.' And it's the flowchart that's copied."

"Given that the Iranian hardware is different—the chips and circuitry—would it have even been possible for the Iranian device to use the same commands to copy the program and make an identical program?"

"No. But you could use different commands and copy the steps, one by one. And that's what the Iranian device does."

"In terms of the electron flow, do the electrons do the same things in both devices?"

"Good point. Electricity is nothing more than a current of electrons. The electrons follow different pathways in these two devices, but they do all the same things in an identical sequence. The Iranian device is copied."

"Mike, a few minutes ago you gave the jury an analogy, using the Bible as an example. Mr. Coleman objected and had it taken away from this jury. Can you tell us that example, now? It's proper now."

"Certainly." Mike looked toward the jury. "The King James Bible is written in English. But it's copied from the Greek, and the Greek version was copied from earlier languages. The words are different, but the Ten Commandments say the same things.

"And that's what's happening here. The individual words are different in the American and the Iranian rollover systems. But the steps in the process are the same for both. The Iranian device is copied from the one that we designed at Nova Aerospace."

"I pass the witness, your honor."

Was it enough? Had he cleared it up for the jury? Robert slumped in his chair and pictured the jurors thinking that he and Mike had tried to flim-flam them. Jurors dread being fooled. He exhaled heavily.

Jimmy's re-cross examination was mercifully short.

"So now, you're comparing your machine to the Holy Bible?" He still radiated the same disgust, or perhaps more.

"Of course not. It's an analogy. The adaptation of the Iranian device, so that it copies ours but fits other hardware, is the same kind of transformation. That's all. Mr. Coleman, answering your questions is impossible."

Jimmy saw his opening.

"Yes sir, I reckon it's impossible for you to answer questions about your testimony." He spat out the words. "It sure is impossible.

"And I got no more questions for this witness."

* * *

"Call your next," said the judge.

"Your honor, the plaintiff calls Romaine Cramshak."

The woman who took the oath to tell the truth had wispy gray hair and a round, wrinkled face. She wore a too-big brown jacket and skirt and a blue-and-white blouse that clashed with it. "They might be the same clothes she wore during her deposition!" Robert thought.

And Romaine Cramshak was nervous. Or rather, scared. Her gnarly fingers curled, uncurled, laced together and unlaced, while her pale gray eyes darted in one direction, then another.

After thirty minutes of shaky testimony, the jury understood Romaine Cramshak's role in the drama. And her relationship to deTravanian Wrenger, their backstory with Nova Aerospace, and their employment by Dravos in violation of their contract. Then, Robert got to the point.

"You and Mr. Wrenger sometimes had the job of dealing with visitors on behalf of Dravos, didn't you?"

"Y—yes."

"And the visitors included a man named Amir Massad, from the nation of Iran?"

"I didn't know his name before."

"Did this man from Iran come right into your high security lab, with Mr. Wrenger's blessing, right past the security that protected a lot of secrets?"

"Yes. DeTravanian and this Mr. Amir acted like good friends, and they laughed and joked."

"And did deTravanian Wrenger show him the flowchart for the rollover device designed by Nova Aerospace? Did he show him the essential plan?"

"I went away for a minute. And I came back and saw deTravanian with this Mr. Amir looking at the flowchart. DeTravanian was explaining it to him. They did this for more than half an hour."

"And then, did deTravanian Wrenger step away?"

"He went away and left Mr. Amir there. Just Mr. Amir and the flowchart."

"And did you step away too?"

"Yes. I had my responsibilities."

"And during the time when both of you were away, did Mr. Amir Massad, this representative of Iran, have full access to the flowchart?"

"I don't know. I guess so."

"He could have photographed every page, couldn't he?"

"I don't know. I guess so. I never saw him do it."

Slow down, Robert told himself. Let's not ask the fatal one question too many. No overkill.

"Let me ask you about a completely different subject. Would this rollover device have been of high value to the government of Iran?"

"I—I think so."

"Worth hundreds of millions of dollars, right?"

"It could be. But I'm not a financial person and I don't know."

I'd better shift my questions again, he thought. If I press, the witness might decide she didn't know anything about the value of this thing, and that would destroy even the slight value of what she'd said.

"The Iranian device is closely similar to the device you and Wrenger developed at Nova Aerospace, isn't it?"

"Yes."

"Does it have all the key features in the same places, or doesn't it?"

"Yes. It does."

"And are there the same functions in the different steps of the flowchart?"

"Y—yes."

"The Iranians must have copied it from the one that was designed at Nova Aerospace, right?"

"I don't know if it was copied." Romaine Cramshak looked down at her feet. "I wasn't there in Iran when they built it."

"But is it true that it's amazingly similar?"

"Yes, it is similar."

"The Iranians must have had the same flowchart? You'd have to say so."

The witness sighed and was silent for a moment. And a longer moment. Then:

"I guess they must have seen it or something kind of like it."

This had gone about as well as he could have expected, with a reluctant witness. "That's all," Robert said.

*   *   *

The next morning, Jimmy got his turn.

"Ms. Cramshak, You know Mr. Wrenger well?"

"Yes."

"And you respect him highly?"

"Yes. Everybody does. He is an amazing scientist and an amazing man."

"If he told you something, you'd believe it was true?"

"Yes."

"You know, don't you, that Mr. Wrenger denies everything you've said? And he says that he didn't show the Iranian man anything, much less show him the flowchart?"

"He just remembers things differently from me, I guess."

"In fact, since he contradicts you, you'd trust his testimony more than your own?"

"I don't know!" The witness's head trembled and her arms tensed. "I've been asked so many questions and pushed around so many times that I hardly know, now."

"I haven't pushed you, have I?" Jimmy's gravelly voice left a credible impression of kindness.

"Not as much as other people."

"Mr. Herrick—he's pushed you?"

"Him and the FBI."

"Now, the fact is, you don't work for Dravos Corporation anymore."

"No. I don't."

"Why not?"

"I didn't like all the security. I never liked it! There are guards every few feet. And they told me once too many times I wasn't following the security rules."

"And that was the reason they invited you to leave Dravos?"

"That's what they said. I don't know."

"All right. Let me ask you this. The chips in the Iranian device are not like the ones in the American device, are they?"

"I don't think so."

"And the circuitry is different?"

"Yes. Yes, it's . . . different."

"The commands are different?"

"Yes."

"From looking at what the commands tell the microprocessor, you know, Dravos says the two devices are completely different. Aren't they?"

"I guess so. I'm—I'm so tired. I'm worn out from this."

"Your honor, I pass the witness." Jimmy's grin was as wide as the counsel table.

* * *

"Jimmy's not a nice man," Tom whispered as they broke from the courtroom at lunchtime.

Robert was looking at the floor. "No. He's not."

"Or honest."

"No, He's not."

"But he's an effective advocate."

A troubled pause. Then: "Yes. Yes, he is."

Robert's hands shook. His face was a pasty white, his collar was banded with sweat, and his words were halting. Distracted.

"Come on, Robert. Let's sit down and eat something, and I'll buy you a drink."

"Well . . . I shouldn't do that. I've got to be sharp this afternoon. We've . . . you know . . . we've got to work."

"All right. Then I'll only buy you one or two."

26

Willie Dudea was a fixture at the corner of San Felipe Road and Kirby Drive. His long white whiskers protruded from wrinkled black skin, and his clothes were a nondescript dirty gray. He walked with a limp, but he could hustle if a passing motorist handed him a dollar bill. He was not particularly articulate—confined, as he was, to the word usage of the street—but he was well spoken enough for any donor to understand that the Deity was being invoked to bless him for his gift.

Willie's sign was sure to please. It was bigger than anyone would think he could carry. Emphasized by shaky capital letters, it said, "Why Lie? Don't Wanna Go Church at Salvation Army."

If a police officer approached, Willie could spot the car two blocks away. And he could make himself invisible.

But right now, he was doing something unusual.

He was flagging down a police officer.

"Willie, what the hell you doing? You know we gotta chase you away from River Oaks. This area is full of big-ass rich folk, and I thought we already ran you off."

"Yes suh, Officer Houghton. I be headin out real quick. Done already bundled up, you know, all a my po' little earthly kinda possession. But I seen something. I seen somethin scary."

"Ahhh . . . All right, Willie. You . . . seen something scary."

"Yes suh, and you know what the folks says. '*If you seen somethin, you say somethin.*'"

Willie was a nuisance, but at least he was entertaining. "All right, Willie, I get it. You're being a good citizen. Tell me what you seen."

"These two weird lookin guys come by here 'bout fifteen, maybe eighteen minutes past. And they stop by where the light be red. Drivin some kinda Humvee car, you know, kind that look like a boxy tank. They got a big kinda gun rack. Weird gun rack. And they got it full. Full. Not with guns you think they gonna be carryin, normal guns. No suh, these dudes—they bad dudes."

"What kind of guns, Willie?"

"I'm not a good expert, you know. But these looked mo' like com-minist guns than the American way a life. Guns outta Russia, maybe. Lotta hardware, mufflers, long barrels, and silencers. Alls I know is, they's the kinda guns that you be put in jail, if you just be holdin one in yo' hand."

Officer Houghton hesitated. I ought to run this guy off and let it be that, he thought.

But he was curious. If nothing else, it was a fun story.

"Is that all, Willie?"

"No. They be mo'."

Silence. Then: ". . . Okay, Willie, spill it! What 'mo' you got?"

"These guys look Ay-rabic. You, know like they come outta places where they got fancy rugs and tents and camels what peoples rides. Ay-rabs. And they got the car windas down fo' some unknown reason and they be arguin. Arguin. And arguin some mo'."

"Arguing in Arabic?"

"No, suh. See, if they been into Ay-rabic talk, Officer Houghton suh, how I gonna know they's arguing?"

"Good point."

"So, this one guy say, 'But the target lives on Willowick.' That's what he say: the target. And the other guy, then, say, 'Yeah, you—and here he said a cussword I don't wanna repeat—you blank-blank, you don't understand. We turn at Inwood to get to the target,' he say. 'Because Inwood turns into Willowick.' And he call him that same cuss word again, but I don't wanna repeat it again."

"They said somebody was a . . . *target*?"

"Yeah."

"Did they get around to saying who this target would be?"

"No suh. They got this Ay-rab music goin on, with all them swirly moanin voices twistin around. Alls I know was, they said something about a lawyer. A *lawyer*, they said, who stay at a house on Willowick. That's the target."

"Anything else?"

"They sounded like they's just casin the place, this go-round. You know, just casin it. Goin in to have a deeper look."

"Okay, Willie. You've done good by telling me. I'm going to give it to gang intelligence. Right after I get through going over to Willowick and casing the joint myself."

"Yes suh." Willie beamed as if he'd just been awarded the Congressional Medal of Honor.

Officer Houghton grinned. "And now, Good Citizen Willie, you get the hell out of here."

*   *   *

"Call your next."

Robert stood. "The plaintiff now will read the testimony of Amir Massad, as recorded by the court in Iran."

"Your honor, I object," said Jimmy Coleman immediately.

"On what grounds?" The judge asked

"This so-called 'deposition' that Mr. Herrick wants to read to the jury—this statement from Iran, of some unknown person who says he's Amir Massad—is not a proper deposition. First thing, it doesn't fit the rules for depositions."

Robert was on his feet. "Your honor, it's not the usual type of deposition, of course. It's testimony taken in a court of a foreign nation. The Rules of Civil Procedure provide for this, just as they provide for depositions, but it's a separate rule."

"Isn't that right, Mr. Coleman?"

"It isn't sworn testimony," Jimmy grated. "There's no oath."

"Your honor," Robert said, "again, it's a statement in a foreign court. And the statement by the court begins by saying that the testimony of Amir Massad is 'in the sight of Allah.' In other words, it's under the Iranian equivalent of an oath."

"It's not an oath." Jimmy was putting on his disgusted act again. "It doesn't swear or affirm anything."

Robert picked up the rule book. "The rule, Rule 603, just says that the proceeding must be '*in a form designed to impress that duty on the witness's conscience,'* meaning the duty to tell the truth. In Iran, you would do that by invoking the name of Allah.

"But really, that's beside the point. This testimony falls under Rule 28 of the Rules of Civil Procedure." Robert picked up a different book. "Rule 28 authorizes testimony taken in a court of a foreign country."

"But not if it's not under oath," Jimmy insisted.

The judge looked puzzled. "This is a new one on me."

Well, new stuff happens, Robert thought, if you're a new judge. And there was silence for a moment.

"All right," said Judge Leeds finally. "My reading of the rules is that testimony taken in a court of a foreign nation is proper if conveyed to this court by the foreign court, and that it does not have to recite an oath. And that's what happened here. But if an oath is required, I find as a fact that the court's statement that the testimony was taken 'in the sight of Allah' would impress the duty of truth on a witness's conscience."

The judge smiled. And shook her head. "Let's take a break. After hearing from you gentlemen, this court might be wise to take something other than testimony. Namely, an aspirin."

* * *

A half hour later, the jury was in the box. The judge was back on the bench.

Robert stood. "Your honor, the plaintiff will read the testimony of Amir Massad, taken in Iran." He faced the jury. "I will read the questions, and Mr. Kennedy will take his place on the witness stand and read the answers.

"May the record reflect that the testimony of the last witness, Romaine Cramshak, referred to Mr. Amir Massad as a visitor to the laboratory at Dravos Corporation."

"So noted." The judge's voice had the mechanical character heard in routine rulings.

Robert picked up a copy of the testimony and read from it. "First question: State your name, please."

Tom, from the witness stand, read the answer. "Amir Massad."

"What nation are you a citizen of?"

Tom, again: "I am a citizen of the Islamic Republic of Iran."

"Do you hold a position in the government or in industry there?"

"Yes, in the Qud Forces, a part of the army of the Islamic Republic of Iran."

"Did you ever have occasion to visit with an American man named deTravanian Wrenger, and if so, where?"

"Yes. In his laboratory at the offices of Dravos Corporation."

"During this visit, did you happen to see documents showing a plan for parts of a spacecraft?"

"Yes."

"How did it happen that these documents were available to you?"

"Mr. Wrenger unfolded a paper containing the plans for a microprocessor flowchart and placed them on the laboratory table. He told me what they were. He then left me. A lady who was his assistant also was present. She left too, and she told me, 'Don't look at this.' But I photographed each page of the document."

"What did you do with what you learned or obtained?"

"I returned to Iran and turned the documents over to my commanding officer."

"Do you know what resulted from the knowledge that you transferred to Iran?"

"Not precisely. All I know is that the documents were furnished to the Iran Aerospace Industries Organization, an entity owned by the Islamic Republic of Iran."

Robert put down the document containing the testimony. "And that is the end of what Mr. Amir Massad had to offer."

A group of men and women hustled out of the courtroom, slamming the door on the way out. Someone in the audience whispered an explanation: "News reporters."

* * *

Robert and Tom laughed and joked as they left the courtroom. "Did you see that one juror in the front row? Looked like a spectator at a tennis match."

"Yes! Kind of bug-eyed, bouncing her head back and forth to watch the questions this way, and then the answers that way."

"And the rest of the jury, they were shell-shocked. Looked like they needed to be scraped off the courtroom wall with a spatula!"

Jimmy walked by and laughed too. "Don't celebrate yet, you fine gentlemen. This Amir Massad is a notorious liar. The evidence is going to explode this testimony you've bought into, like an Islamic bomb."

Something about the way he said it, in his gravelly voice, changed their mood in an instant.

"Oh, no. Here we go again," thought Robert, with his mind conjuring up images of an ambush, the kind only Jimmy Coleman could engineer. The kind that would make a shambles out of his case.

27

The two detectives met him at the federal courthouse.

"Hello, gentlemen!" said Robert. "My two favorite homicide dicks. What are you guys doing here at the Federal Building?"

Officer Derrigan Slaughter was a courtly African American, always sharply dressed. He wore a perfectly cut, pearl gray double-breasted suit with a solid blue tie. His partner, Donnie Cashdollar, sported his usual eclectic trousseau, consisting of a green jacket, brown trousers, a pink shirt, and a skinny off-white tie. What a pair!

Robert grinned. "I always have to laugh when I run into you fine gentlemen. Detective Slaughter, I can see why you're in homicide. But Detective Cashdollar, with your name, shouldn't you transfer to forgery? Or maybe the worthless check division?"

The officers laughed the kind of lame laughter that someone laughs when he's heard that joke too many times before.

"We here because we got a problem," said Derrigan Slaughter slowly. "Or rather, actually, Robert, you got a problem right 'long with us."

Now he was worried. "What? What did I do wrong this time?"

Detective Slaughter smiled in spite of himself. "It ain't 'cause you done anything. We done had a lot of cases together, Robert, you and us. They all been strange. You seem to attract stuff that is just outright strange, my friend."

"Okay . . . what is it?"

"Gang intelligence. Only it don't involve no known gangs. We got gang intelligence in this here situation, mostly because that's gonna be where most rumors about threats go. This one don't involve no known gangs, but it involves you."

"It may be nothing," said Cashdollar.

"It may be nothin," repeated Slaughter. "But then again, it might be somethin."

Cashdollar took over. "One of these panhandlers told a patrol officer, and he passed it on to gang intelligence. You know, he's one of those shabby looking little guys who beg in the street. But the officer believed him. So, this street beggar says he saw two Arabic guys stop at the red light, arguing. And one of them said they were going after a *target*—he specifically said, a target—who lived on Willowick Drive."

"Which is where yo' home is," explained Slaughter unnecessarily.

"Exactly. And this street bum, he said these Arabic folks were heavily armed with assault rifles and silencers. And they mentioned something about the target being a *lawyer*."

"A lawyer," Slaughter repeated. "Like maybe you."

"There's other lawyers who live on that street. But given that you got a tendency to get yourself into trouble with violent criminals, and I don't know why you always seem to do that, but given that you do, we figured you ought to know. You know?"

"Yes," Robert said quietly. "Yes, I know."

"And you know the drill. We can't provide so-called 'protection.' That's in the movies. It would take three shifts of two guys each every day, plus six or eight more for when the first guys were off duty. But we can at least let you know, like we're doing now."

"Not very comforting."

"And more'n that," Slaughter said, "we can alert patrol in the area so that if you call, and we'll tell you how, they can get there real quick. Real quick."

"And keep in touch with us. Robert, given your history with us, you're almost part of the homicide division yourself."

"Ummm . . . Great."

"We gonna be watchin too, Robert." Detective Slaughter fist-bumped his arm.

*   *   *

The Walls Unit of the Department of Criminal Justice is fearsome for its outer perimeter. The walls are enormous, with armed guards at each corner. This is a place for serious offenders. It also contains, in a small enclave deep inside, the execution chamber, where capital punishment is carried out.

Billy Joe Armistead lay on the bunk in one of the six cells just outside the chamber.

He'd had his last meal. Having had a choice of whatever the kitchen could supply, he'd opted for one of the most popular last meals.

A cheeseburger and a Coke.

"It's time," said a guard.

Wordlessly, Billy Joe Armistead stepped out of the cell. There have been inmates who resisted, on very rare occasions, and the prison personnel were ready for it. But the tradition was to "take it like a man," and that was what Billy Joe did.

He had been relieved of his cuffs, belly chain, and leg irons when he entered the enclave, and he would never wear them again.

"No, nobody yells out 'Dead Man Walking,'" explained the guard in response to a whispered question from the condemned man. "That's in the movies." He and Billy Joe both laughed. Gallows humor, literally.

The chamber itself is only a few feet away. The cinderblock walls, incongruously, are painted a bright, cheery blue. Billy Joe sat on the gurney, lay down, and extended his arms.

Almost instantly, the tie-down team had him strapped in. The team actually practices for this macabre task, so that it can be done as fast as possible.

Billy Joe's spiritual adviser was there: a Baptist minister who worked the prison. The warden was there. A doctor was there, although he would have no role in the execution itself, because of the Hippocratic oath: "Neither will I administer a poison to anybody." A technician busied himself with starting an IV in the prisoner's arm.

Meanwhile, two sets of onlookers, in two separate rooms, watched behind glass.

One viewing room is dedicated to the inmate: his family, friends, and lawyers. The other contains the state's witnesses and the family of the victim.

Maria Melendes stood by in the second room. She didn't routinely attend executions. It's hard enough attending even one. But this case was a special horror to her. She felt a need to be on hand if there were arguments for a stay—or, if not, just to see it through.

The warden invited the inmate's last words.

The condemned man looked to the first room. "I love you all. Don't be sad. I'm only getting what I deserve." And then he looked to the second room. Almost inaudibly, he breathed the words, "I'm sorry."

And finally, he turned to the warden. "I'm all set to fly. Flaps down. Let's do it, man."

The warden usually gives a signal, agreed on beforehand. This time, it was that he removed his glasses. Behind the wall, an invisible executioner started a stream of a powerful tranquilizer.

He followed that with a dose that would be fatal.

The prisoner breathed heavily. He strained momentarily against the straps and let out indistinguishable sounds. Then he relaxed. And shortly after that, the shallow heaving of his chest slowed.

Just over two minutes went by before the doctor examined Billy Joe Armistead and pronounced him dead. That was his only reason for being here.

Both observation rooms were silent. Then sobs erupted from the condemned man's kin. According to tradition, prison staff led the state's witnesses and family out first, and the prisoner's observers separately, so that the two groups never met.

Maria, like most of the others, walked in stunned silence.

* * *

As soon as she reached the outside world, which was a few feet outside the barred gates, she dialed Robert.

"I've got some bad news," he told her. "But I'll tell you later, when you get home."

"I'm coming straight there," she answered. "Fast as I can. Because I've had a hard day at the office."

* * *

Robert closed the shutters and lowered the light. And they sat, as they often did, on tan leather couches, facing each other.

"Not this kind of thing again," she sighed. "Why do you get death threats? You'd think I'd be the one to get them, given the kind of work that I do."

"I know. I'm like someone famous, even though I'm not. Like a civil rights activist, or a senator, or a controversial actor who gets death threats."

"It shouldn't be such a frequent thing with you. But here we go again."

"I get into cases where people have done really bad things that affect a lot of other people. And just like a political activist, I make people mad. There are always plenty of people who'd like to shut down this kind of lawsuit. And they tend to be bad people."

"Right. So what're we going to do about it?"

"I thought about checking both of us into a hotel. But that's a bad idea. Bad guys can walk right up to our room. The security is as porous as Sponge Bob Square Pants."

She shook her head. But even with this heavy atmosphere, she smiled at that.

"Since we've hardened the front of the house, it's as good a place to be as any."

"You think so?" And they both thought about the event in the past when a charmer had tried to stop one of Robert's cases by setting off a bomb in the driveway. It had exploded outside a double-brick wall that was outside the fortified front of the home.

"And we'll make it difficult to see where we are in the house," he went on. "Which is what we just did."

"I'm still scared."

"Of course."

They were silent. Finally, he told her, "And Slaughter and Cash-dollar gave me a number to call when we leave the house. We'll both drive out at the same time. A patrol officer will be here in front, watching, when we leave. And when we drive home."

"That'll be so inconvenient. Most days, we come and go at different times. You might have to get there at six in the morning and I get there at 8:30. Or vice versa."

He laughed. "But just think about all those poor folks who have to carpool together every day because they aren't millionaires."

She smiled. "Well, of course."

"Not a perfect solution, I know."

"Can't you settle this case?"

"I tried. I tried. I would have. My clients wouldn't go for what Jimmy offered. And surprise! Jimmy wouldn't pay what they wanted."

"Man, that's too bad. Try again."

"Okay. But hey. Don't I recall correctly that you were one of the people who pushed me to accept this case?"

She looked miserable, but she smiled. "Smart aleck. But I know you're too deep into it now to get out. I'll support you in every way I can."

28

This was going to be money day. A day for proving the amount of damages. The amount of restitution. The amount that Dravos was going to have to pay Nova, if Nova won.

Tom Kennedy was going to handle the witnesses on damages. There were three of them. They had calculated the amount of damages differently, but all their estimates were close to four hundred million dollars.

First, Tom called a woman who was the former CEO of a big Silicon Valley firm. She told the jury, "To figure a market value for this device, you'd have to have a market. But there's no market. The only free-world use of the Nova device is in American spacecraft. And the other markets around the world for the same kind of device are secret.

"But you can make an estimate of value by considering devices of comparable complexity and innovation. I compared the sale values of three similarly complex and new devices, which sold in acquisitions for $305 million, $451 million, and $483 million. Based on that comparison, I estimate the market value of the Nova Aerospace device at 400 million dollars."

On cross examination, Jimmy got the witness to admit that her estimate "wasn't of a real market value. It's what we call a shadow market. But that's the best you can do."

The second witness estimated market value at $380 million. "How did you calculate that?" Tom asked. "That's by using a multiple of earnings model, multiplying the Nova device's earnings per year by seven." But then, Jimmy asked, "Why seven? Why not two, or four?," and the witness lamely answered: "Seven is the customary number, accepted in the trade."

The third witness used a "capitalized earnings method" and testified to a value of $450 million.

One of the jurors dozed off during the first witness. When the third witness finished, almost all of the jurors looked leaden-eyed. The only one who was wide awake was the bank president, and he looked positively excited by the testimony. At times, he had smiled and nodded his head in apparent approval.

The only problem was that the bank president had paid close attention to Jimmy Coleman's cross examination, too, and he had nodded and smiled just as much.

"At first, I was glad we got that guy on the jury," Robert said morosely, when it was over. "But now, I'm scared of what he might do. Ordinary people would just accept our experts' numbers without understanding the reasons. But this bank president, if he doesn't like the methods, he'll be against us, and he'll lead the rest of the jury against us too."

* * *

"Call your next."

"The plaintiff calls Professor Ray Marikeh."

"I object, your honor." Jimmy's voice sounded like an outboard motor that needed a tune-up. "This witness was disclosed only a few days ago! Long after the discovery deadline."

The judge sighed. "Mr. Herrick?"

"Your honor, the plaintiff disclosed this witness immediately, when we first became aware of the need for his testimony. And that happened when Mr. Coleman told us something right after the jury heard the deposition of Amir Massad, who described how he helped steal the trade secret by photographing it. Specifically, Mr. Coleman told me that Amir Massad was, quote, 'a notorious liar,' and that he had evidence that was going to 'explode' Mr. Massad's testimony, quote, 'like an Islamic bomb.' That hadn't been disclosed to us before then."

"Allowing this witness would destroy any kind of orderly procedure!" Jimmy thundered. "We haven't had a chance to take his deposition, for one thing."

Everyone noticed that Jimmy hadn't denied saying what he'd said.

"Given the circumstances," said the judge, "The testimony will be admitted."

The professor took the witness stand. He swore to tell the truth and identified himself. Robert turned toward him.

"And what is your specialty, Professor Marikeh?"

"The governments of the Middle East, particularly Iran and Saudi Arabia."

"Iranian governments have been hostile to the United States for decades. Can you tell us why?"

The professor gave a miniature version of his lecture on the 1953 CIA-assisted coup, the Shah, the popular revolution of 1979, the taking of American hostages, and the continuous sources of tensions between the two nations.

"What part does religion play in Iranian attitudes toward the United States?"

"The external events are secular, but you have to realize, Iran is a pervasively religious Muslim country. The Ayatollah Khomeini is considered the founder of the present nation, which calls itself the Islamic Republic of Iran. He labelled the United States as 'the Great Satan.' Iranian government doctrine is that the United States is evil in a way that Christians consider the devil to be evil.

"In other words, hatred of the United States is not just a political belief, although it is that. But also, hatred of the United States is a religious doctrine. It is believed in, in kind of the same way that Iranians believe in their religious texts. It traces to the government under Ayatollah Khomeini."

"Now, not every Iranian thinks that way, would you say?"

"No, of course not. Young people, particularly, are less likely to feel it. But if you are in the government or the military, you have to at least pretend to it, and the likelihood is that you believe it. You really, deeply dislike and distrust the United States."

"Now, let me bring you to the immediate issues in this case. You have been furnished the testimony of a Mr. Amir Massad, certified by a court in Iran. Have you read it?"

"Yes, indeed."

"The testimony describes an international theft and discloses national secrets. One might think that an Iranian might want to avoid giving this testimony truthfully."

"Yes. One might."

"Why might a witness testify this way and compromise national secrets?"

"The Iranian government has a tendency to gloat over any defeat of us Americans, large or small. And politicians put the worst face possible on every American action. Just as an example, when the Iranians freed the American hostages in 1979, an Iranian spokesman brazenly announced to the world that the Americans had paid 'ransom.' Ransom, he repeated, because describing it this way would embarrass the United States.

"It was a perverse way to act, because the money that went to Iran was Iran's money, and the United States just released a bank freeze on it, under an international agreement. It was sort of like kids saying 'Nanny-nanny-boo-boo' to each other. But the Iranians love to do that. That's just an example. They've done it for years.

"By telling what he did, this Amir Massad presumably acted with the approval of his superiors. And he gave them a chance to say 'nanny-nanny-boo-boo' to the Americans one more time."

"I pass the witness." This is good testimony, Robert thought.

* * *

But Jimmy wasted no time, and he knew where to attack.

"The Iranians don't always tell the truth, do they, Mr. Marikeh? For instance, it obviously wasn't ransom when they released the hostages, but the Iranians falsely called it ransom to put down the Great Satan."

"I think that's true."

"So, bear with me and let's think this thing through. If Mr. Amir Massad never actually stole any rollover device, he would be motivated to lie and say he did, wouldn't he?"

"I don't understand what you mean."

Suddenly, Robert had a queasy feeling in his stomach.

"All right, let me back up. The Iranians deliberately lie sometimes when they can use a false narrative to thumb their nose at the United States."

"Yes."

"Even if he hadn't stolen any trade secret at all, this Mr. Amir Massad might have been motivated to say that he had, just to embarrass the United States. Wouldn't he?"

"Oh, I see. Let me think about that."

"If he hadn't stolen any trade secrets, the truth wouldn't embarrass the United States. But if he hadn't stolen anything, he could say that he had. And that would embarrass the United States. So that would be what he'd be motivated to do, right?"

"Oh, I see. I . . . suppose so."

"So, did Amir Massad tell the truth? Or isn't it more likely that he lied?"

"I don't know."

Jimmy passed the witness.

Robert looked cold and pale when they left the courtroom for the day. "We're worse off than if we hadn't called Professor Marikeh. Jimmy took less than five minutes to completely destroy his testimony. And he destroyed the testimony from Amir Massad, too."

"Come on, Robert," Tom said. "I'll buy you a drink. Or two."

"We . . . really ought to be preparing for tomorrow."

"No. You've got that witness's deposition. You're prepared. He's going to be a hostile witness and we can cross examine him instead of asking namby-pamby questions on direct. Let's go get a drink."

*　*　*

Robert was on his second glass of Scotch and water—MacAllan twelve-year—when his phone rang.

"Oh, no." The display said, "Pepper."

"Hi, baby."

"Daddy, I've drunk too much to drive. I'm sorry."

"Listen, baby. I'm just not able to come pick you up right this second. Can you call Maria?"

"I did. She can't come either."

Tom, listening to half of the conversation, understood what was going on. "I'll go get her. You stay here. I'll loop back and pick you up."

"No. This was bound to happen. We've got a contingency plan. It's time to put it into effect, because we can't keep dropping everything and driving across town."

Into the telephone, he said, "Pepper, please call an Uber. You've got the number. You've got the app. Uber will get there faster than either Maria or I could."

She was silent for a moment. Then: "Yes, Daddy."

He sat for an instant and looked down at the bar. And shook his head. He felt infinitely worse than he had while he had only been thinking about losing his case.

29

A man with mocha skin, purple glasses, and a plus-or-minus tattoo on his check was making his way up the courtroom aisle. At the judge's command, he swore to tell the truth.

And then, deTravanian Wrenger took his place on the witness stand.

"You're deTravanian Wrenger?" Robert said firmly. He was just slightly hung over, frankly, from the night before, but maybe it was a good thing. He didn't have any fear in his stomach or hesitation in his questions.

"Yes. I sure am." The witness was self-assured too.

"You're a vice president of Dravos and an inventor of electronic equipment?"

"Yes to both of those statements."

"You once worked for Nova Aerospace and designed devices for missile guidance. And propulsion. And rollover?"

"Yes. But I quit because of the way the place was run. I couldn't do a good job at Nova Aerospace. I couldn't work honestly there."

"In fact, you'd do anything you could to hurt Nova."

"I wouldn't put it that way. But I wouldn't be sorry if they got hurt."

Robert had looked at the Federal Rules of Evidence beforehand. Rule 611 says that leading questions can be used against a "witness identified with an adverse party." The conventional strategy is to make every question a leading question, and that was exactly what Robert was going to do.

"At Nova, you had a contract, a covenant, saying you wouldn't go to work for a competitor. But Mr. Wrenger, that's exactly what you did when you quit and went to work for Dravos, wasn't it?"

"The lawyers told me that contract didn't apply. It wasn't legal."

"But a lawyer wrote it in the first place, right? And so there was an indication that actually, it was legal, wasn't there?"

"I don't know who wrote it. If he thought that, he wasn't much of a lawyer."

"In any event, you said you wanted to be honest. But signing the contract and then violating it wasn't very honest, was it?"

"I thought it was the only honest decision I could make."

"Nova disagrees, as you know."

Jimmy was on his feet. "I've been patient, but I object because this has become harassment."

"Sustained," said the judge immediately. "Mr. Herrick, get to the point."

"Yes, your honor. I'm doing exactly that. Mr. Wrenger, there came a time when you met at Dravos with a Mr. Amir Massad, from Iran. Isn't that right?"

"Yes. I didn't especially want to meet him, but he kept getting after me, until finally he just came by anyway. Uninvited."

"And he came to your laboratory."

"Somehow, he got around the security."

"And Mr Amir Massad has testified that you showed him the plans for the rollover device from Nova, told him that these papers were the flowchart, and left him alone with it. And he photographed it."

"Mr. Amir Massad is nothing but a big-time liar," the witness thundered. "He has a terrible reputation. He'd say anything that would create trouble for the United States."

"But he told the truth about your leaving him with the flowchart, didn't he?"

"He certainly didn't. It don't think Amir Massad would recognize the truth if it came up and bit him on the bottom."

"And you had an assistant? A Ms. Romaine Cramshak?"

"She's not there any longer, that's for sure."

"And she was also present when Mr. Amir Massad came to the laboratory, and she also left him alone with the flowchart?"

"Nobody I saw left him alone with any flowchart!" The witness's face was red. Good, Robert thought. He's losing control.

"And in this way, you helped the government of Iran steal a valuable piece of missile technology, at the cost of endangering the security of the United States. Didn't you?"

"I object," Jimmy yelled.

Again, the judge was quick. "Overruled."

"It's not all that damn valuable!" shouted the witness. Then he recovered. "No!" he said, this time with the same certainty but a little less volume. The jurors were staring at deTravanian Wrenger with puzzled eyes.

"Yes, actually, I want to ask about the value to the Iranians. Or the market value to any buyer on the open market. The design of this device is worth hundreds of millions of dollars to a foreign country that is an enemy of the United States, isn't it?"

Again, Wrenger lost his temper. "No! It's worth maybe one million. A few million at the most."

Nobody believes that, Robert thought.

Or . . . at least, I hope not.

"You sure did get your revenge against Nova Aerospace, didn't you?"

"Now that is a silly question. I had no intention to 'get revenge' against Nova Aerospace."

"Your honor, I pass the witness."

* * *

Jimmy's examination of deTravanian Wrenger started slowly. But it built quickly in intensity.

"Mr. Wrenger, have you received the Lifetime Achievement Award from the National Electronics Association?"

"Yes. Just last year."

"Is that Lifetime Award given in recognition of, quote, 'excellence in both scientific achievement and personal character' during your entire career?"

"That's in the official description of the award."

Jimmy put on his best disgusted look. "Mr. Herrick implied that you might be dishonest. Would the National Electronics Association have given you this Lifetime Award if you were dishonest?"

"Certainly not."

"Now, Mr. Herrick omitted your education and experience. Tell us about that."

"I have a degree in electrical engineering from Harvard. A Ph.D. from Stanford. I was a professor at CalTech: the California Institute of Technology. And I am a professor at Emery University while I work at Dravos. My patents have provided designs for parts of smart phones, spacecraft, military equipment, medical devices, and consumer items."

"Mr. Wrenger, with your accomplishments, is it likely that you'd need money so much that you'd sell trade secrets to a foreign country?"

"Absolutely not. I don't need the money from my work anymore. I work because I was trained to work, and it's what I do."

"Now that we've got that out of the way, Mr. Wrenger, did you do anything to provide a Mr. Amir with access to the design of a rollover device?"

"No." The witness's voice was firm.

"Did you show him any flowchart?"

"No." Louder.

"Did you do anything whatsoever that helped Iran to get the design or flowchart to the rollover device from Nova?"

"No!" By now, the witness was shouting.

"Before Amir Massad came to your lab uninvited, did you consult with other people in the electronics industry about this Mr. Massad?"

"I certainly did. He was really chasing after me, and I didn't know why."

"What did you find out about the reputation of Amir Massad for truth and veracity?"

"It's bad. Very bad. The message I got back was that he was a big talker and a big liar."

Jimmy renewed his disgusted look. "I pass the witness."

"Let's break for lunch." The judge looked at his watch. "Everyone, be back promptly at one-thirty."

* * *

Robert's stomach bubbled. It hadn't gone as he had hoped. DeTravanian Wrenger hadn't testified the way he had expected. He knew, of course, that even if you have a witness committed in a deposition, details can be put differently so as to turn the entire story around. But he hadn't foreseen this testimony from Wrenger. And the man had been convincing in his denials of the case Robert was building.

One-thirty came too soon.

The judge ascended to the bench. "Mr. Herrick? Re-examination?"

"Yes, your honor." He turned to the witness. "Mr. Wrenger, was Romaine Cramshak present during Amir Massad's visit? Your assistant?"

"Yes, she was."

"You now claim that Mr. Massad came to your laboratory uninvited?"

"That's right."

"He was really a trespasser, you're saying? Or an invader? He broke through security?"

"That's right."

"But you didn't call security when you allegedly saw that he was there."

"Ahhh—no."

"And neither did Ms. Cramshak."

"No."

"And that was because, as she described it, you and Mr. Massad knew each other."

"I guess so. He was trying so hard to meet me, I guess I acted like I knew him. But in reality, I didn't know him at all."

The jurors were watching deTravanian Wrenger's face. Closely. They watched as he rubbed his palms together. They saw him squirming in the witness chair. They saw the slight smirk on his face and his shifting eyes.

Robert watched them for just a second or two.

"But it didn't make any sense to let Mr. Massad stay there, did it? Because no matter how well you knew somebody, the lab was still off-limits. Isn't that right?"

"I guess so."

"And you now claim that Mr. Massad was a liar. And you knew that, so you claim, before he came to you. That made it even more important to call security, didn't it?"

"I . . . didn't see it that way."

"By the way, your flowcharts were stored in a set of cubbyholes within easy reach, weren't they?"

"That's right. I work that way."

"Ms. Cramshak said that, actually, the flowchart for the rollover device was open and sitting on the lab table. That's true, isn't it?"

"No. It isn't true."

"You realize, Mr. Wrenger, that it doesn't add up? You realize, there are all kinds of red flags in what you've said here?"

Jimmy's voice growled with outrage. "I object, your honor. That's a highly improper question."

"Sus-STAINED!" The judge's ruling was prompt. "The jury is instructed to disregard that last remark of counsel and consider it for no purpose whatsoever."

Which served to reinforce Robert's purpose in saying it.

"I pass the witness," he said politely.

*   *   *

"That was a great job of cross examination," Tom said excitedly. He seemed to be genuinely enthusiastic.

Your teammates are supposed to support you. That's what professional basketball players do: they slap palms, even when one of their guys has just missed a free throw. Tom was an experienced observer. But Tom was a teammate.

And he was too enthusiastic. Robert himself had a pessimistic, sinking feeling. He was sweating.

"I hate to say it, but I think Jimmy won this round. We called this witness. We were the ones who put deTravanian Wrenger on the witness stand. If you call a witness, the jurors expect you to prove something by it. If all they have is a mushy impression, you've failed. A tie with the other side is really a loss."

He shook his head. I should never have taken this case, he thought one more time. I knew it was going to be a dog.

And when I try to consider it objectively, I find myself thinking that deTravanian Wrenger's denials were credible. Jimmy brought out the best from this witness. That's why I say, Jimmy won this round.

30

I t was almost an anticlimax when Robert called his principal expert witness. The issues had all been discussed. But it didn't hurt to reinforce them.

"Professor Eisner, do you have an opinion about whether the flowchart for the Iranian device was copied from the flowchart designed at Nova Aerospace?"

"I do have an opinion."

"And what is that opinion?"

"There is no question that the flowchart was copied."

The expert witness explained: The loops, the if-decision points, and other pathways in the two devices were identical.

And Jimmy's cross examination was predictable. The actual commands were different, the chips were different, and the trajectories of the electrons were different.

Robert's re-direct examination again hammered away at the simple fact that the flowcharts were near-identical, even if the hardware was forced, by Chinese components, to be different.

Some of the jurors were yawning.

"Now, we've got to recall Mike Martin," Tom reminded him. "To testify about damages."

"Oh, yeah." After this many days in trial, Robert's brain was mushy. Day after day in trial is like taking a difficult college exam for an entire week. It leads to a punch-drunk feeling.

"Keep it short. The jurors are bored."

Robert's direct examination took less than ten minutes. The market value of the Nova rollover device was at least $ 400 million. The value of sales of devices of comparable complexity showed that the value was at least this much. So did development costs for the device.

Jimmy also sensed the jurors' fatigue. He asked only six questions, all designed to point out that none of the witness's comparable sales were for this product.

Robert stood. "Your honor, the plaintiff rests."

"Ladies and gentlemen of the jury, we will be in recess until Monday morning." The judge was tired too.

* * *

Maria was waiting for him at home. She held out a glass of Talisker and water. "I need to tell you something. Not essential to your case. Just an interesting sidelight."

"Good, if it isn't something heavy duty."

"It isn't. Derrigan Slaughter and Donnie Cashdollar arrested the switchboard operator at the hospital. The one where deTravanian Wrenger was recuperating, and the one where that shootout killed those Iranian invaders."

"I though the FBI was investigating that."

"They were. But the Justice Department decided to defer to the state authorities. The Feds handed over the case to our homicide officers."

"Oh, yeah?"

"Yes. The Feds decided that the state criminal courts would have better laws for this particular crime. There were federal crimes committed too, of course, but they involved more complicated elements to prove. For example, the Feds would have to prove that the killers were trying to get rid of Wrenger as a potential witness to a federal crime. And that would be hard to do. The state has more direct pathways toward proving the case."

"What are the crimes that the state will charge?"

"One is attempted murder. For that, it doesn't matter whether Wrenger was a witness."

"So Slaughter and Cashdollar tracked down the other people involved."

"Yes. They found out that this switchboard operator had originated a bunch of calls to this guy with an Iranian name. And that guy, in turn, made a bunch of calls to a phone that was in the possession of one of the invading killers, a phone that was in his possession when he was killed.

"The switchboard operator had deposited a thousand dollars in a bank account a few days earlier, which was a strange amount compared to what she usually took in. The detectives drove the lady downtown and interviewed her. I understand she denied it at first, but she wasn't used to being in this kind of trouble, and she gave it all up pretty quickly."

"And don't tell me. They arrested her Iranian telephone friend after that."

"Yes. And a couple of other characters too."

"Well, I guess this means that some of the heat is off deTravanian Wrenger." Robert sounded hopeful. "Not my best friend, but I'm glad he hasn't gotten murdered yet. And maybe some of the heat is off me, too."

"Don't count on it." There was resignation in her voice. "I talked to the detectives about that too. And they say there are probably plenty more Qud Forces out there waiting—you know, the Iranian military outreach that does the dirty work, is the Quds—so don't count on it."

*   *   *

"You did *what?*" Now, Robert was talking to Pepper. "You drove home anyway? After calling and telling both Maria and me that you'd had too much to drink?"

"I didn't exactly tell you I'd had too much to drink. That may be what you thought I was telling you, because you're used to thinking that."

"I sure as heck didn't just think it. I knew it. You were slurring your words and—listen, it was unmistakable. You just had no business driving a car."

"I didn't have any trouble driving home. I didn't have any trouble at all. I just wasn't too drunk to drive. I wasn't even drunk!"

"The fact that you didn't have trouble on this one occasion doesn't mean it's safe. If you drove home ten times in this same condition, how many times do you think you'd have a wreck? Two or three? Even one is too many, of course. You can't tell me that if you drove home ten times in that condition, you wouldn't have a wreck at least once."

"But that is what I'm telling you! That is what I'm telling you. I wasn't drunk enough so that I couldn't drive."

"What about our agreement that you'd call an Uber? It's inexpensive. It's easy. You've got the app, right on your phone. Why didn't you get an Uber, as we discussed?"

"Because there was no problem with driving home."

It is impossible to argue meaningfully with someone about drug or alcohol abuse. If you're trying to persuade someone who argues with you about that, your conversation is always going to go around in circles, Robert thought unhappily.

"Pepper, listen. I want so much for you to go to Alcoholics Anonymous. You've been arrested repeatedly for driving while intoxicated. You had a wreck that injured someone. You've been convicted for that. Every time, you spent at least overnight in jail, and you've had a jail sentence that kept you in on weekends for several weeks. Aren't those events a wake-up call?"

"Of course. They've convinced me that I've got to use will power."

Robert was ready to pull out his hair.

"I really, really want you to go to AA. Please, Pepper. Make it part of the waking up that you've gotten from the wake-up call."

"I've gone before. A couple of times. Because you wanted me to. And the answer is, I didn't get anything out of it."

"Which is too bad. Please go back. I'm hoping that you *will* get something. At some time. Einstein didn't get it at first when he was an early student. St. Paul didn't get it until one day, he was struck with an experience on the road to Damascus. Alexander Graham Bell didn't get how to make a telephone until he tried and tried and finally got it done by accident. It took Jonas Salk many times trying to make his vaccine before. . . ."

She had to laugh. "Never mind. No more examples. I get the idea." Then, she was serious. "I just don't think it applies to me."

"I have lots more examples. People who didn't get it at first but finally found something valuable. Please, Pepper. I want you to go back to AA. More than once more. I want you to try a little harder."

He was quietly out of arguments, at least for the moment.

She was silent.

"All right. I'll go to AA at least once more. I'm pretty sure I'm not going to get anything out of it this time, either."

She hesitated. "I don't need to go to AA. I have nothing in common with those losers and what they talk about. It's almost like they're bragging about claiming to be alcoholics. It's like they're saying, 'I'm a member of the club because I have this valuable thing—I'm a drunk.' That's not me. And I don't need it. If I go there, it's only for you."

*　*　*

Tom sounded impatient. "Robert, we've got to be working this weekend. We're back in court Monday. Just because it's Jimmy who's going to be doing the direct examination doesn't mean we don't have to get ready. We've got to think about cross-examination."

"I know. I've just had family stuff going on."

"Well, let's get to work."

"Jimmy seemed to be hinting that he was going to call his expert on the Iranian missile program. The guy who isn't an electronics guy, but he knows what the Iranians are doing with their rockets and stuff."

"Yes. And we've got his deposition summarized. Thirty pages of summary. You ought to read that first. I'll be studying it, too, and outlining ways of attack."

"All right. Then what?"

"Well, there's the President of Dravos. He's on Jimmy's witness list too. And Jimmy's electronics expert. The guy who's going to say what we already know, namely that the hardware is different and the commands are different. That's two more that we're pretty sure are coming up soon."

"I bet he recalls deTravanian Wrenger."

"You think so? What for?"

"We might have gotten to deTravanian when we called him during our case. We might have lowered his credibility just a little. By raising red flags."

Tom nodded. "I think so. But recalling him will just allow you to cross him again and reinforce the red flags."

"But it will also let Jimmy get his story told again, nearer to the end. And now, with all the background the jury has, he can emphasize the highlights. And deTravanian is a more experienced witness now. We'll have a harder time getting bad stuff out of him."

"Maybe so."

"I don't think they'll recall Romaine Cramshak."

"No. That would re-tell the jury about the contradictions between them."

"How long you think we're going to be here at the office?"

"Not too long. We're sleep deprived. It's been, like, work in court all day and prepare half the night. Robert, I'd like for you to get some sleep tonight."

* * *

On a morning in April, when the grass around the bayou shone with overnight rain, it happened, and Robert got a call from the two detectives.

"Those guys in the Hummer done come by yo' place on Willowick," Derrigan Sluaghter told him. "It was befo' you taken off for yo' office. Officer Houghton was set up there, waitin for you to leave, and these two strange lookin gentlemen drove by, real slow, watchin yo' house."

"And so, what happened?" Robert's voice was tight.

Donnie Cashdollar took up the narrative. "The bad guys saw Houghton's car and they kept on driving by, like they were just on the way somewhere. Houghton followed them and stopped them within a couple of blocks, and he called for backup, because he knew about the guns they had."

"And a bunch of patrol officers responded," Slaughter continued. These two detectives were like Tweedle-Dum and Tweedle-Dee, Robert thought, the way they told a story. "They threw down on the bad guys 'cause they had weapons modified to automatic. They's Iranian citizens on visas, legal in the country, but Houghton turned 'em over to the feds 'cause of the illegal guns.

"They names, for what it's worth, are Mahmoud Dabiri and Ramshad Tehrani."

"You can just call them Mahmoud and Ramshad. But the bad news is, they've already made bail," Cashdollar lamented.

"You mean, the Feds just let them go?" Robert shouldn't have been surprised, but he was.

"Yeah. It's just a piddly gun charge," Cashdollar said. "Sorry."

"The only good news is, we hear they done taken the guns away from these jive turkey hoodlums," Slaughter said flatly. "They don't hafta give back the illegal firearms even if the guys make bail."

Great, Robert thought. I wonder how long it will take them to get new ones?

Meanwhile, I'm on my own. And just incidentally, I've got this not-so-easy trial starting up again on Monday, and I really ought to be putting some of my concentration into that, instead of worrying all the time about being shot by Iranian terrorists.

But "Thanks, gentlemen. I really appreciate it," was all he said.

31

Monday dawned clear and bright. On the square in front of the courthouse, a thousand redbreast robins grounded their journeys north momentarily, looking as purposeful as a phalanx of Roman soldiers marching up through Gaul. Even the lawyers slowed their time-conscious steps on this beautiful day to watch the perennial signal of spring.

Robert Herrick was one who tarried less than others.

He frowned. "I wish we knew who Jimmy's going to call first."

Tom smiled. "Robert, you're a bigger overachiever than the emperor Caesar himself. We know the witnesses, and we're ready for them."

They shucked everything necessary for the metal detector, picked up their luggage, and replaced their shoes and jackets. The elevator seemed to Robert to take forever. His squirming amused Tom and, at the same time, worried him.

The eighth floor. They were early. But they went into the courtroom and plopped their bags on the counsel table.

Jimmy wasn't there, but a handful of his minions were. And the presumptive next witness, the expert on the Iranian missile program, sat in the back of the courtroom. "See," said Tom, "we did know, or we guessed who the witness would be. And we're ready."

"I'm not sure anyone's ever ready for Jimmy."

At that moment, the great man himself waddled into the courtroom, resplendent in a blue-and-white striped seersucker suit that embodied spring itself. "Good morning! Good morning. What a marvelous day. Too bad we're indoors."

Nobody ought to be that cheerful at a moment like this, Robert thought.

* * *

Finally, the judge's law clerks, both of them, sauntered into the courtroom and took up positions in the well fronting the bench, like sentries in a foxhole. Next came the bailiff, in his marshal's uniform, then the court reporter, and during it all, a room full of spectators.

One law clerk stepped out. And then, he opened the door with the cry: "Order in the court. Everyone rise, please. . . ."

Judge Shanice Leeds, straight as a ramrod and thin as one, too, walked smoothly up to the bench.

"Get the jury." And the bailiff hustled off.

"Mr. Coleman, you ready to rumble?"

"Yes, your honor. And rumble is right. We're ready to roll right over the bad guys on the other side of the courtroom."

"All right." The judge shook her head and grinned. "Spoken like a true advocate. Call your first."

The jurors were filing into the box as Jimmy grated it out. "Professor Lincoln Hernandez." And the jurors watched as the newest witness was sworn and stated his name.

"And how are you employed, Professor Hernandez?"

"I am the Hayden Richardson Chaired Professor of Government at Columbia University. I concentrate on Middle Eastern Studies."

"And does that include Iran?"

"Of course. Iran is maybe the most interesting nation there. But interesting in a bad way. It's the black sheep of the family."

"Later, we'll have to hear why you say so. But for now, tell us your qualifications."

And the man was indeed qualified. Degrees from Columbia, UCLA, and Stanford. Middle-east desk at the State Department. High level at the CIA. Assistant, associate, and full professor at Columbia. Six books and countless articles, of which he named a few, with suitably long and complicated titles.

And current holder of the Hayden Richardson Chair in Government. Which no one had heard of, but as Robert told himself, it sure does sound impressive.

"The government of Iran is of what kind? A theocracy?"

"The society is mixed, of course, and the government is difficult to classify. I myself regard it as theocratic. The principal founder of the current order was the Ayatollah Khomeini, who obviously is a religious figure. And it calls itself 'the Islamic Republic of Iran.' The judiciary is headed by an ayatollah who definitely has religion. During the 1980's, he sat on a panel that sentenced thousands of people to death, both men and women, for crimes that involved apostasy. In other words, the death penalty for heresy.

"And yet in some respects Iran is a secular government. The president, for example, is elected. Of course, you can't get elected without being Muslim, but that's just like the United States, because it's hard to get elected here if you're an atheist."

"Professor Hernandez, some people might think of Iran as backward. Not technological. Not scientific. Is that true?"

"Not at all. Remember, Iran was close to developing a nuclear bomb. And although they obtained raw materials and equipment from elsewhere, the Iranians did it mostly on their own. They also have a sophisticated missile system."

"Now, that's not a good thing, of course."

"No. It's not good at all. As I was saying, Iran is a black sheep. It is the biggest sponsor of terrorism in the Middle East, and it has exported war to Syria, Yemen, and Iraq. The Iranians have a working mid-range missile program. And it's not good that they do."

"Have they received assistance in setting this program up?"

"Yes. Most industrial countries won't trade missile technology with Iran. But some have. Most significantly, the Iranians have gotten help from North Korea and China."

"What kind of help?"

"In the past, Iran has gotten whole missile systems from North Korea. For example, the Kharramshar missile, which is a well-known two-stage craft in Iran, originally came from North Korea."

"Do the Iranians still get hardware from North Korea?"

"No. Well, the honest answer is, we don't know for sure. But we think we have stopped North Korea from shipping technology to Iran."

"So, the Iranians have the basic missile designs, and they test them. But do they get the spare parts they need, or innovations, from North Korea?"

"No. And that's crucial. A missile has a surprising number of components. Hundreds of thousands or even millions. You've got to have replacements. And as for innovation, if you don't innovate, you're falling behind. But the Iranians are technologically savvy. They've filled the gap with their own technology."

"Are they able to design and manufacture guidance systems for missiles?"

"Oh, my, yes."

"And rollover controls?"

"Yes, again. We've reached the stage by now where Iran can do all these things itself. It is a sophisticated industrial nation, even if it is something of a pariah. As I said before, it's not a good thing. But we're better off knowing about it, and that's what I study."

"Pass the witness."

Robert had watched the professor, now, for most of the morning. His testimony made sense. He was credible. I bet the jury believes this, he thought.

Of course, it wasn't strong evidence on the real subject, which was whether Amir Massad had connived with Dravos personnel to steal this trade secret. But jurors' thinking is funny sometimes, and they might imagine, "Why would the Iranians go to so much trouble to get the secret from DeTravanian Wrenger? They didn't need to."

And Jimmy could combine this testimony with a lot more evidence, of course. Including Wrenger's own testimony directly denying that there was any theft of a trade secret.

Robert was thinking of lines of attack on cross examination when he heard the judge say, "Let's break for lunch. It's a little early, but I've got things to do.

"Everyone, be back and ready to roll"—and she looked at her watch—"at one-thirty this afternoon."

*   *   *

Judge Leeds was punctual. At one-thirty, she was sitting at the bench. At one-thirty-three, the jurors were all in the box.

"Mr. Herrick, you may cross examine."

"Good afternoon, Professor Hernandez."

"Good afternoon."

Courtesy works sometimes, he thought. Especially if you're going to start a line of questioning that the witness will agree with.

"The Iranian government is a murderous regime. That's true, isn't it?"

"Absolutely."

"And the Iranian government is dishonest, isn't it? For example, in avoiding sanctions by labeling banned imports as something they're not?"

"Yes. Absolutely."

"Their missile program blatantly violates international law, doesn't it, since they're testing spacecraft that are capable of launching nuclear weapons?

"Yes. No question about it. They're international outlaws."

When you cross examine an expert witness, there always are some points where the expert will have to agree with you. It's best to cover those first, before attacking.

And he had done that. But now, Robert was ready for some disagreement.

"Given the crimes that the Iranians are perfectly willing to commit, there's no reason why they wouldn't also steal trade secrets, is there?"

"Ahhhh . . . I don't know."

"If they could get a design for free, like a design for a rollover device, these international outlaws would go for it, wouldn't they?"

If the witness uses terminology that helps you, he thought, you should use it too. "International outlaws?" That's a good one.

The witness squirmed. "I . . . suppose so."

"Now, let me ask you something slightly different. You don't question the fact that Amir Massad visited deTravanian Wrenger and Romaine Cramshak in their lab at Dravos, do you?"

"I don't know."

"Well, all three of those people have said it happened. You don't know of any facts to the contrary, do you?"

"No."

"You weren't present when Amir Massad visited?"

"No."

"So, we'd have to rely on those people who were present to know what happened when Amir Massad visited, right?"

"Well, sure."

If the witness says he "doesn't know" something that's obvious to everybody, reason it out with him. Take your time. The witness will show the jury that he does know, and he's just trying to avoid telling the truth.

"So, if an Iranian agent stole trade secrets with the help of Mr. Wrenger, you can't tell us anything about that, can you?"

"No. Not directly."

Sometimes, you can nullify far-out circumstantial evidence just by pointing out that the witness wasn't there when it happened.

"No further questions." Robert did his best to sound as disgusted as Jimmy had pretended to be.

* * *

Jimmy's redirect examination was only three questions, all repeating his earlier theme: The Iranians didn't need to steal anything because they could design it themselves.

Pretty lame, Robert thought. For the first time in a long time, he actually felt good for a moment.

But as they left the courthouse, he realized how small this victory was. Really, how irrelevant it was.

"We didn't do anything to advance our case," he said to Tom. "All we did was to shoot down one of Jimmy's so-called experts. And that doesn't prove anything. Or win the verdict."

32

Call your next."

Jimmy stood. He had on an off-tan suit, almost gold-colored, that stretched across his belly like a trampoline.

"Dravos calls Melinda Gratzmor. The president of Dravos."

After a half hour of preliminaries, it turned out that this witness was nothing but window dressing: a spokesperson for the company, to claim that it was solid and responsible. Dravos had been founded in the early 1900's by Bruno Dravos. Today, it had a big international reputation. According to this spokesperson, Dravos had designed thousands of components for the American space program.

"Now, you've got trade secrets yourself, right? And you take pains to protect them?"

"Yes. We contract with every new employee, that they will keep trade secrets. We enforce a clean-desk policy. Sensitive materials are marked with red cross-hatching covers prominently saying, "Trade Secret." They are retained under lock and key and returned immediately after use. Those are just some of our trade secret policies."

"After their experiences with these policies, can you even imagine an employee stealing anyone else's trade secrets?"

"Certainly not."

Robert's cross examination was brief. "Can you imagine any legitimate reason for a visit by an Iranian agent to a guarded laboratory?" "Ahhh . . . no." "You realize that Amikr Massad visited deTravanian Wrenger's laboratory and went around your security to do it?" "I don't believe it." "You were not present, if he did, and you can't tell anything about what happened?" "I just don't believe it."

And then, Judge Shanice Leeds felt called upon to say something, and she acted decisively. "It's lunch time. Everyone be back at one-thirty."

"The judge knows one thing very well," Tom said as they left the courtroom. "She has an inner clock that tells her when to tuck into her midday meal."

* * *

The next witness was as important as the earlier one had been un-important. Jimmy stood just after one o'clock and announced the man with a flourish.

"Dravos calls Professor Emeritus Marcus Denshire of Harvard University. To tell this jury how different the Iranian rollover device is from the Nova Aerospace rollover."

The witness was indeed impressive, Robert realized. Degrees from Berkeley, Pennsylvania, and Chicago. Had held more than a dozen patents before he graduated. A member of too many prestigious societies to count, including the British Association for Science, to which it was unusual for an American to belong. Consultant to the CIA, the DIA, the Commerce Department, NASA, and EPA, in addition to a wide range of Fortune 500 companies.

"And have you had occasion to compare the Iranian rollover device in this case to the one designed by Nova Aerospace?"

"I have, yes."

"And are they closely similar or completely different?"

"They are completely different. Do you want me to explain why?"

"Please."

"The commands are different, from beginning to end. The chips are different. And the order of the significant events is different."

"Now, it's true, isn't it, that there are some similarities? For example, what are roll, pitch, and yaw? What does that phrase refer to—roll, pitch, and yaw?"

"These are the movements of a spacecraft in three dimensions. Roll, pitch, and yaw are just labels for the three dimensions. Every program for guidance of a missile has to deal with roll, pitch, and yaw."

"So, are there Do Loops and If-Decisions for each of these three dimensions—roll, pitch, and yaw—in both programs?"

"Yes. And they're similar. They have to be."

"Aside from this kind of similarity, and other similarities that are required, are the programs and flowcharts different?"

"Yes. In my opinion, completely different."

"Now, let me ask you this. It's been suggested that Iranians simply ripped off the flowchart for the American rollover device and followed it identically with different hardware. Would it be practical to do that?"

"No, it would not."

"Why not? Please explain."

"First, you can't do that with different kinds of chips. American chips can do some things that Chinese ones can't, and vice versa. Second, it would be almost as difficult to re-design from the American flowchart as to design your own device in the first place, using your own hardware. It just wouldn't make any sense."

"No further questions." Jimmy announced it in a rough but honeyed voice, as if he were saying, "cross-examine if you want to, but it won't do any good."

*   *   *

Robert started his cross examination politely. "Good afternoon, Professor Denshire."

The professor frowned. "Good . . . afternoon."

"The calculations that are made by either program—Professor, they can't be exact down to the last possible decimal point, can they?"

"I don't understand what you're asking me."

"Let's put it this way. If you want to make a motion in space in a particular direction, and you calculate it, it's ultimately just an estimate, isn't it?"

"Oh, I see. Of course. A calculated movement is an approximation of what's needed. In this case, a very close approximation."

"Right. And that's what some of these Do Loops do, right? They might refine the calculation fifty times, or 99 times, or any multiple of times, to get the number to the closest decimal point that you need, and maybe past the decimal points that you need."

"Exactly."

"And if the two flowcharts were different, and the two devices didn't follow each other, the number of loops in any given Do Loop calculation wouldn't be exactly the same, would they?"

The witness was wary. "I suppose . . . not."

"But there's a curious similarity in the number of loops in each Do Loop in the two devices, isn't there?"

"I didn't see any similarity."

"All right. Let's compare the Do Loops in the two devices closely. Look at the first Do Loop in the American device. It does fifty-one repetitions, or fifty-one 'iterations,' doesn't it?"

The witness fumbled with the chart. "Ahhh . . . it says, '*Do . . . i equals 1 Dash 51*.' . . . Right. Fifty-one repetitions of the calculations."

"It's the same in both devices, isn't it?"

Professor Denshire frowned. "Yes."

"Now, Professor, please look at the next Do Loop in the American flowchart. This time, it's a hundred and one repetitions, or a hundred and one 'iterations,' right?"

"Hmmmm . . . yes."

"And the Iranian Do Loop in the same place also has a hundred and one iterations, right?"

". . . Yes."

"Pretty amazing coincidence, isn't it, Professor?"

"I don't know if I would say that."

Wow, Robert thought. This expert witness is really a partisan for Jimmy.

"All right. Now, notice that the first Do Loop in both devices has an If Decision, but the second doesn't, in both devices?"

"Yes."

"And an If Decision just means that the program compares the results of a calculation to some other number, and directs the flow in either of two directions based on the comparison?"

The witness smiled. "That's a pretty good description."

"And there's no reason why the comparison number has to be the same in the two flowcharts, is there?"

The witness thought for a moment, hedging. "No, but I guess it could be."

"And the comparison number in both flowcharts is 0.0000001, isn't it? A 1 with six zeros before it, after the decimal point?"

"...Yes."

"Again, it's a pretty big coincidence, isn't it?"

The witness smiled and looked relaxed. "I don't know that I'd agree."

"Well, I can tell you that more than eighty percent of the Do Loops and If Decisions use the same numbers in each program. And the rest, amounting to about fifteen percent, can be accounted for by differences in the hardware. Isn't that a big coincidence? Or—actually, it shows that the Iranian device is copied, doesn't it?"

"I wouldn't say that necessarily follows."

The jurors were watching the professor through squinting eyes.

This time, Robert's disgust didn't have to be acted out. "Pass the witness."

* * *

The judge looked amused as she said, "Mr. Coleman? Redirect?"

Jimmy sprang to his feet. "Yes, your honor!" He sounded enthusiastic. Robert knew that the enthusiasm wasn't real, but he thought, I bet the jurors are expecting Jimmy to explain it away.

"Professor," Jimmy began, sounding like sandpaper rubbed on an oak board. "These numbers aren't a coincidence at all, are they?"

"I don't think so." The professor smiled again.

"For example, are fifty and one hundred used often in Do Loops?"

"Yes. They're nice round numbers." The professor faced the jury and smiled. "The microprocessor, of course, goes through a hundred iterations in less than a millionth of a second, so it's okay to have a hundred calculations even if you don't need that many."

"And what about fifty-one? Or a hundred and one?"

"It's a convention that some programmers use. You go one iteration beyond the number you're aiming for. And so fifty-one and a hundred and one are common numbers to find."

Jimmy stood and extended his arm, the way a herald might introduce the Queen of England. "No further questions, your honor."

* * *

"We start at ten tomorrow." And everyone stood up as Judge Shanice Leeds stepped away from the bench.

"It only took Jimmy three questions to destroy my cross examination." Robert whispered it while they packed up, but there was no mistaking the pain in his voice.

"I think it's all right." Tom sounded a little more steady. "I'm sure the bank president wasn't fooled."

"Good for the bank president. But now—tell me about the other six. The taxi driver, the waitress, the postman, the mechanic, the flight attendant, and the school secretary. If they understood this bunch of chatter about internal computer language, I'll be really proud of them."

33

Everyone felt the case ending. Or at least, approaching its end.

For Robert, the rest of Jimmy's case went by in a blur. There was an expert on damages, who improbably put the value of the Nova Aerospace device at only forty thousand dollars. Robert cross examined him for an hour, going over calculations based on the mechanism's income potential. The witness admitted that "if you figure it that way," the value was in the hundred millions.

And Jimmy called Dravos's head of security to testify about how closely the company guarded its secrets. But he was easy to cross examine: He wasn't there when Amir Massad avoided security to visit Wrenger's lab and couldn't deny that the Iranian agent had photographed the flowchart.

On rebuttal, Robert called Mike Martin, Nova's president. Not for anything new, but to repeat the essentials of the plaintiff's case, so that the jurors would have it fresh in mind when they deliberated.

There was an audible sigh in the courtroom when both sides rested.

* * *

"We should have had some shadow jurors," Robert said to Tom.

"We didn't think it was a very good case, to begin with. And it wouldn't have seemed like it justified the expense."

Big cases usually justify hiring three or four courtroom observers who are called shadow jurors. They wouldn't know which side had hired them. They would report their impressions throughout the case to an intermediary who would pass on their guidance.

But not in this case.

"I know what you can do, though," Tom said. "The bailiff and the clerk are as good as shadow jurors. Maybe better. They sit through case after case, and they know how jurors think."

"Of course. I've spoken with the bailiff throughout this trial. He'll know which side he's advising, and that's a drawback, but I bet he'll tell me."

The next time he would need advice would be for final arguments, but Robert decided to ask right away.

"What do you think, Lieutenant Nowlin? Am I winning or losing?"

The bailiff leaned back in his chair. His sheriff's uniform was creased and starched, his boots were shined, and his white hair and mustache were close cropped. "I don't know. I'm not sure."

That was bad news.

"How would you call the odds? If you had to guess, what would you say?"

"Maybe . . . fifty-fifty."

That was very bad news. If you were ahead, if you were winning, a bailiff would tell you so. He'd say, "You've got nothing to worry about." But if you were behind, the bailiff would be noncommittal. He would avoid a specific answer. He would say "I don't know," or he would say "fifty-fifty."

"Among Jimmy Coleman's witnesses, who did you think was the best?"

"I guess I'd say, maybe . . . like . . . the expert witness who talked about how good the Iranians were at designing missiles."

"You mean, Professor Lincoln Hernandez?"

"Yeah. That guy. If the Iranians could design it themselves, why go to all the trouble of stealing it? He made a lot of sense."

"Okay. Thanks. Now, can I ask you about my own case? Who was best?"

"I liked Mike Martin. The president. He knows what he's doing, and he just came across as a good guy. But I don't know if he's enough for your side to win."

"What about this? Mike Martin and my expert, Professor Eisner, reinforced each other. They both said the Iranian rollover was copied."

"Well . . . that's true."

"What did you think of deTravanian Wrenger?"

The bailiff laughed. "He's a slimeball. He treated his lady assistant real bad, too."

"But still, you think I might be losing this case."

"I don't know. Honestly, . . . I just don't know."

*　　*　　*

Robert trudged back to the office with Tom at his side. He was as depressed as he had been in as long as he could remember.

Lieutenant Nowlin had helped him figure out how to argue his case to the jury. But the bailiff had also refused to take sides. All he would say was a mouthful of "I don't know." Translation: the bailiff was telling him he was going to lose.

Tom didn't share his pessimism. "I've got our version of the court's charge to the jury, and it's ready to go. You ought to read it over in final form once more, before we argue to the judge about the charge."

"What? . . . Uhhhh. . . . Sure, Tom. Right."

"What's the matter?"

"I tried one more time to get Mike Martin to authorize me to settle this case. He won't settle. He's gung ho. Believes in his case. He's dead solid certain we're going to win."

"And Robert . . . you don't think we're going to win?"

"No. At this point, I don't. Bailiff wouldn't tell me we're winning. Just said he didn't know. But from his body language, I know what he's really saying. 'You're gonna lose.'"

"Well, I've been through a lot of trials too. And I don't read it that way at all."

"You said it yourself, Tom. He's more objective than you or me. And the bailiff always knows. He knows what the jury is going to do."

*　　*　　*

It didn't take long for the judge to decide on the charge. "I'm not going to ask the jury about your antitrust claim, Jimmy. There's no proof even remotely supporting it, and you know it. And Robert, the same for your covenant-not-to-compete claim. The covenant just isn't enforceable under the law."

Both lawyers recorded their objections, but both knew the judge was right.

"And the rest of the case is the real lawsuit," Judge Leeds went on. "The trade secret claim. I'll use the standard wording in the Pattern Jury Charges. It fits perfectly. That makes for a clean case that the jurors can decide. A case that you two gentlemen can handle in good, solid final arguments to the jury.

"And we'll do that tomorrow morning."

*   *   *

It wasn't a good idea to drive to court today in the Duesenberg, Robert thought to himself. But he'd taken it from the garage without thinking. This was the car he most enjoyed driving, and he needed a little diversion—because these days were miserable.

He opened the gate and nosed the Duesenberg through it. Officer Houghton was waiting in front by the curb in his patrol car.

But the Iranians—Mahmoud and Ramshad—were there too, in their Hummer. And they had timed it perfectly.

Robert was ready for a leisurely drive down Willowick, onto Inwood, and then onto Kirby Drive, on his way to the courthouse. He passed by Officer Houghton and waved to signal that his sentry should go on to other business.

He watched as a Hummer came up behind him. He didn't realize what was going on until Mahmoud and Ramshad tried to pass him and cut him off. When that happened, he floored the accelerator and got ready to make an unexpected right turn at Mockingbird Lane. He would spin the wheel at the last second and hope that the Hummer didn't make the corner.

By now, Officer Houghton had begun to follow the Iranians. Robert in his Duesenberg, Mahmoud and Ramshad in their Hummer, and the officer in his patrol car were all racing through this tony residential area known as River Oaks.

Robert made the corner at Mockingbird. The Hummer stayed with him. So did Officer Houghton.

It was only a short block to Del Monte Drive. Robert made another sharp right turn there. By now, the Iranians had caught on and made the turn too. Officer Houghton was right behind.

The Iranians had pulled out their hardware. Ramshad leaned out the window and sent a stream of bullets toward the Duesenberg. Fortunately, he hadn't had time to modify his assault rifle to automatic, and the sound was rat . . . a tat . . . a tat, each shot requiring a trigger pull. That, plus the moving vehicles, plus stretching out the window, made it hard for him to be accurate.

The end of the block crossed Larchmont Lane. Robert made another sharp right. A short block brought him back to Inwood, and then he turned onto Willowick, heading home.

He had opened the gate, and he made one more sharp right into his own driveway. He was glad he had paid for the rapid-closure version of this gate.

Outside, Mahmoud stopped the Hummer in confusion. Robert heard Officer Houghton's loudspeaker commanding the Iranians to exit their vehicle and lie face down on the street.

Within seconds—literally, seconds—the street was full of cars with flashing lights. River Oaks is nothing if not well patrolled.

"This time, we gonna keep 'em," Detective Slaughter told him later. "Attempted murder is a pretty good state crime to charge 'em with."

"We'll be there when bail gets set," Cashdollar added. "But even if we get it set as high as we'd like to, I wouldn't count on us holding these two charmers unless we can get a no-bail order, which we'll try for. Short of that, I reckon these outlaws are wards of the Iranian state, and the Ayatollah will pony up whatever's necessary to get them out."

As soon as he could, Robert called Tom.

A few minutes later, Tom stood before the judge. "Your honor, I need to move the court for a continuance until tomorrow."

"On what grounds?" The judge was impatient, naturally, as any judge would be.

"On the ground that Mr. Herrick just called. He's been the victim of an attempted murder by Iranian operatives."

". . . Oh."

"And he's probably going to spend the rest of the day being interviewed and filling out forms. Right now, I understand, he's counting the bullet holes in his car."

34

The next morning brought one of those gloomy days down on the city, with clouds like gray cotton covering the whole sky. Instead of rain, there was a wet mist falling. Robert felt reasonably good in spite of it. Mahmoud and Ramshad were still in the county jail, and bail still wasn't set.

If these Iranian outlaws did get a bail number, it would take a little time to post it. And they would try to leave the country if they got out. He'd make sure there was a writ of ne-exeat—literally, "don't let them out"—which they would either elude or which would put them in jail again, perhaps without bond. And Robert would have a peaceful time, at least until the next band of assassins showed up.

He drove to the courthouse with fewer worries.

Except that he was worried about losing his case.

An hour and a half later, he stood in front of the courtroom to give his jury argument. He faced the seven familiar citizens without notes.

"Good morning, ladies and gentlemen of the jury." And they answered with a hearty "Good morning," which was a good sign.

"You've been fine public servants here. You've taken your valuable time to do this job. We've noticed that you've paid close attention. Believe it or not, it's common for jurors to fall asleep during a long trial. But you jurors have watched and heard everything."

He took a step to his right. "I believe in the jury system. In totalitarian countries, a commissar from the ruling party decides what's best for the commander, not for justice. Serving on a jury is something only free people can do."

The standard wisdom, Robert knew, is that you start a jury argument by praising the ideal of trial by jury. And more importantly, by praising the jurors. Psychologists call it the "audience reward" theory. We like people who like us back.

But won't jurors dismiss this kind of praise as hypocritical? Again, the psychologists have an answer. They call it the "fundamental attribution error." We attribute the actions of others to their genuine motivations, and we tend to discount situational influences. The jurors were most likely to accept the lawyer's praise as genuine, not as a contrivance to win the case—even though that was what it was.

Then: "This case is very simple," Robert told them.

If you have the burden of proof, you want the jurors believe your case has clarity, not complexity.

"I'm going to speak from here on out about what the judge tells you in her charge to you, because if we all follow the law, it's a simple case."

Appeal to a recognized authority, the psychologists say, is a powerful motivator. Here, the judge was that authority.

"The judge starts out by telling you what a trade secret is. She gives you a two part definition. First, the secret has to have, quote, 'economic value.' Mr. Coleman says that this wasn't a trade secret, but you know what? His own witness actually testified that it had economic value. They deliberately lowballed it—remember, forty thousand? Which was silly—but it shows how dishonest it was of Dravos to deny it."

He noticed that some of the jurors smiled at the forty thousand number. Good. It was an absurd figure. Jimmy had made a mistake by lowballing it beyond all reason.

"Second, to be a trade secret, the judge says there have to be, quote, 'efforts that were reasonable to maintain its secrecy.' Well, Nova had guards all over the place. There were all kinds of policies about secrecy, and there was a big security department to enforce them. DeTravanian Wrenger and Romaine Cramshak had to sign contracts to protect secrets, and they had to sign contracts not to go to work for a competitor. Both of them violated both contracts, and Dravos knew it when it hired them. But Nova did all it could reasonably do.

"The judge also tells you that it's illegal to, quote, 'misappropriate' a trade secret. And misappropriate just means you 'wrongfully acquired' it. Notice how hard Mr. Coleman is trying to say that the Iranian rollover mechanism wasn't copied. Notice how hard he's trying to claim that the devices are different because they use different hardware. The answer is, they use the same flowchart. It's copied, period.

"And notice how hard Mr. Coleman is trying to say that what happened didn't happen. According to him, Amir Massad didn't visit Wrenger and Cramshak at their lab at Dravos. The trouble with that is, all three of them tell you he did. And deTravanian Wrenger had the flowchart out and unrolled. He says he didn't explain it to Amir Massad, Romaine Cramshak says he did, but anyway, both their testimony shows that he said something to Massad and left it there for him to photograph to his heart's content.

"The judge also tells you something that's obvious: that a corporation acts through its agents and employees. Their actions are the responsibility of the corporation, What deTravanian Wrenger and Romaine Cramshak did—that all was done by Dravos."

Robert paused and walked to the other end of the jury box.

"Then the judge asks you, very simply, for your verdict. 'Did Dravos Corporation misappropriate a trade secret from Nova Corporation?' There is a blank for you to check with your answer, Yes or No. And I humbly suggest to you . . . the evidence is overwhelming, and the answer is, 'Yes,' it did.

"Then, the judge asks you how much Nova has lost in damages. There is a blank for you to write in the number. So, what is the evidence? The only real testimony is that the value is four hundred million dollars. Mr. Coleman's witness says forty thousand, but that's ridiculous, and it ought to be ignored. That same witness admitted that this rollover device would earn a stream of income that would be worth hundreds of millions. That's the real market value.

"And I humbly submit to you that the only credible figure that you have heard is four hundred million dollars."

The conventional wisdom is that the opening jury argument should be unemotional. The plaintiff's lawyer should stick to logic and rationality. Otherwise, the defendant's best arguments will be about points that you exaggerated. You should go over the court's charge and the questions the jury has to answer, and you should marshal the evidence that answers the questions. You'll get another chance to argue, in rebuttal, after the defendant's argument.

And so Robert faced the jury and ended without flourishes, or fanfare, or flashiness. "That's what the evidence shows, ladies and gentlemen of the jury. We humbly ask you to return a verdict consistent with the law and the evidence."

He sat down, slowly and heavily. It's not going to be enough, he thought. He remembered the bailiff's prediction.

And Jimmy Coleman would be standing before the jury next. I'm going to lose. I just know it, he said to himself. This is an important case, and I just didn't do enough.

*   *   *

An hour and a half later, the lunch break was over, and Jimmy rose to address the jury.

His clothes announced his attitude. He was a bull in a china shop. A gold-lamé shirt with a curving collar. A bright silver tie. A brown suit with a fine orange check. The jurors blinked. He had their attention.

"Ladies and gentlemen, I want to thank you for your jury service. It's an honor to be here with you. You all have superb backgrounds. You're a fine jury, much wiser than those I've talked to before."

Jimmy's voice creaked, as usual, but he dripped honey into it.

"But it's my unpleasant duty to tell you how Mr. Herrick has bent the evidence and the law in that bombastic speech of his."

Jimmy pointed. His index finger seemed unnaturally long as it extended toward Robert.

"Mr. Herrick told you that Mr. Wrenger showed the flowchart to Massad and explained it to him. But he conveniently left out the most important evidence about that. Which is, Mr. Wrenger himself denies it completely.

"And Mr. Herrick told you that the Iranian rollover device must have been copied because it was just like Nova's. But what he left out was that every single command in the Iranian program is different from the Nova program."

Jimmy was following the conventional wisdom. Don't let your argument be dictated by your opponent's. Don't try to answer all of it. Pick one or two points—issues that can be restated in one sentence and answered convincingly in one sentence. And then go on to your own argument.

"But Mr. Herrick's argument is all over the place, like a shotgun. I can't possibly run after all of his rabbit trails. I have to depend on you to recognize the things he's misrepresented and exaggerated.

"So now, let me turn to what this case is really about."

Jimmy's gold lamé sparkled. He was doing his best at sounding disgusted with his opponent, and his best at that, Robert had to admit, was pretty good.

"Your first question asks whether Dravos Corporation stole a trade secret from Nova Aerospace. The evidence is clear. Dravos didn't do anything of the kind!" Jimmy's voice ground hard and rose in volume for an instant.

"De Travanian Wrenger told you it didn't happen. Romaine Cramshak remembers it differently, but she agrees that no one could say that the Iranian visitor stole any secrets. The president of Dravos came before you to say how much Dravos tries to keep internal secrets, and how it tries to respect other people's secrets.

"And then, there's another whole reason why it didn't happen. The program is completely different. You heard that. You heard that from this witness stand!" Jimmy pointed. "The commands are completely different, from beginning to end."

Jimmy paused. And then he shifted into high gear.

"Dravos is a fine company. It's served the United States space program for decades. It's helped America innovate, push the envelope, and keep its world lead in space. Sometimes patriotism sounds corny today, but I tell you, Dravos is a patriotic company. And proud of it.

"But now it's being accused of something it didn't do. Do you know how awful that is? Dravos is accused of a crime here, and it's the victim of a shakedown scheme where one of its competitors wants to beat hundreds of millions of dollars out of it. Nova Aerospace hasn't really lost anything, and it wants to bankrupt Dravos if it can. And Dravos is not guilty. It's *not guilty!*"

Jimmy was shaking his finger and pointing at Robert. His voice croaked and shivered.

"I'm asking you with all my sincerity. I'm *begging* you. Go to the jury room and render a swift, sure verdict that says Dravos is not guilty of this imagined crime. Render a verdict consistent with the law and the evidence, saying that Dravos didn't misappropriate *anything!* And I will be grateful, and so will Dravos, and so will your—*your*— American space program."

Jimmy finished with an artistic wave of his arm. And he sat down with surprising agility, given his corpulence.

Robert was appalled. He had just watched a masterful performance. And for the thousandth time during this case, he said to himself: I'm losing.

35

The next morning was another one of those gray days. Robert got to the courtroom early, as usual. His gut bullied him with a dull, persistent pain, and he knew it was because he didn't want to be here at all, in this building, or in this courtroom, or in this case.

Finally, the jurors filed in. And the judge turned toward him. "Mr. Herrick?"

He imitated alertness and did his best to spring to his feet. When he started to speak, he was into the moment, with an edge of enthusiasm. "Thank you, your honor!"

He faced the jury. "Ladies and gentlemen, I need to ask once more for your attention. Soon I will sit down and the case will be yours and yours alone. But I need to dispel some of the errors that Mr. Coleman has made."

And just as Jimmy had pointed at him, he pointed back.

"Mr. Coleman tells you that there's no evidence that Amir Massad saw the flowchart. That's dead wrong. Romaine Cramshak tells you that deTravanian Wrenger showed it to him and explained it. They seemed like old friends. And Mr. Coleman completely ignores the testimony of Amir Massad himself, which we went halfway around the world to get and petitioned a court in the Middle East. That Iranian agent admitted that he photographed everything.

"And Mr. Coleman tells you that nothing was stolen. Only four hundred million dollars, that's all. And it ended up in an Iranian missile. Where it can carry bombs to Israel. Where it can carry death and destruction to Qatar, where there's a huge American military base."

He held up his hand. "When you answer question number one, remember what the judge tells you. A corporation acts through its agents and employees, and their actions are the actions of the corporation. DeTravanian Wrenger and Romaine Cramshak were Dravos. They personified Dravos, as far as the law is concerned. And so, when question one asks, Do you find that Dravos Corporation misappropriated Nova's trade secret, the answer is Yes, Dravos did misappropriate it. Acting through Wrenger and Cramshak, Dravos gave Nova's rollover device to the Islamic Republic of Iran."

He stepped to the other side of the jury bar. "The second question asks you about damages. I noticed that Mr. Coleman didn't try to argue to you about that strange forty thousand dollar figure. The only credible evidence you have is that the damages are four hundred million dollars, and it's not challenged by anything Mr. Coleman's given you that's at all believable."

Robert was wound up. He was ready to set off his fireworks.

"And let me tell you, I was shocked—shocked!—when Mr. Coleman talked about patriotism, after all the evidence that showed how Dravos gave this secret to Iran. In all the world, that's one of the two or three countries we have the most reason to fear. The biggest sponsor of terrorism that exists. A brutal regime, one that abuses its own people, and one that's sure to have a nuclear weapon one day. And Dravos has helped them build missiles that can carry it."

Jimmy was on his feet. "Your honor, I object. This is outside the record, and it's an appeal to passion and prejudice."

"Well," said the judge in a puzzled voice, "Mr. Herrick's just answering an argument that you made yourself. About patriotism. Mr. Coleman, you opened the door to these remarks!"

Robert didn't miss a beat. "And so Dravos's employees gave the Iranians a critical component for missiles that are capable of carrying nuclear weapons. And Mr. Coleman has the gall to ask you for a verdict saying that Dravos is patriotic, and it didn't misappropriate a trade secret. Don't do that! Don't do that, I beg you! Can you imagine the horrible scene we'd all see on the news, when the Iranians celebrate? I picture the chief Iranian ayatollah laughing at the United

States and chanting along with the mob that is always present, and all of them shouting, *'Death to America!'"*

He paused. Then, more quietly: "Ladies and gentlemen of the jury, thank you for your kind attention. Godspeed your verdict."

After the jury filed out, the bailiff nodded at Robert. "I think now you've got a better case than what I thought earlier."

* * *

Lawyers call it "sweating the jury." It takes no physical effort, but it really takes it out of you physically. And otherwise.

"The court's given them a simple charge, with only two questions," Robert said. He and Tom waited in the courtroom for three hours in case the jury came back quickly.

"You know how to reach me, right?" he finally said to the court co-ordinator, who nodded and smiled, because she was used to lawyer anxiety.

Six o'clock came and went. Back at the office, Robert tried to work but couldn't. He kept imagining what he would write in a Motion for New Trial after the jury returned what he expected would be a zero verdict.

Seven o'clock. The court coordinator called to say that the judge was sending the jury home. "We hoped for a verdict today. But we're calling it a night."

* * *

Next morning, early, the court coordinator called. "No, it's not a verdict. The jury has sent out a question. The judge wants everyone in the courtroom right away."

It took three hours before all of the lawyers assembled at the courthouse.

"This is the screwiest question I've ever seen from a jury." The judge frowned as she stared at the handwriting scrawled across a piece of lined notebook paper. "Everyone can look at it if you want, but let me first read it out loud. . . ."

"If we don't believe deTravanian Wrenger, do we have to award our verdict to Dravos Corporation?"

She looked down from the bench at a group of lawyers with blank faces.

"In the first place," the judge went on, "if you don't believe Wrenger, it doesn't make sense to think you have to favor Dravos Corporation. Wouldn't it be the opposite?"

Nobody answered her. The lawyers were all racing through conflicting thoughts, trying to figure it out. And failing.

"In the second place," the judge went on, "these jurors don't seem to understand that they are the final authority on these questions. They are the exclusive judges of the evidence."

Silence. The lawyers couldn't decipher it either.

"The charge tells them that. It says, flatly, *"You are the exclusive judges of the evidence."* And it tells them they're to decide *"the weight to be given the testimony."*

Judge Leeds threw up her hands in a gesture of surrender. "I'm inclined to bring them into the courtroom and direct them to refer to the charge they've already received. And maybe re-read the part about them being the exclusive judges of the evidence."

Jimmy was beginning to enjoy this. In his perverse way, he thought it was amusing. Also, and not incidentally, he liked the idea that the jurors might decide they "had to" award their verdict to Dravos, even if their reasoning was crazy.

"I think that's a good idea, judge."

Robert whispered back and forth with Tom. "This jury is loony." "Yes, but what do we do about it?" "Telling them to judge the evidence might be better for us."

Finally, Robert stood and said, "Judge, we have no objection."

And so the jurors trundled into the courtroom, all of them avoiding eye contact with both sides. And Judge Leeds charged them again with some of the words she had already given them, both orally and in writing.

* * *

When they were gone, Tom turned to him. "Robert, maybe you should consult the bailiff again. The Greeks used to head for Mount Parnassus and get advice from the Oracle at Delphi. You've got this bailiff you can ask for clairvoyance. Same thing."

He did ask, and the bailiff smiled while shaking his head. "I don't have any idea what's hanging these jurors up. But I still think you've got them with you."

Tom liked that. "It's as solid a prediction as the Oracle gave to Oedipus Rex. And a whole lot nicer."

* * *

The third day of jury deliberations brought Robert a small measure of comic relief.

"Have we heard anything?" It was Tom.

"Nothing. Nothing at all."

"Maybe no news is good news."

"No, I doubt it's good news. This isn't a difficult case—that is, not if the jury is going our way. I figure, the longer they're out, the worse are our chances."

"Oh, well, I was thinking that there's one, or maybe two, jurors that are holding out because they're with Dravos, and the bank president is the presiding juror and he's working to persuade them for us. And so are the other jurors, who are all with us. That's my scenario."

"That sure would be better than what I'm thinking."

"I know. You're just a big-time, gloomy pessimist."

"Right. Ever since this case waltzed into my office."

Two minutes later, Donna deCarlo buzzed him. "It's your two favorite homicide detectives. Slaughter and Cashdollar."

He flipped the switch. "Hello, Detectives?"

He heard laughter from the other end of the line.

"Robert, we tryin to keep you on top of all the happenins be goin on with yo' friends Mahmoud and Ramshad." Slaughter was full of merriment.

So was Cashdollar. "They're both residing in the Harris County jail. So far, no bail's been set and maybe it won't be."

"That's a relief. Can't somebody send them home?"

"No. We gonna get these marplots convicted and sent up for ninety-nine semesters. Ninety-nine full rodeos. Or somethin like that."

"Anyway, we're getting off topic." Cashdollar put on his official, television news anchor voice. "We want to keep you up on the headlines, Robert. It seems there's an Israeli guy who's right there in the can with these two Iranians. In the same block."

"He be in there for some kinda small-time weapons charge." Detective Slaughter snickered. "And this Israeli fella, he's a little guy. Them Iranians found out where he was from, and they gave him a little bit a lip. Death to Israel, you know. And some other stuff that was a whole lot worse."

"Anyway, this Israeli guy, he just lets it roll off his back. But then the Iranians, they be frustrated cause he don't get riled up, and they start tryin to push him around. Which was a major kinda mistake." Slaughter laughed.

So did Cashdollar. "What Mahmod and Ramshad didn't know was, this Israeli guy is a champion at cage fighting. He's little, yeah, and he's like featherweight class or something like that, but he does this all-holds-barred fighting for a living, and he put both of the Iranians in the hospital. He dressed 'em down real quick, before the deputy sheriffs could get to them."

"Well, I'm not for anybody getting beaten up." Robert thought about it for an instant. "Even guys who deserved it as richly as Mahmoud and Ramshad.

"Ahh, the . . . Israeli man . . . he's okay?"

"Not a scratch. And it's pretty clear he was doing it in self-defense. It's just that his version of reasonable force was more'n Mahmoud and Ramshad expected."

"I appreciate you two gentlemen keeping me up to date."

But the news didn't help him feel better. And another day went by without a word from the jury.

* * *

"It's unusual," said Judge Leeds. "We're near the end of the sixth day. Almost a week. And there's been nothing from this jury saying anything about a deadlock. Six days isn't all that unusual, of course, but with only one question and no note about deadlock?"

"They must like where you're sending them to lunch, Judge." Jimmy could appreciate the humor in the situation.

Not Robert. "Nothing to do but keep them working, Judge."

"That's right. Tomorrow makes a week. Maybe we'll hear from them tomorrow. You watch—we'll see them coming in at five o'clock sharp. It happens all the time. They act like they're on the job, and they stay at work for the day, but they knock off at quitting time. It's like they heard a whistle or something."

36

On the seventh day, the jury had a verdict. Not at five o'clock, but just before noon.

"Same idea." Judge Leeds was cheerful. "They're on a different shift and they knock off at noon. We'll call everybody to come in and send the jurors to lunch."

At two o'clock, the lawyers milled around in front of the bench. A gaggle of well-informed spectators formed an audience.

"Bring in the jury." And the courtroom pulsed with barely-contained anticipation. The jurors shuffled into the box, all looking at the floor. So did Robert. He couldn't read anything in their faces.

"Mr. Presiding Juror, have you reached a verdict?"

The bank president stood up with a page of paper in his hand. "We have, your honor."

"Please hand it to the bailiff." And the courtroom seemed to shift to slow motion.

Judge Leeds studied the verdict, the way all judges do. Thoroughly. "I've seen judges try to read the edges of the papers," Tom whispered.

"Come on, Judge! Come on," whispered Robert.

Finally, the judge announced that "the verdict seems to be in order."

Then she paused and studied it some more.

"The first question . . . asks, 'Do you find that Dravos Corporation misappropriated a trade secret of Nova Aerospace Company, as those terms are defined in the law?'"

The judge paused again. "To which the jury answered . . ."

Another pause.

Robert's hands covered his eyes.

". . . Yes."

It didn't register with Robert. Tom grinned and tried to shake hands with him, but he still didn't quite get it. Finally, his hands came off his eyes. Tom grabbed the right one.

"It's okay, Robert. We won. You can come back to earth."

But they both knew they hadn't won. Not yet. There was another question. To which the answer could be zero, or four hundred million dollars, or anything in between.

"The second question," intoned the judge, "asks, 'What sum of money, if paid now in cash, would compensate Nova Aerospace Company for the misappropriation, if any, of its trade secret, if any?"

As was her established custom by now, Judge Leeds paused.

For what seemed like forever. Then:

"To which the jury answered . . . three hundred million dollars."

"Wow." The judge put down the verdict sheet. And shook her head, while grinning.

"Now, see?" Mike Martin grinned too. "It's just like I said. We've got a good case. And it's been an easy case, Robert."

Robert didn't think it had been easy at all, but he didn't argue.

Tom looked happy, but puzzled. "How'd they get *three* hundred million? The only evidence, other than forty thousand, was *four* hundred million."

Mike Martin nodded. "That's right. We need to appeal. And get our full four hundred million."

"I have a suggestion." Robert was waking up, finally. "If the three hundred million survives Jimmy's appeal, you ought to just take it to the bank."

* * *

Jimmy was cheerful as he sashayed out of the courtroom. "Yes, we certainly will appeal. This trial was shot through with errors. Admitting the unsworn so-called deposition from that Arabic guy in that Arabic court. And that flagrant appeal to prejudice that ran all through Herrick's final argument.

"But those two examples are just the tip of the iceberg. The court of appeals is gonna reverse this crazy verdict bigger'n . . . bigger'n . . . bigger'n three hundred million dollars."

Tom had invented a proverb for it. "The defense lawyer who loses big doesn't lose anything himself, personally."

By now, Robert was talking to the bank president.

"Why did it take seven days?" The man pulled at his chin. "Well, it didn't for me. Or for most of us. But Elmer Lynann—that's the fellow who drives a taxi—he got hung up on one word. 'Misappropriate.' He thought it meant something like 'to make a mistake.' And he kept saying, 'They didn't make a mistake,' And Lizette—she's the one who's a secretary at the high school—she agreed with him for a while.

"It took forever, with us showing him the definition that the judge gave us, over and over. And finally, I think the two of them just got tired and wanted to go home."

"How'd you get three hundred million? The testimony said four hundred million."

"Yeah. I know. But everybody thought four hundred million was too much for this little bitty component."

"So instead of four hundred million, you settled on. . . ."

"Right. Three hundred million. I know, I know: If four hundred million is too much, why isn't three hundred million too much? But that's what we settled on. To break the logjam."

"A compromise."

"Yeah. I guess."

*   *   *

The call came to his cell phone as he was leaving the courthouse. "Will you hold, please, for the President of the United States?"

What should a person say to that? "Ahhhh . . . sure," was what Robert blurted out.

"You'll hear a silence, then another operator. And just keep holding."

That sounded real. Too complicated for a prank call from one of the Viet Nam guys. So he held.

Then: "This is the White House communications system. Please hold for the President of the United States."

And he held some more.

"Robert? Is this my dear friend, Robert Herrick?"

"I'm here, Mr. President."

"Robert, I always appreciate your support in terms of money contributions, but now you've helped your country in a whole 'nother way. Robert, you've shown the world how the Iranians cheat and steal. Good. We're going to use this verdict you got to shore up our allies who are slacking off on the sanctions against Iran."

Well, Robert thought, maybe there's a whole additional reason I should be glad I took this case. "Thanks. . . . I'm pleased to hear that."

"Give me your best judgment, Robert. Is this verdict going to hold up while it travels through the court system, including the appeals?"

"I'd be guessing. But if I had to guess, I'd say yes sir, it'll hold up."

"Good. Now, remember to send me some of the money you get out of this case. For my re-election."

He laughed. "You don't miss a beat, Mr. President."

"Well, Robert, a whale sweeps it all in by swimming around with his mouth open, and us politicians, we've learned to be just like those whales." And the President laughed too.

*　*　*

He drove home in the Duesenberg with the top down. Half a block on Rusk Street to Smith Street. South to Lamar, at a leisurely speed. A few blocks west on Lamar to Allen Parkway. A mile or so to the gates where the Parkway turns into Kirby Drive and River Oaks begins. Right on Inwood, then onto Willowick, and home.

He watched the colors in the afternoon sky as the clouds inched by.

Maria was waiting for him. "When you called, I took the rest of the day off."

"I'm . . . tired," was all he said at first. "You know what they say. 'It's five o'clock somewhere.' I'm ready to act like it's five o'clock right here."

She laughed.

A moment later, he faced toward her in the living room and lifted his glass. "All's well that ends well. That's what Shakespeare said.

"But you know what else? It sure can wear you out while you're getting to that place that ends well. . . . And that's an old saying I just made up."

And she laughed again. "You're full of wisdom today."

"Mostly, I'm tired."

"And what did you learn from this experience?"

"I'm back to where I like being a lawyer."

"Well, good. Because I don't think you can change careers now."

"And there's more."

"What? Really? More?" She was in the mood to tease him.

"If I take a case, from now on, it's going to be one I believe in."

She stuck both arms up. "Alllllll right!"

"And if I believe in it, I'm going to keep working even if the case turns out to be an uphill battle."

"That might be bad for your health."

"Well, smart aleck, speaking of health, Slaughter and Cashdollar say the gang intelligence doesn't seem to be threatening our health any more. They think that the Iranian repercussions have died down, now that the case is over."

"Wow. I like that."

"And Jimmy already called. He says Dravos will give up its appeal and settle with us if we discount our judgment. He knows it's not a very good appeal he's got, even if he'd never admit it. He even said, we'd have to discount the judgment '*a little*.'"

"But will Mike Martin go along with that?"

"I think so. We'll have to negotiate hard with Jimmy. It's got to be less of a discount than he probably wants. But there's something else that might persuade Mike. If we settle, he gets the money now, instead of two or three years from now."

"But our life can't all be coming up roses. There's got to be something wrong out there."

"Right. There's Pepper. She dutifully went to one AA meeting. Just one. And she says that meeting was just for me. She didn't need it. And she doesn't want to go back."

"There's another old saying. 'You can only be as happy as your unhappiest child.'"

"That old saying is sooooo true."

"Anyway, you got something out of this case. A little bit of contentment as a lawyer. And a way to start believing in your cases." She laughed. "And so it's also true: All's well that ends well."

"Yes. It's good if it ends well. But remember what's also true. It sure can wear you out while you're getting to the place where it ends well."

———————

Postscript

I've always included a postscript after my novels to explain what's real and what's not. My trademark is reality. The lawyers in my stories act in the ways that lawyers really act, and the law is shown accurately. The critics have all picked up on this.

But to write a novel that's readable, you have to follow certain obvious conventions. For example, a lot of the practice of law is plain old, boring, grind-it-out work. But I don't want to write a boring novel, and you don't want to read one. Sometimes, I just suggest the grind-it-out hours and days, without dragging them out realistically. And there are other conventions that novelists have to follow about characters and stories.

There aren't many realistic courtroom dramas out there, which is too bad. Most people get most of their knowledge of our justice system from fiction, and it misleads them. For example, John Grisham's biggest story was *The Firm*. It features a law firm that is an integral part of organized crime, and the partners will kill anyone who leaves. It's a novel that draws you in, but I've never known a firm like that.

And I don't want to write a novel like that.

This postscript is a guide to the places where I've deviated from reality. It's necessary to do that. But I want to correct the record here.

*   *   *

Jimmy Coleman is the consummate bad guy, and he comes from the big bad law firm. In reality, big firms are not more evil than smaller ones or solo practitioners. Actually, I think being among a group of talented lawyers in a big firm imposes a higher standard of conduct. But people like picturing a large organization as evil, especially if it opposes a smaller firm.

As for Jimmy himself, he's a composite of bad guys. I've never been acquainted with anyone just like him, but I've seen the tricks he pulls sometimes, just not all crammed into a single figure. This is one of my compromises with storytelling. People like to hiss at the bad guy, and Jimmy invites it.

*   *   *

On December 27, 2019, Iranian missiles attacked two United States air bases in Iraq. The explosions resulted in injuries to 34 American soldiers. Iran, of course, exaggerated the effects of the missile attacks and boasted that the United States had been powerless to stop them. This novel was nearly completed by that time, but it anticipated Iran's program to develop missiles that would support strikes against the United States.

*   *   *

The lawsuit that Robert wins is, in reality, probably unwinnable. You usually can't recover damages when you haven't lost anything. Nova Aerospace doesn't try to prove a real loss, and it probably can't. A judge probably ought to grant a Judgment as a Matter of Law for the defendant, if Nova doesn't have any other evidence.

Sometimes a plaintiff can get around this problem by pleading for "restitution" instead of damages. The difference is subtle, but it can make a difference. Simply stated, restitution calls upon the defendant to disgorge its ill-gotten gains and pay them over to the plaintiff. This remedy works if the plaintiff can't prove a loss but can prove what the defendant gained. It probably wouldn't work here, because Defendant Dravos didn't make money from its misconduct.

I wrote Tom's complaint so that it asks for not only damages and restitution but also for a "constructive trust." This remedy is not really a trust, but simplistically, it's a way of recovering when there's no other way. The constructive trust is poorly defined and amorphous. The court is said to "impress a constructive trust" on ill-gotten gains as an expression of the "conscience" of equity. I don't think a constructive trust is viable here, but it might be the plaintiff's best guess just because it's so vaguely designed.

Then, there's the matter of the trade secret, here, having no definable market value. This is a common problem, and often, it means the plaintiff can't recover. So, for all of these reasons, there's a big question in the story: a claim that, in reality, probably couldn't be proved.

There is one possibility that might make the proof viable. My state's supreme court has said, "Absent proof of a specific injury, the plaintiff can seek damages measured by a 'reasonable royalty.' . . . '[B]ecause the precise value of a trade secret may be difficult to determine, the proper measure is to calculate what the parties would have agreed to as a fair price'" for the secret if they were negotiating in an imagined market. This is what Tom Kennedy's witnesses were doing. Maybe, just maybe, this method could make my fictional case realistic, though I'm skeptical. In any event, maybe it's close enough for a novel.

* * *

Sometimes readers are surprised to hear that plaintiff's lawyers prefer to be in state courts, not federal. They assume that federal courts are somehow "better." Not so, for the average plaintiff's case.

Federal judges are appointed for life, and state judges usually aren't. Federal judges can be more high-handed. They also can make you go through more complex and confusing procedures, which are expensive and more suited to defendants, who benefit from obstruction. Federal judges have two recent graduates as law clerks, and state judges usually don't. Those two eager beavers love procedural issues, and they can really tie up plaintiffs without having to consider the cost.

* * *

The court's charge to the jury is simple, in this case. I've winnowed it down to two questions. Those questions are legally correct and would correspond to the core of the charge. But in reality, the instructions would be more complex, and so would the questions.

* * *

I'm not confident that I've realistically described the electronics that guide a missile rollover. Actually, let me put that differently: I'm confident that a knowledgeable specialist at a NASA contractor would find my description of the electronics unconvincing.

I know a little about it, because I was an aerospace engineer at NASA before I was a lawyer, and I did computer programming for the division responsible for the Orbital Attitude and Maneuvering System—the "OAMS." But I worked on the wet chemistry side of it, not the electronics, and it was long enough ago so that things have changed. I got help from a real electronics expert: my brother Steve, who worked at Bose Corporation and helped invent noise-cancelling headphones, among other products. I remember seeing American tanks on TV when they went into Baghdad, and Steve pointing and saying, "Look. They're wearing my headphones!"—the ones he'd just worked on for the military.

With Steve's help, I can tell you that the basic idea that—the device is a microprocessor—is real, along with the description of Do Loops and If-Decisions. I worked with those back in the day, and they're still around. And a flowchart is the first step in setting a program up. So there's something of reality there, in this work of fiction. My basic goal, however, is to tell a good courtroom story.

*   *   *

The government of Iran is described harshly here, but unfortunately, I think accurately. The death penalty for heresy has been a historic punishment there. And that kind of instinct hasn't disappeared. As these words are being written, there is an American citizen under a sentence of ten years for crimes including insulting the Ayatollah.

The Islamic Republic of Iran is the biggest sponsor of international terrorism in the world and a major exporter of war, as the description says. Saudi Arabia is not a model society, but it furnishes something of a buffer against this outlaw regime. And the Iranians have a viable mid-range missile program, just as this story describes. Their missiles violate international law because they are nuclear-capable, just as the story says. And they have the range to reach the American base in Qatar.

*   *   *

Tom tells Robert that talking to the bailiff is like consulting the oracle at Delphi. This oracle was the subject of a favorite Greek myth. She actually was known as Pythia, the high priestess at the Temple of Apollo, the god who, in addition to driving the flaming chariot that was the sun, was associated with forecasting the future. Consulting the oracle at Delphi was a task of such complexity that it has to be studied at length, before the possibility can be believed that anyone ever believed it.

Tom also tells Robert that the bailiff's prediction is nicer than the one Oedipus Rex heard. In the Greek drama by Sophocles, *Oedipus the King*, the oracle at Delphi predicted that Oedipus would kill his father Laius, the king, marry his mother, Jocasta, and become king himself (after solving the riddle of the Sphinx). It all comes true without Oedipus's realization, and the play is about his search for the killer. When he learns of his patricide and incest, Oedipus blinds himself and Jocasta commits suicide. Yes, the bailiff's prediction is a lot nicer.

*   *   *

My description of the last steps in a capital murder case is mostly realistic, I think. There is no real case that I know of that is like Billy Joe Armistead's crime, but it's realistic, unfortunately, because these are horrible, nightmarish crimes. The way the case winds its way through the courts is accurately described. If the trial produces a conviction and sentence, there is an appeal, then a petition to the Supreme Court, which the Court usually refuses to hear.

But then the *habeas corpus* process begins. The case goes back to the original state trial court and goes through state appeals. Then the convict's lawyers can petition the federal courts: first a district court, then the court of appeals, and then the Supreme Court. It takes years, of course. And sometimes, there are multiple habeas loops through the court systems.

In this novel, I show the case when it reaches the federal court of appeals. The procedure is accurately described, except that the parties' written briefs are more important—usually, much more important—than the oral argument, but the argument is what makes the stuff of a novel. One deviation from reality is that in my state an assistant attorney general takes over in the federal courts and replaces the assistant district attorney who's had the case, but I made a composite person, Maria Melendes, handle both jobs. I don't want this to be like one of those Russian novels with a thousand characters.

My friend Larry Fitzgerald, who was the public information officer for the prison system, took me through the death penalty chamber. It really is (superficially) cheerful with its bright blue paint, there really is a tie-down team, they really do practice, and the gurney is, indeed, really disturbing to look at.

* * *

The Riemann Hypothesis, which deTravanian Wrenger uses to confuse everyone, is real. It was proposed more than 150 years ago by Bernhard Riemann, and it remains one of the most prominent unsolved problems in all of mathematics. I bet when you picked up this novel, you thought there'd be no math.

* * *

The complaint, discovery, analysis of electronic documents, mediation, evidence, arguments, and judge's rulings are all realistic, I believe, although they are presented in shortened form.

* * *

Robert Herrick, the famous "lawyer for the little guy," is pictured in this story as uncertain about the case. And nervous, really nervous, about trying it. Some readers have thought that this depiction is unrealistic. He's an experienced professional, they say, and he would be calm and cool.

In the first place, a case you want to take doesn't waltz up to you and announce how good it is. In fact, you don't know much about the case when you take it on. I once accepted a case only to have the other side send me a release signed by my client—one he hadn't thought to tell me about. You develop instincts about type of cases and clients, but it's an imprecise art.

And then, what about Robert's anxiety? There are some lawyers— a few—who don't experience fright when they start a trial. But most trial lawyers are nervous. This condition may manifest itself on the lower end of the scale, as butterflies in the stomach, or it may be as pressing as a desire to go to the restroom and lose one's lunch. I myself was somewhere in between. I tried somewhere between seventy-five and a hundred jury trials, and the fear never went away. (Back in the old days, we tried more of them than lawyers do today.) I always thought that the measure of your willingness to go to trial is your willingness to go to trial, and not the fact that you did it with a stone cold attitude.

And so I picture Robert Herrick as nervous—not just nervous, but scared—when he goes to trial. But he does it and does it well. I think that's normal, even for a professional.

Just ask a trial lawyer.

— David Crump
January, 2020

Also by David Crump, in the *Robert Herrick Series*

Visit us at *www.quidprobooks.com.*

www.ingramcontent.com/pod-product-compliance
Lightning Source LLC
Chambersburg PA
CBHW051636260626
47170CB00004B/1204